PRACTICAL SINS FOR COLD CLIMATES

"A strong plot and engaging (fted mystery, and Val's humorous a   less do much to lighten the tension. The core of the story is Val's discovery of her own self-worth."

— Publishers Weekly

"Costa hits all the right notes—vulnerable but likable characters, a compelling plot, a clearly drawn setting, and a tangled web of past and present events."

— Sheila Connolly,
New York Times Bestselling Author of *A Gala Event*

"Taut, well written and suspenseful, *Practical Sins for Cold Climates* draws readers into a community where the past haunts the present and residents' motives are buried deep...just like the truth."

— Kylie Logan,
Author of *And Then There Were Nuns*

"An engaging, deftly-plotted mystery with a smart, tough-minded heroine. Shelley Costa delivers a terrific series debut."

— Daniel Stashower,
Author of *The Hour of Peril*

"Very well-written...this book reads as longer than typical cozies because it needs to, for honest character evolution. The mystery has a very satisfying conclusion...This is the first book I have read by Shelley Costa, and I am very impressed."

— Librarian at Jefferson-Madison Regional Library System

"A brooding, atmospheric story, you can almost feel the weight of a blizzard bearing down. Highly recommended."

— For the Love of Books

PRACTICAL SINS *for* COLD CLIMATES

Books by Shelley Costa

PRACTICAL SINS FOR COLD CLIMATES
A KILLER'S GUIDE TO GOOD WORKS
(September 2016)

CAL
SINS *for*
COLD
CLIMATES

A MYSTERY

SHELLEY
COSTA

HENERY PRESS

PRACTICAL SINS FOR COLD CLIMATES
A Mystery
Part of the Henery Press Mystery Collection

First Edition
Trade paperback edition | January 2016

Henery Press, LLC
www.henerypress.com

ISBN-13: 978-1-943390-41-0

Printed in the United States of America

For Miriam
All of the moments
All of the years

ACKNOWLEDGMENTS

Thanks to editor Kendel Lynn for warmth and latitude; editor Rachel Jackson for just the right touch; agent John Talbot for a couple of superlatives when I most needed to hear them; Marnie Albers for putting her estimable mind to the plot; Jessica Bloomfield for her close, early reading of the book; Tom Kelly for the float plane side of things; and my husband Michael for pushing the envelope on our canoe trips. Thanks, finally, to the great silences of the Northwoods. Lake Wendaban is fictitious, and so are its inhabitants. But northern lakes like it exist. It's good to know there are lakes clean enough for drinking, and forests old—and protected—enough that we can still make discoveries in them about our world and ourselves.

You have to meet the enemy to appreciate him.
– Grey Owl

1

Val Cameron stepped off the Ontario Lakeland train from Toronto and onto the wooden step the conductor had slung into place. He grabbed her elbow when her heel got caught in a space between the boards and held on while she wiggled it loose. It had been a six-hour ride north to this place called Lake Wendaban, where her assignment was to get a signature on a book publishing contract. The train came through, in either direction, just once a day, and Val planned on making the return trip to Union Station in Toronto the day after tomorrow. From there, Pearson Airport, from there, LaGuardia. And finally, a cab back to her place on E. 51st St., where her plants were waiting to be watered and life was beautiful all day long.

She had passed the time on the train by eating two toasted cheese sandwiches in what was loosely called the dining car and, after watching a road trip movie about the buddies' hilarious scrapes, she napped. Then she spent the rest of the trip wondering one more time why she had agreed to this particular assignment. But that line of thought only flung her right back into the murky gumbo of her personal life.

Brushing off her skirt, she watched the train speed northward at a pretty good clip, like it couldn't wait to get to its final destination, a place the timetable told her was actually called Moose Factory. While she stood wondering whether that was where they either processed or assembled moose, Val adjusted her purse, her briefcase, and her small overnight bag. Then she picked her way across the gravel parking lot in her Prada shoes.

She slowed down as she eyed the place.

There had to be some mistake. Where was the town?

When Peter Hathaway, her boss, first told her she had to get to the town of Wendaban, Ontario, she figured on awnings and sidewalk café seating. Some charming cross between Fire Island and Bedford Falls. Signs pitching all-you-can-eat fish fries every Friday night. Barbershops and garden clubs. People. At the edge of the parking lot she set down her briefcase and overnight bag and looked around.

Had the train let her off prematurely, say, at a whistle stop? Some little pre-station station where you just had to wait while the moose crossed the tracks? She had sudden misgivings and whirled around. No, it was definitely a train station and the sign said WENDABAN. The town looked like the outskirts of itself. But, then, she had got out of her bed that morning in Manhattan and, happily, had very little basis for comparison.

She looked up and down the main drag, which was also the only drag, called Highway 14, just as a semi flew through like a windstorm, kicking up dust and tossing around her Donna Karan skirt. Apparently, if she wanted to buy moccasins, a fishing license, trolling motor, tackle, or something called a Bee Burger, she was in the right place. But her next iced decaf quad venti three pump soy no whip white chocolate mocha would just have to wait until she got home. And she wasn't even going to think about where to find a good kosher dill.

Across the road, a couple of elderly tourists tottered into a restaurant painted black and yellow and called HONEY BEE MINE. And two doors down, a burly, bow-legged guy in baggy shorts emerged from a place called LCBO clutching a case of Labatt's to his sizeable chest. So maybe this wasn't The Town That Time Forgot, after all. No, Val rolled her eyes, in two days that would be *her* job.

Just get yourself to Bob's Bait Shop on the municipal dock, Peter Hathaway had said. For a man who micromanaged everything including which sugar packets to stock in the office break room, he was curiously unhelpful on the big stuff. Work, for one. Love, for another. And, as usual, she was left having to fill in some pretty important blanks. But get herself to a bait shop in this weird little fishcentric Brigadoon? This she could do. And it wasn't like she had to buy anything. She preferred her fish smoked, slathered across half a bagel, and slapped down in front of her on a plate at the Carnegie Deli. Any other choices in terms of fish apprehension and delivery held no interest for her.

Bob's Bait Shop was just a means to an end in this two-day assignment to sign a bestselling old hermit. It was there she was supposed to meet up with her ride to the Hathaway family cottage that Peter had arranged for her. Still, there was a glimmer of a bad feeling that hanging out around bait—bad as that was, considering she had an *ick* problem with invertebrates—could turn out to be the least of her problems.

She crossed Highway 14 and headed toward the place where sun glinted softly on a body of water, which seemed totally promising. Could a bait shop and a dock be far behind? Her deductive skills were something to behold. On her way down the boardwalk, Val passed a gas station, where she figured fishermen could gas up their bass boats, a public library, where they could read about "angling," and a community center, where they could get together and exaggerate the day's catch.

Truly a breed apart.

A glass-covered community bulletin board sported hand-scribbled signs advertising boats for sale, psychic readings (will I catch fish?), taxidermy (can you stuff my fish for me?), and a Friends of the Lake meeting on August 10 (Camp Sajo Lodge, 7 p.m., come discuss our mutual interests and bring your ideas!). No matter where you went on the planet, Val decided, jiggling her foot, someone would be having a meeting. Was her heel possibly a little loose, after all? Since the likelihood of finding a shoe repair shop in this Wendaban place was nil, she'd ignore the slight wobble until she could hold the shoe in one hand and the heel in the other.

Rocking softly at the dock were two houseboats—one called *The Love Boat* and the other *Rock Me Baby*—painted in psychedelic swirls, next to two small planes and half a dozen banged-up motorboats. At the end of the boardwalk, there it was: Bob's Bait Shop. It was a hut with rough-cut shingles, slanted boards, and the kind of windows you prop open with sticks. She could think of at least three books she'd edited in which the kinds of things that happen in places like Bob's Bait Shop usually include dismemberment.

Val stepped inside and lingered near the door as her eyes adjusted to the dark. Behind a sagging wood counter was a stocky young man placidly reading a magazine. "Hi." She was surprised to hear herself sound quite so chipper. "I'm looking for Wade Decker." With her luck, the guy balancing a case of Labatt's on his gut.

The young man looked up. "He went to the bee for poutine."

After a moment, she murmured, "I see," kicking herself for not bringing along a Canadian phrase book.

His eyes flickered at her, and Val knew he had figured she wasn't a bait-buying kind of gal. She could tell he was about to add something. How long could she pretend before she had to admit to this kid that she didn't understand? She could be missing something vital, like where to get a Reuben sandwich. The kid's eyes suddenly got wide as he discovered something helpful to say. "You can wait for him on the dock." Which came out sounding like *dawk*.

If the language barrier didn't go much beyond *bees* and *poutine*, she'd be able to pull it off. She smiled at him like she had caught it all, and sauntered over to the rack holding brochures about houseboat vacations, which only some combination of bondage and chloroform would get her to try. But she felt bad for the kid behind the counter, trapped with old issues of *Walleye World* in a dark hut on a summer afternoon.

Val shot him another smile meant to convey something about how city girls with expensive Italian leather briefcases really do take an interest in any Canadian wildlife less than two inches long, and she swaggered over to the smelly bait tank. She lifted the lid and got past the stink just long enough to stare at what was inside. Some kind of flatworms undulated their way through the water. "What are these?" she asked in a way that nicely suppressed her gag reflex.

The kid grunted. "Leeches."

The lid slipped out of her hand and clattered into place.

When the kid turned away so she couldn't hear him giggle, which she did anyway, Val noticed that across the back of his head someone had shaved the words GO JAYS. She wondered if he was aware of it. With a breezy "Well, thanks," Val stepped back out into the afternoon sunlight and walked twenty feet to the municipal dock.

She crossed her arms and leaned against the piling. There was a stillness to late afternoons in August, past the heat of the day, when everything seems suspended. Wind dies, the air settles, and voices are drawn away to other places. She watched a family in a boat the kind of white you only ever see in rich people's teeth purr into a vacant slip. Past them, beneath a spread of low, flat-bottomed clouds, the lake began.

Where it went from there, she didn't care. In the briefcase at Val's feet was a book contract from her place of employment, one of only a handful of publishers in New York City that had yet to be bought out by a cookie conglomerate, where twelve years ago she had landed her first job straight out of college and had finally become a senior editor.

Nearly all of her work life at Schlesinger Publishing had been in the adult trade division, where she had plodded alongside her colleague Peter Hathaway. Until six years ago when he had the luck to acquire that blockbuster, *InCubeOps: America's Secret Program to Destabilize its Allies*, by Anonymous, a well-placed source who turned out to be the Deep Throat of the Millennial Generation.

Twelfth printing and a Pulitzer Prize in the firestorm of government outcry—and Peter Hathaway was deemed a wunderkind, rocketing to the top of the editorial heap. In short order he became such an institution that CEO Henry Schlesinger had finally given him his own imprint, *Fir Na Tine*, which Peter chose for some obscure reasons of personal ancestry.

It took Val by surprise, just how philosophical she was about Peter's success. Her business in this outpost of civilization, which was located somewhere between the CN Tower and God, was to sign the reclusive old Charles Cable, who was writing a big novel about a celestial disaster, when he wasn't monitoring the effects of lake water levels on loon nests. For whom, no one knew. What she did know was that the man didn't even own a telephone and only came into town—presumably, this mother of all backwaters—once a month to collect his mail.

Val looked up.

Down the boardwalk came a tall man dressed in a faded teal t-shirt, khaki-colored nylon shorts, and blue Adidas slip-on sandals. Between his teeth was a long, thin cigar. The man moved with the kind of loose grace that comes from everything hanging together in just the right way, stepping back instinctively a few times when the brown mutt dashing around his feet stopped short to snap at horseflies.

When Val straightened herself away from the piling, the man noticed her, and squinted.

"Are you Wade Decker?" she asked him.

He came over to her, slid the cigar out of his mouth, and shook her hand. "That I am," he said. "And you're..." he drawled as he unfolded a crumpled piece of paper he had pulled out of his pocket, "Valjean Cameron."

"Val."

"I figured." His light olive skin had tanned and peeled and tanned again, with a raw pink spot along the long ridge of his nose, where a dried line of Nosekote didn't seem to be doing any good. He had hazel eyes, a wide mouth, and light brown hair cut long in the front and combed back. He glanced at her briefcase and overnight bag. "Is this all you've got?"

"That's it. Two days, two nights."

A slow nod. "So here you are," he said, sizing her up, "for an errand in the frozen North." Decker's voice had the same musical quality of all the Canadians she had heard since she'd arrived north of the border. They always sounded surprised—surprised she wanted a ride from the Toronto airport to the Royal York Hotel, surprised she wanted to change American money, surprised she was taking the train north. It must be nice to be shot through with the kind of wonder that has nothing to do with senility.

"Believe it or not," she told him, "there aren't all that many of us who think you get around on dogsleds." Her own more practical view of the neighbors to the north was that they drive like lunatics, smoke with abandon, and wear funny hats, only she wasn't about to say that to the man who was loading her briefcase into one of the small planes. She couldn't tell whether she was swaying from stepping onto the floating dock or being overcome by the kind of fear that homogenizes her internal organs.

"I thought we were going by boat." She sounded accusatory.

"Oh, did you?" he said, thrusting her briefcase in the space behind the pilot's seat. She casually walked alongside the plane, wondering whether she should just sandbag him and call a water taxi and trying damn hard to look as jaunty as Amelia Earhart. The plane looked like it had all its rivets, although she wasn't sure she could say the same for the pilot. But she wasn't about to come off like some kind of Yankee baby, so when Decker held out a hand, Val grabbed it, stepping onto the float and through the open door. She slipped across the pilot's seat to her own, where the red leather was old and cracked.

Decker swung himself into the plane and immediately filled the space. When he reached for his seat belt, she reached for hers like she knew what she was doing and they spent a companionable five seconds strapping themselves in and adjusting their belts. He flipped switches, checked gauges, and pressed buttons, all of which looked disturbingly fake.

To take her mind off the toy plane, she tuned into the thrum of the engine and watched the propeller speed up to a haze. Val jerked back as he leaned across her and checked the silver door latch. She felt a sudden wild black anger at Peter Hathaway, this Decker person, and all men everywhere who make half-baked arrangements they think are just fine.

He smiled. "Your first time up?"

"Well, actually," she said, "yes."

"You'll like it." She was relieved to see him put on a headset. At least now he wouldn't be able to hear her whimper. They backed away from the dock and floated an easy turn westward, then picked up speed as they taxied around a small island housing a brown cottage with a proud white flagpole flying a Canadian flag. When the plane cleared the island, the lake opened up before them like an endless corridor of water flanked by pine forest and rocky shore. She could see for what must have been a few miles, until the distant mainland disappeared into summer whiteness.

An errand.

He was right: she was doing an errand. Like picking up the dry cleaning—but someone else's, not even her own. It was one of those times when she had to shore up her ego with a self-inventory. She was a senior editor with a perfectly respectable 401K. She owned an apartment with twelve-foot ceilings and wainscoting to die for in a co-op building off Second Avenue. She was thirty-four years old and—according to her Aunt Greta—still reasonably attractive, although her wardrobe could use some work. Yet here she was proposing to get airborne with a stranger who, from the looks of him, had probably done most of his flying inside his own head.

So, 401K aside, what she was doing was just another in a long line of errands for Peter Hathaway that started two years ago, when, at the age of forty-two, he took to wearing unbleached cotton tunics and pajama pants that made him look like a serf. He had his hair cut short, grew a trim Van Dyke beard, and pierced an earlobe. In two places. The effect was one of concentrated decadence that she found disturbing. He also developed what she considered an abnormal interest in space junk.

Peter, whose family owned a cottage on this lake, knew

Charles Cable from thirty summers of fishing for pickerel in all the same places and protesting illegal access roads. When he got word that Cable, whose breakout book, *The Nebula Covenant*, stayed on the *Times* bestseller list for thirty-two weeks, was working on a thriller called *The Asteroid Mandate*, it tickled the space junk gland in Peter's brain. But when he learned Charles Cable had inexplicably fired his agent, he sent Val north with a contract.

Partly she went as a self-inflicted penance for the debacle over the author of *Downy*, a sensitive novel about an old man's friendship with a young girl, when, just a week from the book's publication, his name showed up on the National Sex Offender Registry as a sex offender in her midtown neighborhood. For weeks thereafter, blame was liberally flung around the Fir Na Tine offices like rose petals from a toddling flower girl. It didn't escape Val's notice that anytime Peter Hathaway muttered about *a failure of due diligence*, his eyes always settled on her. It didn't help matters that the sex offender down the street was now actually suing the company for breach of contract.

But the real problem was what she and Peter Hathaway had discovered with horror nearly a year ago, sometime well after Peter left his wife Tish, after a four-week courtship and a three-week marriage. He moved to a loft in Tribeca with nothing but a laptop, a lamp, and a futon. Here, one night, he'd hand-rolled sushi for the two of them and Val uncorked a bottle of Barbaresco so they could bicker happily about Fir Na Tine's latest acquisition, a novel by a writer who had invented a new language. They were both reasonably sure this writer wasn't turning up on any embarrassing registries and that she hadn't stolen whole pages of *Finnegan's Wake*.

So, out came the Barbaresco. And after the third helping of tekka maki, without another word they found themselves setting aside their clothing with the same powerful ease that had characterized their working relationship. The sex that followed contained sensations she thought only laboratory rats got to enjoy. Their second time together they dispensed with the sushi, drank the wine, and set about determining whether what had happened on the futon was really as good as they thought. The third time they dispensed with everything, including the futon.

Wade Decker lifted the plane off the water, so light and easy, Val couldn't feel the precise moment they left the lake and took on the sky. Cottages were dropping away. Decker reached under his seat and pulled out a worn map he handed to her. "We're flying down the East Arm of the lake," he said.

The air was unresisting, the sun poised and golden. She watched clouds gather and drift and shift from pink to gray near the horizon. There was no need to talk. He had seen it all many times. She had never seen it. There was no word bridge possible between those two degrees of experience.

"How high are we?"

"Twelve thousand feet."

Val turned her head just enough to check him out. When Peter had sensed in a phone call that Charles Cable could be persuaded to sign, he called his Canadian friend Wade Decker and asked if he could get Val to the writer's cabin in the wilderness. This Decker person was happy to oblige. According to Peter, his pal Decker had been married to the beautiful Leslie Selkirk, who died unexpectedly a couple of years ago, and he owned a cottage on the lake, and maybe another property in Toronto, where he lived. Peter wasn't sure.

Men had an appalling lack of curiosity about each other.

As Val and Decker moved through the beautiful blankness of the air, he pointed out the shadow of the plane on the water. Ahead of them the lake was opening up, and what she could see in every direction, all the way to the horizon, was that it was really a system of lakes, shapely and silver in the late afternoon light, separated by dense green islands and mainland.

She settled into the silence, listening to the steady thrum of the engine, shooting a quick look at the pilot. If they went into a nosedive, she could at least focus on his heaven-loving great legs. Take the edge right off the whole death experience. By dinnertime two days from now she'd be landing at LaGuardia. By bedtime, she'd be fed and showered, telling herself one more time that there was nothing better on the face of this Earth than sleeping alone.

2

Caroline Selkirk leaned the extension ladder against the front of the boathouse and climbed up with a paintbrush and a quart of brown paint. The sun stiffened her back, let her see in the cracks between the boards, let her pretend whole microscopic civilizations were thriving in there out of sight. The sun even brought out the faint old pungent smell of the cedar. Near the top of the boathouse was a stringy cobweb, and next to it a white beetle-like casing, like a scarab, that a dragonfly had crawled out of, unfolding its wet, new wings.

The metal handle of the paint can dug into her palm, and whoever used the brush last hadn't cleaned it well, so it was hard, but maybe not too hard. She dipped the brush into the brown paint that had been leftover from some other job around the camp and pushed the unbending bristles into the C of Camp Sajo. Her whole life suddenly seemed to teeter on just how fast she could touch up the letters in the Camp Sajo sign, with its three-foot-high letters that her father, Trey Selkirk, had carved into planks of red pine when he had inherited the camp from other Selkirks all those years ago.

It was ten o'clock and she had waved goodbye to the last of her few campers, but not before she had heard a couple of parents whispering how rundown the place was looking. So what would that mean? Five fewer campers next summer? Could she afford to lose even one more?

Suddenly she saw it all—or at least all the things she had

overlooked because, without the money to change them, for her they had ceased to exist. The Camp Sajo sign over the boathouse. The buckling steps to the lodge. The camper cabins that went unused because Sajo's numbers had been dropping for the last ten years, after Trey died. Even her lovely handyman Luke couldn't keep up with the work.

What she saw—what she always saw—was the Camp Sajo of 1993, when she was eighteen. Twelve wilderness acres, a fleet of two dozen yellow fiberglass canoes, two hundred and fifty campers from a dozen different countries, a bustling waterfront program, breathless romances, campfires, camp songs, camp cheers, the clatter of voices and dishes at mealtimes—and her father.

A cowboy-booted, crazy embroidery hippie-shirted man, her father, with his never-ending windburn and kind green eyes. It was Trey Selkirk who became the face of Ontario youth camping because he wasn't just a guy with an inherited hobby camp and a soft spot for kids—he was a mountaineer, and a competitive sailor, and he played one hell of a blues harmonica. For a kid to spend a month at "Chez Trey," as Sajo was called in those glory days, was to come into the presence of a man who figured in all the best books about northern adventure.

She still had the camp—here on what was called Selkirk Peninsula because her Selkirk ancestors had come to the region one wagon ahead of the mapmakers—but the canoe fleet had shrunk to ten (eight she'd trust), and the campers to twenty-five. The SARS scare of '03 had hit them hard, her cook Kay would remind her. And the microburst of '07 had hit them harder, the lovely Luke would remind her. And don't forget how youth camps go in cycles, her friend Martin would scoff, always seeking the big picture, the big vague picture, reducing all her efforts to some vast inevitability.

But what had hit them hardest, Caroline knew as she dabbed brown paint into the faded letter *A*, was her sister Leslie. The dead Leslie. Because it takes a special kind of parent who's willing to send a child to a place where one of the camp owners herself met such a bloody and mysterious end.

*   *   *

The West Arm of the lake, Decker told Val as he brought the plane around and headed into the wind for a landing, had the trickiest shoals, which is why boat traffic was low and cottage values were high. Val threw on her sunglasses so he couldn't tell her eyes were squeezed shut, and she concentrated on not stiffening herself into a complete plank while he continued the goddamn geography lesson.

This part of the lake had several large secluded islands with maybe no more than a dozen cottages, well hidden from view, that had been in their families for three generations. Decker's plane plonked down almost imperceptibly and skittered across the water. The Hathaway cottage, on an island at the beginning of the arm, was built sometime between the two World Wars. Desmond Hathaway, who had been camping and renting on the lake since he was in his early twenties, bought it from the original owners when Peter was ten.

Farther down the arm was Selkirk Peninsula and what was left of Camp Sajo, where Decker had worked for several summers, owned by the Selkirk family. Over the last thirty years, summer camps suffered a long dry spell, and many folded. Trey Selkirk, who brought his wife and two daughters up from Peterborough every summer to help with the camp, fought to keep the camp open, selling off two sizeable islands close to the peninsula to Martin Kelleher, an American businessman from Philadelphia.

The sale bought him some time, but not much, and he started looking into leasing the mineral rights to Selkirk Peninsula to a Sudbury copper mining company. When the early drilling didn't turn up enough copper to make a damn tea kettle, as Trey put it, the miners closed up shop—and so, nearly, did Camp Sajo, although the Selkirks managed to hang on to the property. The daughters, Leslie and Caroline, inherited it, finally, but it's Caroline who keeps opening it up summer after summer for the handful of campers they still get.

"Why?" Val called to Decker as he scrambled out to secure the plane. "What happened to Leslie?" She clung to the wing strut as she let herself slide onto the dock, the closest she had ever come to feeling like a paper doll, a flat, flapping, falling over thing.

"Well, I guess you could say *I* happened to Leslie," Decker said, coming around to help her. "We got married seven years ago."

So the Selkirks' Leslie was Decker's wife. Val ran shaking fingers through her hair, trying to stay in the conversation. "And Peter tells me—"

"Right." Decker lifted her bag, shooting Val a look she couldn't read. "She died," he said, almost oratorically, the way she imagined Galileo sounded when he announced the Earth was not flat. As Decker turned on his heel and headed up to the Hathaway cottage, she found herself wondering whether his wife had met her end through some terrible accident, some crazy Northwoods misadventure—death by black bear, death by hypothermia...

Val pressed her sleeve against the foam at the corners of her mouth and looked around. If death in this godforsaken place could happen to Leslie Decker, who presumably had some wilderness skills, then what were her own chances? The cottage where Decker was depositing her was in a cove where the lake water looked green, cold, and deep. The front of the Hathaway island was an expanse of exposed gray rock. Where the rock leveled out, the cottage stood, back from the water by maybe twenty yards. There were several islands nearby, but only one had a small cottage, which looked uninhabited, judging by the dull red shutters snapped in place over the windows.

She could tell from the contrast between the tan and yellow boards under her feet that the dock had been recently repaired in four places. Maybe Peter's freeloading nieces weren't so useless after all, although she had a hard time picturing girls named Muffy and Lana wielding hammers and chainsaws.

Val picked up her briefcase—Decker must have taken up her overnight bag—just as a white boat with blue bumpers sped by out in the channel. The man at the helm raised his hand at her. She waved back, grimly happy that she'd be back home in Manhattan before she'd ever have to wave at anyone in this watery nightmare place ever again, and headed up to the cottage. It had rough-cut cedar shingles the brown of rich, wet soil, a dull green roof, a fieldstone chimney, and casement windows that had been cranked open.

She hated it already.

Decker held open the door.

She stopped on the threshold. "Who fixed the dock?"

He looked her in the eye. "I did."

"Why you?"

"It needed it," he said, "and I had the time."

"Is that what you do?" She went past him into the cool darkness of the Hathaway cottage, half looking for a futon.

"Am I a Northwoods handyman, is that what you want to know?" Decker smiled. "I live in Toronto," he said, letting the screen door close quietly behind them, "where I manage a commercial building downtown."

"Oh. Right." So far, nothing this man did was anything she knew how to talk about. Flying planes, managing properties, getting married.

"This is where I spend my summers." He nodded toward a small hall. "Bedrooms are this way," he said, and she started after him.

Decker stood aside for her to go into the bigger of the two bedrooms. It was an L.L. Bean kind of place, with a white Hudson Bay blanket smoothed over a sleigh bed that would have cost her a month's pay. There was a green braided rug over the plank flooring, a single highboy dresser against an empty wall, and a low Shaker rocker. A light breeze rippled the edges of the sheer curtains. For sure this Down East look had preceded Peter Hathaway's libertine shepherd monk days.

Decker stood in the doorway, looking at her like he wasn't quite sure she was level or plumb. "So you work for Peter," he said in an appraising way.

Well, that was the fact of it, but it didn't make her like it any better. "We're colleagues," she answered with a primness she couldn't help.

"Which is why," he said slowly, crossing his golden arms, "you're doing his errands in a place that terrifies you."

"It's more—complicated than that."

Decker cocked his head at her. "Ah." Got it in one. To his credit, Val saw he didn't look her over.

When she caught him eyeing his watch, Val offered him a beer. He tried not to smile—"You'll be fine, you know," he told her—but he was kind, thirsty, or just plain damn Canadian enough to take her up. She opened her hands as if to say it couldn't matter less. No words were necessary. Decker's finger flicked at his Nosekote like he'd just discovered it. On the far wall were some polished wooden pegs for clothes—Val pulled two things out of her bag and hung them up—and an old framed map of the lake. She grunted at it.

Where he lived, Decker told her, steering her by the shoulder over to the framed map, "just so you know," was in Lightning Bay. By boat, half an hour from here. Suddenly it felt far to Val, considering this loose-limbed Canadian pilot was the only soul she knew here and nightfall had all the appeal of a colonoscopy.

He ambled back into the main room to show her how to work the marine band radio. The Hathaway call sign was Knickerbocker, his own was Aero, and the kid who mans the station always sounds like he's transmitting from behind enemy lines, so don't mind him, he works for room and board.

They stood with their bottles lifted, silent for a minute, and Val considered barring the door while he answered every frantic question she could think of about the propane, the gas lights, the motorboat, the shoals, and whether the Blue Jays had a shot at the Series sometime this decade. Then she finally felt the beer seep all the way to her feet, shorting out every nerve along the way, and she knew Decker was right, she'd be just fine.

Especially if she could keep him there through the next round. While Decker twirled his nearly empty bottle in one hand over his crossed arms, she spoke up. "When can I see Charles Cable?"

"And get back to Toronto."

"Right."

He pulled his phone out of his pocket, and she took some comfort in his tapping because it meant information, a plan, a schedule for getting the hell out of there. "Tomorrow's the day he comes to town for his mail and generally makes the rounds."

"So you won't have to get me to his cabin." Altogether good news.

He pointed the empty bottle at her. "I guess you lucked out, Valjean," he said, slipping the empty into a Sleeman's beer box next to the kitchen stove. "Looks like you'll catch your man at lunchtime tomorrow, at Caroline's."

"And she would be?"

"Caroline Selkirk. My sister-in-law." And then he added, "Camp Sajo."

"Oh. Right." She held her breath and wheezed it out. "Anything sooner?"

Decker's eyes were wide. "Sooner than lunch?"

"The night is young." Did she actually just bat her eyes at him?

He looked at her quizzically, like he wanted to say *too bad about that eye tic thing*, and headed toward the front door. Val followed, noting the vertical line of sweat tracing his backbone under his shirt. In someone she actually liked, she'd find it oddly appealing.

Outside the cottage, shadows were already hitting the far shore. "Listen," Decker turned, "I can send someone over here to stay with you, if—"

"Thank you, no." She'd lock and bar all the windows and doors, pull the covers over her head, and cower until morning. Even that was better than having to make conversation with some sleepover buddy she'd never see again. The only thing that would make the nine hours of blackness endurable would be the silky pleasure of knowing she could deposit the signed contract, like a mouse, at Peter Hathaway's Jesus-sandaled feet. "Any chance at Charles Cable tonight?"

"Well, there's a meeting he might have come in early for, a community development group. I'm going."

Her heart sprang. "Can you take me?"

"Be ready at seven," he called back to her as he jogged toward the plane. And she thought she heard him add, "What a shame," softly, more to himself, even.

After he left, Val rummaged through Peter's shelves and came up with a can of Campbell's clam chowder. She was drawn to the word *Manhattan* on the label, and two minutes later she was downing the soup like it was a potion that could transport her there. While she ate, she thumbed through an old family album of madly smiling Hathaway forebears holding up stringers of fish, brandishing walking sticks, or hugging any of a number of big old black dogs with tongues the size of tennis shoes.

In one photo, a much younger Peter, from the days when he still had hair that required a brush, leaned against a red Jeep with one arm around a beautiful blond in a halter top and shorts, the other arm around a less obvious beauty, this one a redhead in a sarong. He wasn't madly grinning like his dog-loving parents, but it was a kind of in-the-moment expression that took whatever was on offer because he never had to go looking for it. Beautiful breasts just naturally nuzzled against him, and slender, rounded hips invited his hands.

Now she knew.

It was just how the world worked.

She teased the picture out of its photo corners. *Peter with Les and Caro*, someone had written. Not Peter. Someone, maybe his mother, was the chronicler of the life he was too busy living to have a moment's anxiety that maybe it wouldn't always be that way, young and strong in front of a jazzy car with two beauties, that maybe hanging onto a photo could at some point be inexpressibly sweet. It might be a key to understanding the baffling connection she and Peter Hathaway had been working on since that first night on the futon, but she had the train and plane rides home to ponder it.

What had happened between them was so shockingly uncomplicated that neither of them trusted it, of that she was lay-down-your-money sure. He had quickly taken up with a schizophrenic poet named Daria Flottner, who shaved her head, and Val found herself a widowed Irish undertaker who lived in Brooklyn and had three kids. While the love had been uncomplicated, the failure to love became a matter of exquisite torment. When Peter wanted Val's sympathy, he would stand looking moodily out of his office window on the twelfth floor and tell her that it wasn't easy being hooked up with a poet. She didn't mention that the Irish undertaker lasted only two months, since she didn't like his children and he didn't like the commute. When she could tell Peter was feeling rejected, he told her that she feared rejection and then he refused to sign up any author she recommended. So she pursued Peter's writers of space junk, never certain whether it was more to please him or to get away from him.

3

Mosquitoes bounced softly against the screening, and because she and Martin were eating dinner in silence on the porch, Diane Kelleher could hear the little *tick, tick, tick* the insects made. She had made what their friends on the lake always called "Diane's chicken"—the tamari and plum wine marinade—although, as she cut slowly into a boneless breast, she always thought she'd be known for something more lasting than chicken. There is something that happens to a woman, she thought, when she makes this kind of a good marriage, and she wondered if there would be more finished work in her pottery studio if there were fewer jars of caviar in her pantry.

Hunger, she thought, pushing a forkful of chicken through the sauce on her plate in a little figure eight, keeps ambition keen. But she was fifty-four and just yesterday she had figured out a surprising statistic. After thirty-three years of marriage to Martin Francis Kelleher, who ate silently across from her, one finger lovingly keeping his place as he read through his daily stack of faxes, the number of dinners she's cooked up herself came to 9,642, taking into account things like vacations, takeout, business dinners, holiday family meals, and so on. Maybe she'd shoot for an even ten thousand, present herself with a gold oven mitt, and just—disappear.

She impaled a few garlic green beans. "Are you going to the meeting tonight?"

"Of course." He didn't look up.

"Where is it?" She already knew the answer.

"Sajo."

He had a broad, well-shaped head, and the kind of crinkled eyes and quizzical brows that always made him look skeptical. At fifty-six, he still looked good in t-shirts and shorts, which he always wore belted, and the sun had bleached the hair on his arms white. His skin was rough from years of shaving a tough beard, and his hair was thinning, but on him it hadn't mattered. He was a man whose face you noticed, not his hair. To Diane, he had the presence of a union leader, square and scrappy, not the CEO of Cintorix Corporation—and these days, who knew what else?—that he really was.

One night while he slept, she took a mini-flashlight out of her nightstand and shined it absurdly on his left ear, counting the hairs that had been sprouting there in recent years. There were seven. His breath came like rustles, and his arms were crossed, maybe while he monitored the bullshit of his subconscious adversaries. Seven golden ear hairs, so far. She twirled the mini-flash, picturing a hair forest thickening up over the next couple of years, cutting off whatever lay behind it, like the charmed briars around Sleeping Beauty's castle.

Things were different in the twenty months since Leslie Decker's death, and Diane turned it over in her mind. There was a discomfort Martin felt, she could tell. For, just a mile away, poor Leslie had been killed. Beaten and hurled out a second story window. It had been early in October, and first the nights went cold, and then the days went cold, and finally the case went cold. Someday soon maybe her own suspicions would go cold as well.

Lake and town people said they missed Leslie Decker because of her smile—which always seemed to Diane a ridiculous reason to care for somebody, smiles are so easily made—or because Leslie had worked hard to keep Camp Sajo solvent after the death of Trey Selkirk out in the Rockies, that senseless way. Or even because—and this was Martin's line—she had done so much to save the lake environment. And anyone listening at that moment took it to heart because everyone knew that Martin Kelleher cared very, very deeply about the environment.

The sun was heading toward the treetops, and Diane stood up from the table, the mosquitoes backlit, the sun shining just about pink on the seven golden hairs in Martin's left ear. She swallowed a smile, blinking. "Is the meeting in the great room?" She picked up her own dinner plate.

"I guess so. The meetings always are." He scowled at his papers, made a violent note.

She wanted to make him look up. "Even when Leslie ran the show?"

He met her look. "That Leslie," he said, and here it came, Diane could tell. "What an environmentalist."

"Martin, *please*," she came back, faster than she would have liked.

She beamed at him, at his surprised look, and held out a hand, rippling her fingertips at him, glancing at his dinner plate, as though she had just asked him for it—instead of scoffing at his comment about the dear dead Leslie. He handed her his plate with a quick, sheepish look like now he understood what she had meant—when he hadn't, at all.

But Diane turned away with the empty plates from the 9,642nd dinner she had made and—covering her laugh with a couple of coughs—decided she would deduct this evening's, lowering that total by one, because something about it had been delicious, and if anyone ever asked, she would have to tell them it must have been the plum wine marinade. What else could it possibly be?

They got to the meeting thirty minutes late, but for Val it was an extra half hour of dithering time while she kept an ear open for the drone of his float plane. The aqua top with the print skirt? Or the brown top with the khaki-colored drawstring pants? And why in God's name did she pack a good skirt for this Northwoods gig, anyway? Did any of it really matter?

"Why don't *you* go?" Val had asked Peter a week ago, shuffling through a stack of office mail, only half-listening as she ripped open the latest whizz from Human Resources, telling them all one more time how their health insurance was being slashed *to serve you better.*

Peter wagged his shorn head. "Charlie Cable knows my stuff too well. In person I'm still the screw-up who drove the boat over the fishing lines and we had to watch the mother of all pickerel swim off, and if that wasn't bad enough," here he opened his arms wide, never missing an opportunity to display himself, "I'm just another sellout to the great urban whore."

"How *is* Daria?"

"I meant my personal style."

"Of course," she murmured. "My mistake."

"And Cormac?" he countered.

The undertaker.

She fanned herself with her mail. "Oh, you know, New York in a heat wave. Lots of handguns, no air conditioners—"

"So," Peter filled in the blanks, "he's busy?"

How would she know? She shrugged noncommittally, disgusted with herself. She was going to have to leave for Toronto on the next flight just to get away from the baffling thing she always became when she was with Peter Hathaway. "So you and Charles Cable—"

"—are phone friends. Out of sight, he loves me. I have mystique."

They looked at each other a second too long.

Any other man would pull her in.

Any other woman would go.

He walked around to his desk drawers—his serf pants flowed nicely around his Jesus sandals—as he explained he didn't want any time to elapse for other editors to start sniffing around Charlie, and he sure as hell didn't want *The Asteroid Mandate* to go to auction. Neat, sweet, and complete. That's what he wanted, and that's what Valjean Cameron could deliver. He himself had already made a six-figure offer to Charlie Cable, which had been accepted. All Val

Cameron had to do was get a signature and make nice.

"Look, Val," he said, squeezing Purell on his hands. She knew what was coming: the usual threat. "Do you not want to go?" He sanitized his hands vigorously, then fluttered his fingers dry. "Is that what you want? I'm sure I can find some nice memoirs for you to work on. There's that five-hundred pager from the former undersecretary of defense—"

The one thing Valjean Cameron wouldn't touch with a ten-foot pencil was memoirs. Mem-WAHRS. The self-indulgent ramblings of the formerly busy. Before she went to have all of her wisdom teeth extracted a few years ago, she made herself read the mem-WAHR of the ex-head of a soap manufacturing company, figuring some swirl of rage and boredom would take the edge right off her pre-op anxiety. She was right. There was simply no excuse for autobiography. But this, she knew, was a minority opinion.

"Threats," she told a sanitized Peter, using the voice of the sixth grade teacher she had loathed, "are beneath both of us." Here she was lying: they were beneath her, certainly, but these days she was no longer sure what exactly was subatomic enough to slip in between Peter Hathaway and the pursuit of pleasure.

"Very well, then," he said, enunciating carefully. "I take it you mean you will go."

"I will indeed go." You obtuse and maddening flake.

"Indeed. I believe that is wise."

"What it is," she looked at him pointedly, although she wasn't sure she had a point, "is necessary."

His eyes flickered at her. "Just be sure to do your due diligence," he said, and never missing an opportunity for a parting shot, added, "this time." He always saved references to the *Downy* debacle for those times when he was feeling particularly bested by Val.

By the time Decker arrived, she was waiting on the dock, sitting in an Adirondack chair, dressed in her drawstring pants, and going for the fifth time through her briefcase to be absolutely certain she had the contract for Charles Cable. When Decker dropped her back off later, she'd call the airline and see if she could switch her ticket for a flight out of Toronto tomorrow. That was the first piece of good news. The second was that Decker, wearing a red baseball cap that had faded to a battered pink, pulled up to the Hathaway dock in a small silver boat with an outboard motor. He idled while she climbed in, wobbling, and then tossed a life jacket to her to use for a seat cushion.

It was a ten-minute ride west, farther from the center of the lake, to Camp Sajo. Decker pointed out a loon peacefully riding the eddies flicked by the breeze that hadn't quite settled down yet for the day. As their boat breached the water, coming just a little too close, the loon slipped under, head first.

Ahead of them the mainland seemed to rise, where the terrain turned into low, craggy cliffs, and the forest appeared denser. But as Decker swung wide around what she thought was mainland, she could see it was deceptive—it was a sizeable land mass that jutted out into the channel, and the lake continued beyond it.

"Selkirk Peninsula," Decker shouted over the engine.

Val gave him a couple of big nods. Decker slowed down as they threaded their way between two islands. The one on their left had a dock in good shape, but on the shore there was a sizeable pile of wood debris that looked like it had been left to weather for a few seasons. A construction site that fell on hard times? Standing behind it was a permanent sign that read TAX THIS!

She looked at Decker, who flashed a wry grin. "Charlie Cable's property. Two years ago he was so enraged at his property tax increase, based on a boathouse he tried telling them was forty years old, that he took a pickax to the thing. He tore it down board by board and left it there, calling it his permanent exhibit. Then he moved to the wilderness."

They threaded quickly between two islands, where docks seemed extensive and new, but no other buildings were visible. Then she saw Camp Sajo, rising like a funny old Canadian pueblo, dark cabins ascending the land that had rock fortifications around the periphery, disappearing into woods that tolerated everything.

Val counted over twenty boats strung together haphazardly like beads, rocking in the wake she and Decker made, *thunking* softly against each other. He tooled around, puttering, looking for a slip, gave up, and pulled up against a gleaming white boat with a pristine canopy and a wooden steering wheel. No clunky outboard there. Decker lashed his boat to what he told her was Martin Kelleher's new plaything, being sure to set the bumpers between them.

Val tried clutching her briefcase first against her chest, and then under her arm, but couldn't clamber from one boat to the other, not with all the bobbing. Finally, with Decker watching, she threw her briefcase into the Kelleher boat and climbed in after it, catching the hem of her pants on something metal. As she tugged it free, she realized she was still two boats away from the Camp Sajo dock.

Decker passed her, lightly springing from one deck to the next, finally setting her briefcase on the dock and, in a quick swing she wasn't expecting, herself alongside it. "Hey, Arlo," he said, shaking hands with the young man Val recognized as the clerk from the bait shop.

Half bent over her knees, Val tried to catch her breath. "Go Jays," she wheezed. Arlo pumped the air with a grin, and for some reason started carrying Val's briefcase up to the camp like a bellhop at the Ritz.

At the far end of the camp docks was a two-story boathouse with an extension ladder leaning against it. High over the door that looked locked up tight for the day was a sign, *Camp Sajo*, where everything except the *ajo* was dark enough to read. At the place where the docks met the land, a pole from the trunk of a tall pine, the bark stripped away, had been mounted a long time ago in a concrete foundation, and flew a Canadian flag, where only the edges fluttered. On that far side of the camp property, the rock dropped away into softer, denser forest.

High overhead, a bird with broad, level wings floated in a thermal—"maybe a golden eagle," Decker said, shading his eyes to see it better—and then disappeared over the treetops. Val grunted and then hustled to catch up with Go Jays, who was disappearing into the main part of the camp. Ordinarily an eagle might hold some interest, but tonight she was on a mission.

4

They heard the meeting well before they got to Camp Sajo's main lodge, a low sprawling cedar-shingled building in a clearing at the center of the camp, with rows of crude plywood window shutters that swung upwards and were propped open with sticks. Mosquitoes dusted at the screens, and Val swatted at the ones that landed on her as she followed Decker up the single swaybacked step to the wide porch that seemed to wrap around the entire building. He chose that moment to whisper that they were stepping into a perfect storm of all the lake's factions: cottagers, youth camp owners, permanent residents, outfitters, and Ojibways, the local Native American tribe.

A heavyset older woman in loose black capris was pulling weeds in a small vegetable garden. "Kay Stanley, the camp cook," Decker told her. Val watched her gently release a handful of weeds into a bushel basket, unaware of the raised voices sailing out through the double screen doors. Someone was wielding a gavel to bring the group back to order.

Val and Decker went inside.

What hit her first was the smell of nachos, old fish, and Deep Woods Off spread among the fifty or so men and women, reminding her of a really lousy weekend she spent tent camping in the Catskills about twelve years ago with a puritanical boyfriend who thought Madonna was the Antichrist.

Benches were set out like pews in a Quaker meeting house, and it was clear that people had come to the meeting straight from whatever else they were doing on the lake. A trail of sawdust boot prints led to one tight group of workmen who stood around with their arms crossed, daring everyone else to make sense.

Decker steered her around to the side of the great room. Cottagers with pastel t-shirts that said "Canoe Head" or "The Near North" were sitting in proper little rows, tired from a day of blueberry picking and birdwatching, their hands clasped around their crossed knees. They had an expectant look, like someone was going to give a talk on edible mushrooms or the virtues of composting.

It was hard to tell the outfitters from the youth camp owners. They both sported straps to hold their glasses in place, like they had to be prepared for anything nature could, at any conceivable moment, dish out, and wore nylon cargo pants that were the kind of sartorial nightmare you can zip off at the ankle, knee, thigh, and hip, although what you then do with all the litter of pants parts, Val couldn't tell.

What Val figured were the local Ojibways didn't have to wear shirts that stated a damn thing.

There was an older guy up at the front with flyaway gray hair that appeared to have its own agenda, who was wearing a shirt with a collar and a bolo tie. There was a nondescript woman wearing a summer suit who seemed to have been directly airlifted from Toronto, and Val had thirty bad seconds wondering if she was a competitor, someone from HarperCollins Canada, say, whose own briefcase held a sheaf of papers requiring Charles Cable's signature, too—although the expression on her face seemed to shift from a kind of hard-won bureaucratic patience to a low-level snarkiness that said *let them yammer on all they want, these goddamn lake trout, but I know the law.*

From a room off the side of the great room stepped a woman who spotted Decker right away. She was a tall redhead, her hair in shoulder-length layered waves, her hand pushing absently at a forelock as she came over to them, smiling. She was wearing a long artsy shift made out of thin cotton in a pattern of dripping teals and ochres. Val recognized her as an older version of the redhead from the Hathaway family photo album.

A quick look told Val she was braless, but then, breasts that trim didn't need the packaging, and there was just a hint of French-cut panty line that said this was a gal who still shopped at Victoria's Secret. She had those pretty Brit lips that were shaped like the most delicate lines of India ink. Her eyes were pale green, her collarbone awash with sun freckles, all twenty finger and toenails were unpolished, and her nose was severe.

She was beautiful.

Caroline Selkirk gave Decker a peck on the cheek, which he returned, all very careful brotherly love, and then she shook Val's hand. "Peter Hathaway." She leaned into Val, raising her voice in order to be heard over the meeting that was escalating all around them. "He's your boss?"

Val slid a look at Decker, who was fanning himself complacently with his hat, waiting to hear how she answered. "Right. My boss, my colleague..." Where should she stop? Certainly before the events of last night, when at 5:25 he had spontaneously asked her to dinner so he could give her some final instructions about the trip.

Over drinks and bruschetta he had presented her with a set of keys and a raft of papers. She would be staying at the Hathaway family cottage—no renters right now, and his nieces, those lovely little freeloaders Muffy and Lana, left the lake early to go to a Lightning Dust concert in Montreal. The fridge is stocked and the girls say they changed the sheets.

He's assuming there's still furniture and pots and pans—he hadn't been to the cottage in four years, not since his lady friend at the time came across a garter snake in a cake pan. That did it for her. And as for him, Val noticed, since he started dressing like the shepherd of SoHo, he was suddenly having to go very far away—to places like Crete and the Galapagos—in order to work on his "centeredness." In that strange Hathaway mind, getting to the family cottage in Canada didn't involve enough suffering to bring him peace of mind.

Caroline went on, "Peter and I had a thing about twenty years ago, but then..." Wrinkling her nose, she waved it away with a secretive smile like she had cast a charm over it and happily moved on. How old was Caroline? Forty? Little crow's feet, her skin a final creamy softness before the comedy team of sag and droop make their entrance. Val's own friends in their forties enjoyed trotting out their sexual histories for the general entertainment, either because nothing much was happening in the here and now, or because discretion was just another thing that didn't matter very much when you come right down to it, like chewing with your mouth closed.

Pretty soon, Val could see herself collaring total strangers in Times Square and telling them about leaving the restaurant last night with Peter, both of them awash with wine and remembrance, chattering away as he walked her home. And into the building. And into the apartment. And into her bed. Daria had never happened. Cormac was pure fabrication. They actually found themselves saying things like *Oh, Peter, Peter*, and *Darling, I've missed you so much*, words they would slash mercilessly wherever they found them in a manuscript, but not before they'd call them out jubilantly to each other. *Val, wait 'til you hear this one!*

Suddenly all that twaddle coming from their own lips sounded like the mysteries of the universe revealed. At one point she was weeping. At one point he looked like a man who had staggered into an oasis with just one breath left in him. That patchouli smell of the man, the glint of his earrings in the candlelight—she never wanted to be anywhere else in the world. Suddenly he was leaving, she was retreating without going anywhere at all, and she wondered whether that same old gauze of idiocy and equivocation was back. And she had gotten up at five a.m. for a flight. *Peter and I had a thing about twenty years ago, but then...*Well, Caroline Selkirk, we had a thing less than twenty-four hours ago.

"It's getting nasty," Decker murmured.

Caroline just shook her head fondly at the meeting, like a first-grade teacher doing playground duty, watching the little scamps get out of hand.

"Which one's Cable?" Val asked Decker. He angled his body around until he could pick Charles Cable out of the crowd, drawing Val's head closer to him so she could see where he was pointing. Charles Cable was up at the front, the older man with the flyaway hair like a stand of sea oats in a hurricane.

The goal was in sight.

Val felt herself settle into her game head. More people were standing. Only the most elderly—bony in their straw hats and fishing caps spangled with fishing flies—were still seated, part of a generation that still waited decorously for the opportunity to vote, assemble, worship, make their point, or storm a beachhead. All the others were youthful philistines.

"Well, there won't *be* any more wilderness if we don't put a stop to these damn—"

Someone topped him. "And what about the lumber mill, hey?"

"—to these damn—"

"Martin," a voice shouted over the din. "Martin, is that you?" Like he wanted to pinpoint the exact location to operate his handheld rocket launcher.

"How are we supposed to make a living? Tell me that."

"If you can't live here, then fucking move, I say."

Collective gasps from cottagers.

"Move? *Move?* My whole family was living here, winter and summer, for three generations before you even got here, you silly piece of summertime shit."

"Now, Dixon—"

The gavel was half-hearted, like a woodpecker on a bug-free tree. "Look, the town council will listen to all—"

"Shut up, you hypocrite—"

"—*all* sides of the issue before we—"

"What's the issue? Tell me that. What one, single, end-of-all-time issue are you bunch of two-faced councilors going to—"

Generalized huff was setting in. "I'm an elected official—" he was struggling to get to his feet, like he was tripping over his own bluster, "—working for the public good—"

"What about the good of the lake?" a cottager piped up.

"The lake pays the taxes!" A Canoe Head jabbed the air.

A workman rounded on him. "The town damn well services the lake."

"Well, if *that's* what you want to call it," someone sneered, which led to a minute of loud incoherence. Then the pushing started, and the sudden eruption didn't prepare anybody for Quaker pews falling like sinners all around them. A few polite old cottagers started to struggle to their feet, perhaps to register an official protest in the general anarchy. Val watched what she could make out of Charles Cable at the front of the crowd, his head steadily moving toward the back door, his arm hurling fed-up, Zeus-like bolts behind him.

Val pulled the papers out of her briefcase and headed into the mêlée, ignoring Decker's *"Wait!"* and clutching her briefcase like a lifeline out of Hell, keeping the flyaway hair in her sights. An outfitter whose pants were zipped off at the thigh fell into her, but she stayed on her feet, driven by the need to locate once and for all the space junk scribbler whose signature was the only thing that stood between Valjean Cameron and her own almighty bed on 51st Street in a place where nobody had to count loon chicks at all, ever.

The gaveling got louder, like a jackhammer in her brain, and she was making real headway toward the back door, elbowing a brawny workman in painter pants, when there were strangled cries, and someone yelled, "Give me that, you sellout," *sellout, sellout, sellout to the great urban whore*, and it wouldn't strike her until much later that the last thing she thought of as the brawny workman grabbed the gavel and lost his balance, his fist hurtling toward Val's face, was Daria the baldheaded Flottner.

5

Val sat up, groaning, and something fell away from her face. Her right cheek, her eye, her nose? Nothing would surprise her. Groping around, her hand settled on an ice pack. Then her fingertips dabbed at the place where she had last seen her right eye, only now it was sunk somewhere between her abnormally large cheek and her eyebrow, which seemed somewhat lower than before. Like every cell on the right side of her face was pumped full of cheap whiskey and then ignited. Her tongue slid quickly over her teeth—all present, none loose. In her worst nightmares she had a mouth full of loose teeth, like a honky-tonk piano whose ivories had seen better days.

She looked around, started small, took note of the couch where she'd been deposited. It was a leftover from the '70s, Scandinavian style, with a screaming Bargello fabric that felt pretty much like the inside of her head. She was in the office at Camp Sajo, judging by the rolltop desk and file cabinets. Someone had lighted the oil lamp, which let off a faint citronella scent. Outside the open window, it was dusk, so she hadn't been out for long. She heard feet crunching on a trail nearby, in a way that sounded like normal life resumed, and her one good eye saw a bat streaking by. Her eyelashes felt like they were gummed to her face. She checked her hands in the dim light: no blood. So aside from a face like Orson Welles and—she looked down at herself—the nachos she was wearing, she was good to go.

Val held onto the doorway and stepped up into the great room. The gaslight chandelier was burning, and Decker, Caroline, and the camp cook, Kay, were cleaning up. Now that all the others were gone, she could really see the place. It had to be the heart of whatever this camp had once been, with the open rafters, cavernous old stone fireplace at the far end, trophy cases, and camp memorabilia. Large framed pictures of campers in their cabin groups were all over the walls.

The year 1932 was closest to where Val was standing. The girls with their Carole Lombard bobbed locks, the boys with their hair cut long in front and skimmed back without brilliantine—kind of like Decker's, all these years later. All their squints in the sunlight, their grins at the photographer, arms filled with paddles and each other, before a World War would keep some of them from ever coming back. It meant something to have them live forever on the walls of Camp Sajo, preserved in the soft amber light.

"Hey, you're up." Decker looked over at her, setting a long bench back on its low feet.

"I wasn't exactly taking a nap." From behind the ice pack clamped to the right side of her face, she managed a small smile. She wondered whether Decker had singlehandedly moved her to the couch, or whether it took all three of them to do the job, but at that moment in time she couldn't take another blow, so she didn't ask.

Caroline handed him her broom and came over. She braced Val's shoulders, and looked her over optimistically. "Well..." She finally pursed her lips, and they both watched a clod of nachos flop from her chest to the floor.

Val couldn't help a mighty sigh. "Damn, I'm hungry."

"Come on, we'll get something to eat."

Val squinted at her. "What happened?"

Caroline's neck got even longer as she dropped her shoulders. "I adjourned the meeting after you went down."

"You threw them out, is what you did," said Kay, holding a dustpan while Decker swept broken glass into it.

"Well, I'd never seen such bad behavior. Dixon Foote, Martin, the others."

Sweeping, Decker didn't look at her. "And it's getting worse, Caro." His voice was quiet, and Val watched him move the broom in wide, precise arcs, like he was trying to outline the shape of the problem. Val grabbed a thirty-gallon trash can with one hand and dragged it over to them as Caroline said nothing for a minute and went over to the table at the front, near the fireplace.

"Well, what am I supposed to do, Wade? Not let them meet here?"

Kay emptied the dustpan, her fingers suddenly pushing gently at Val's swollen cheek like she was testing a cake for doneness. Her nose was flat and broad, her eyes dark, and she had the kind of face that seemed to be smiling even in repose.

"Three days," she wrinkled her nose at Val, "the swelling will go down. Keep icing it."

"Well?" Caroline turned with a sheaf of loose papers in her hands.

"I don't know." Decker seemed restless.

Caroline stacked the papers, shaking her head. "Just let them all fester in their own little places, without ever seeing one another, without—"

"I don't know!" He sent the broom sliding across the floor, then he dropped onto one of the long benches and ran his hands over his face. "They don't do anything for you. They break your glasses, they eat your food, they damage your stuff, and when it comes right down to it, Caroline, they won't do a damn thing to save your camp." He swiveled around to look at her, straightening up. "No, dear, saving your camp is the very last thing they'd all get together—somewhere—anywhere—to have a meeting about—"

"That's not true," she said coolly, brushing past him.

"—and you'd be a fool to think otherwise."

Caroline handed Val the stack of papers. "I'm sorry, Val. These are yours." It was Charles Cable's blank contract, warped from food that had soaked into the pages, and smeared with the prints of work boots. Caroline turned slowly to face Decker. "I know these people, Wade," she said with her chin high. "There isn't one of them who'd hurt me."

"Caroline, you remember them from when you were a girl. From when you were Trey Selkirk's kid. You and Leslie. But you don't know who they've become—"

"Why are you talking this way?"

"One of them killed Leslie."

"That's crazy. Someone broke in. Someone broke in and killed Leslie, Wade, and broke things, and stole—"

Wade looked hard at her. "The door was open." Val could tell it was old, old ground. And a futile effort.

"You're never going to let it go, are you?" Caroline Selkirk stood in the great room of her lodge, where Val had been knocked out in the brawl, where Kay was moving a broken bench into the shadows, where beer bottles were smashed underfoot, and food had been swept into the garbage can, and it was only then that she looked broken to Val. Broken and an easy ten years older suddenly.

"She was beaten up, thrown through a glass window, and fell two stories to the rocks."

"I know!" Caroline yelled at him, her voice filling the shadows.

Looking squarely at his sister-in-law, he said quietly, "Kind of hard to let it go."

So much for a Northwoods misadventure, thought Val, trying to breathe through the image of Leslie Decker's murder. Something worse than black bears and hypothermia was at work here. Her eyes slid to Caroline Selkirk. In the great room at Camp Sajo, where the campers of 1932 had talked about hemlines and Greta Garbo and the Lindbergh baby, the only movement was the rise and fall of Caroline's chest.

Val held the ruined blank contract and heard crickets rasping in the new night and stared at the closed back door where she had last seen Charles Cable as he left, disgusted, and what she found herself remembering was Peter Hathaway, making some offhand comment about Wade Decker's wife dying "unexpectedly" a couple of years ago. Somehow Peter's comment didn't do justice to the woman's violent death, and Val wondered whether there was anything her colleague, her boss, her lover, her love, couldn't belittle if it hadn't happened personally to him.

Val folded the papers—tomorrow she'd call Peter's office and get new ones faxed—and walked slowly to the garbage can, where Kay had pulled it over to the front doors, and let them flutter inside.

The three of them sat together on stools at the gleaming metalwork station in the Camp Sajo kitchen, while Kay dished up some quick bacon, eggs, and hash browns. At nine forty-five on a summer's night, the air was draped with the smells of a good breakfast. Val forked the food with her left hand while her right kept the ice pack pressed to her eye. Maybe it was the fact that Peter's pantry wasn't as well-stocked as Muffy and Lana had led him to believe, but she was ravenous.

Caroline nibbled at some triangles of buttered brown toast in a contented way, and Decker, one bare foot propped on the stool next to him, tried to glean something from the depths of his red wine. In the hungry silence, Kay scraped forcefully at the grill. Then, wiping her hands on a dish towel, she told Caroline the double sleep cabin could take overnight guests. "Good night, my darlin's," she finished, and walked away from them. "Just leave the dishes next to the sink."

"I can get you back to Peter's, Val, if that's what you'd like," Decker said, but he seemed tired.

She looked straight ahead, out into the dark, empty dining room, and shifted the ice pack. "I don't think I can get down to the boat." It was a strange exhaustion, like everything about her that had any weight at all had floated away, out of sight, and all she had left were the thinnest, lightest of membranes still attached in the vague shape of Valjean Cameron. "Who else is here?"

Caroline was looking better. "Oh, the maintenance boys, and the handyman." She cuddled her cup of rooibos tea, blowing happily across the top of the steaming cup, sending the spicy bark smell Val's way. It seemed to Val that naming those camp jobs was enough to send Caroline back to the glory days, when "maintenance boys" meant maybe ten, and not two. Still, it was *staff*. Val eyed Decker, who had a shrewd look like he didn't know how Caroline was going to meet her next payroll or ever come to terms with her sister's murder. Then his eyes widened at Val and he finished his wine.

"So, the meeting," said Val, cleaning her plate, and wanting to prolong the company. "What are they fighting about?" She felt like she was back at her desk on the twelfth floor in her happy office jumble of Matisse prints and Florentine glass and Fir Na Tine books mounting toward the ceiling, with a difficult author sitting across from her who can't quite say what he means.

Decker waited for Caroline to start, but when her hand stayed midair, where it had strayed, and she lifted her eyebrows, perplexed, he began. The permanent residents, lake and town, want a livelihood, which here in the Northwoods has always meant lumbering, mining, construction. The seasonal people—cottagers— pretty much don't want so much as two more boards nailed together anywhere on the lake because they see it as the old slippery slope leading to the destruction of the environment, at which point all of them—lake, town, seasonal, permanent—all of them lose.

The Ojibways want to make a livelihood, preserve the environment, and have their traditional tribal lands returned to them, many of which are sitting under tents, cottages, restaurants, and gas stations. And the outfitters, houseboat vacation merchants, and youth camp owners, seasonal businesses that depend on a beautiful environment for their living, push for ecotourism.

But ecotourism lets out the guys wearing the tool belts. Returning native lands lets out the folks who want to gawk at the loons and the sunsets from their cottage docks. Incorporating the lake community pulls the tax base out from under the town, but the environmental impact of twenty new cottages or lodges a year lowers the property values on the lake. There are the occasional flashpoints—claims get staked, illegal access roads get ploughed, whole stands of trees—Decker opened his hands wide—disappear, like a sleight of hand.

It's all provocation, and then meetings like tonight's ensue, although not usually with quite the same outcome. Bottom line? "For Dixon Foote, a three-generation lake man, who's a carpenter, to feed his four kids may mean new neighbors with dock lights and generators like a carnival sideshow right in the face of Martin Kelleher, who comes up here every summer from Philadelphia to get away from it all."

Caroline spoke up. "Wade, you're reducing the whole problem to—to—"

"What?"

"Individuals." Caroline leaned toward him, her eyes bright. "Whatever happens here will be a matter of law, finally, and community will. It won't come down to the actions of a couple of," she pronounced each syllable with good-natured mockery, "individuals."

"Of course it will." Decker gathered up the dishes. "It always does." He set them in the sink and Caroline turned off the lights, and the three of them found the screen door by the pale moonlight that was just enough to light their way. Val dropped the ice pack into her briefcase and fell in behind Caroline, who looked insubstantial on the path that wound slowly uphill. Behind her, Decker was lighting a cigar, the tip glowing with each draw. Caroline stopped, flashed her mini-light toward a double sleep cabin, where two rooms shared a common wall, then handed the light to Val. "This is yours. Sleep tight," she added, squeezing Val's arm, "and ice that cheek."

Decker came slowly up the path, saluting them, then moved around them on the porch of the double sleep cabin. "I'm just next door," he told Val. She watched him disappear into the adjoining room. "That's not an invitation," he added, whistling to himself, "in case you were wondering." A small toad hopped in and out of the circle of light from her flash. When she turned to thank Caroline, she was gone.

The aromatic smoke, the Big Dipper, the waxing moon. Val wondered whether things were less distinct, or more. Why couldn't she tell? To see landscapes of stars bursting backwards into the wilderness of the night sky, it means you've lost the moon for several days. She knew you couldn't have all of the moon and all the stars at the same time, but it felt small, and somehow human, to want to.

He was wrong.

Caroline leaned against the door inside her cabin, thinking about Wade. She set her Coleman lantern down on the table, and in the small circle of light, closed her muslin curtains. Somewhere outside she heard the crazy warble of a loon—the danger call. *Maybe we only think it's meant for other loons. Maybe we just need to read the signs.* But nothing frightened her anymore, if anything ever really did, not violence, not failure. Not even Wade's gloomy talk about lake and town people she had known all her life.

Her fingers pulled together the muslin wherever it gapped, the very same curtains her parents had at the windows when they ran the camp. Not even the lack of love, the lack of real love, in her life at forty, frightened her, because there were sweet compensations. And the possibility of long-lasting love was what kept her on her feet and in her right mind, against all the sorrows about her ghost camp, her crow's feet, and her sister's murder.

When Caroline and Leslie took over Camp Sajo, after Trey died and then their mother less than a year later, Leslie had made the old boathouse hers, and hired locals to make the renovations. And so on the second floor of the original boathouse built out over the water there came new flooring, bigger windows, skylights. Jobs for year-rounders, Leslie had said with pride.

Jobs for three weeks, Caroline noticed.

Caroline moved into their parents' cabin, where she would

never change the dark green Jotul wood stove, the colorful braided wool rugs, the log furniture that had held lucky young staff members invited in for an evening. Shelves for books had been hammered between the exposed studs, and finally there were so many books, shoved in, double-stacked, that she just left them alone, the out-of-date atlases, the discolored paperback mysteries, the hopelessly quaint nature chronicles. The funny old mustiness that happens, finally, even without water damage. The book-lined perimeter of the Selkirk living room had become part of the Camp Sajo history, no less than the framed camper photos in the lodge.

They won't do a damn thing to save your camp.

She didn't need them to save her camp. All the questions about Leslie would become tiresome, finally. Questions do. Given enough time, the lean times would get pulled away by the ice that always takes docks along with it, that day in the spring, usually in May, when the ice breaks up and the lake turns over. The ice goes, the frigid water returns, and life abides. Leslie's death, too, would go out with the ice, someday. It would have to. And the campers would return in numbers.

She set the Coleman lantern down beside the steamer trunk at the foot of her double bed. Family legend had it that the trunk had come all the way across Quebec with her ancestors after they had landed in Halifax in 1804. It wobbled, but the metal hinges still kept it all together, and the padlock Caroline had installed wasn't really necessary. No one else could possibly care about the contents.

She looked quickly at her watch. Ten minutes, maybe less, until that sweet man arrived, now that she could hear the deep nighttime silence that sinks into the ground on Selkirk Peninsula. Soon, then. While she waited, she lifted the heavy lid. First she pushed aside the t-shirt she herself had been wearing the day she and Leslie had been playing as kids on the ore crusher at the abandoned mine, when she had fallen and a piece of rusted metal swung free, cutting her across the belly. The dried blood had mostly flecked off, but the shirt was still creased from it.

She pushed aside the neck gaiter her father had been wearing the day of the avalanche, the neck gaiter that could keep out the cold, but not the suffocation. She pushed aside the periwinkle blue silk robe her mother, Hope, had been wearing when she got the news about Trey. She pushed aside an old glass jar with a sliver of steel in it, like a specimen, or a relic, extracted from a grandfather's eye. A rag doll from a great aunt who died of polio. A rosewood box that held her father's ashes in a plastic bag, like Miracle-Gro.

Then she came to the object that stood for Leslie, wrapped in what Caroline remembered was her sister's baby blanket that Hope Selkirk had knitted in the yellow and brown colors of Camp Sajo. Caroline was three, and had liked it very much, although Leslie, as she grew, did not. Caroline took it out and unwrapped it on her knees, coming to the eighteen-inch core sample, a gray rod of pure rock—although no copper—extracted from the earth, leftover from the brief mining explorations on Selkirk Peninsula.

In the light from the Coleman lantern she gazed at the core sample that Leslie used, for some crazy, Leslie reason, as a paperweight. It wasn't what had crushed Leslie's collarbone or femur or skull in three different places—the rocks below her window had done that—but it had been in the room with Leslie when the robber broke in. She could have defended herself with it, if only she could have reached it in time. Or thought of it. Or maybe even wanted to. But the cops had found it thrown into a corner, discarded, nothing but muddled fingerprints, when the robber trashed Leslie's place. Weapons, even Caroline knew, who had none of her own, were only as good as their nearness to hand.

All she had in the face of the cops' never-ending questions about whether she could determine what had been stolen, was the stark truth that her sister was broken and dead. So Caroline had been no help, no help at all, because she really didn't give any sort of a damn about what had been stolen.

You're never going to let it go, are you? she had said to Wade rashly.

And as she looked at him she felt like the old steamer trunk itself, holding the steel sliver, the stiff bloodied shirt, the useless hedges against that final airlessness, the orphaned doll, the clothing that never defends against despair, and the ashes, ashes, we all fall down. This core sample didn't need the trunk. It didn't deserve the trunk. This core sample was just a reminder of Wade's intransigence. Tomorrow she would take it deep into Selkirk Peninsula and hurl it away from herself and maybe her arm would go too. She set it, wrapped in the baby blanket, on the ladder-back chair, and closed and locked the trunk.

It was a small sound, but she had been listening for it, the sound of feet springing up her steps. Caroline Selkirk opened the door to the figure outlined in the weak moonlight. He was her finest consolation. Then she stepped back, both of them pulling her shift over her head, as she let in the very lovely Luke.

6

Waking up to the sound of a chainsaw, Val uncurled herself from the tight little congealed mass she had rolled herself up into in order to stay warm. Under the two thin blankets Kay had left folded on what had to be a counselor's bunk in this eight-bunk cabin, Val made herself a hard tight invisible object against the nighttime roving depredations of bears or Decker. But even keeping her clothes on hadn't helped against the morning cold. She liked Augusts that behaved like Augusts, the way they did back home on 51st Street—hot during the day, oppressive at night. Now that was a climate she could get behind. Not this sly Northwoods summer heat that pulls the rug, and apparently the blankets, out from under you when the sun goes down.

In the daylight, this Camp Sajo cabin was a blank space, plain square frames of bunks and shelves, everything stained dark sometime in the past, everything immovable from weight and habit and years. But it was a camp history the same as the lodge with all its framed camper pictures, because the rafters and walls and bunks were carved with graffiti, ghost campers memorializing themselves forever with signs and names, some just carved, darkening with time, some filled in with paint or charcoal or what looked like nail polish.

Steff, one girl had dug deep into the wood of the rafter.
Tressa, followed by a heart and the name *Keith.*
Mattie & Margo 4-Evah.
Leslie every summer til dead—swear.
Hagit '92-94. Shalom.

Brianne '65
Paloma '73-78
Wadin' in Wade. Oh, baby!
Foxy tripper boys.
Carvings of canoe paddles, shooting stars, and puckered lips. Pierced hearts with initials. Winged hearts with initials. Broken hearts with initials.

Trey is RAD.
Jean-Pierre—Awesome Tripper God
Moose muck!
The petroglyphs of teenage girls.

Val picked up the ice pack, which had flopped onto the floor during the night. Now it was just a sack of room temperature water. Which pretty much described herself. A cheap drugstore mirror was hung on a nail next to the bunk. Val unfolded her arms and legs and moved slowly into place to inspect the damage, squinting. Somehow the alternating rips and growls of the chainsaw outside fit the picture. The right side of her face had all the bloat and colors of a beached jellyfish.

The last time she had looked quite this bad was a couple of years ago on a miserable January day when she had been coming down with the flu and gone to the office anyway. Running to catch the crosstown bus after work, waving her bus pass, Val slipped on the ice. She took down the guy in the Army surplus jacket stomping next to a rickety metal display stand on the corner, where he was selling black velvet "artworks" of the Empire State Building. *'ey, look out, whatta you, crazy?* was his trenchant commentary as she plunged into him, and as they toppled toward the sidewalk, his head battered her cheek, and her boot caught the end of the display stand.

By the time they got their footing and a couple of passersby winched the two of them upright, her hair was wet from slush, which also didn't improve the looks of a few of his better velvet masterpieces. She ended up standing there, shaking, her hair dripping as though it was ink running right off her head, writing him a check for a hundred bucks. They argued. She felt her forehead: fever for sure.

She pointed out the sales he was making off four Japanese tourists in camel-hair coats who had been attracted to the spontaneous street theater Val had launched, the kind of thing you can expect in America. Finally, when she couldn't find her bus pass, a little Japanese girl with the tourist group pulled her over to the curb, where she nodded at the storm sewer.

Very carefully, Val kneeled down and lowered her head—her flat wet winter hair, her lips swollen from the rock-like skull of the purveyor of New York crap—to look into the storm sewer. Nothing. A yellow cab screamed by, close enough to spray her, and she could swear that it was Peter Hathaway lounging warm and dry in the backseat, and she cried for her lost bus pass in the black maw of the city storm sewer, where the only sounds that roared back at her were melted torrents of captured water.

In the cool Lake Wendaban morning, Val wrapped a blanket over her shoulders and stepped outside. Not quite eight thirty. The sunlight shot low through the trees, scattering like doubloons on the paths. At that moment Kay and Caroline came by, carrying an old, water-stained mattress between them. Caroline was wearing light cotton cargo pants and a bright green t-shirt. Her hair was still wet from a shower. "Bagels and coffee in the kitchen." She grinned at Val, then bit her lower lip. "Wade's gone, but he'll be back. Charlie's not coming for lunch."

Val shrugged the blanket tighter. "So, when—?"

"Wade said he'll see what he can do. Listen, there are a couple of jackets hanging in the office," she jerked her head, "so help yourself. And there's a fax machine. Use the landline, Val. Cells don't get a reliable signal here."

They shifted the weight of the mattress and then disappeared down the trail, walking into the scattered sunlight. The chainsaw ripped and growled and idled, and through the dense trees, closer to the lake, Val heard a loud crack and saw a small pine do a header toward the ground. "That's Luke," Caroline called back.

Back inside the cabin Val folded the blankets at the foot of the bunk where she had clenched the night away, grabbed her briefcase, the ice pack, and the flashlight, and headed for the chow. The mere offer of a cup of coffee made the hairs on her arms think about lying back down. First she'd tank up and then call the office. Ivy League Ivy, Peter's secretary, could fax her a new contract for Charles Cable. Not without some eye-rolling bad attitude, but she would.

I didn't graduate come loud from Brown for this, Val had overheard Ivy say on the phone to her mother, petulantly gnawing a thumbnail. As she breezed by, Val mused that the girl had an academic honor she couldn't pronounce, and Ivy League Ivy slung her an unusually well-wrought whipped-dog look—the one Val called poster child for Oppressed Workers of the World.

Val had no sympathy. Peter Hathaway was a dream boss, unless, of course, you were either sleeping with him or his equal. Toward Ivy he was undemanding, couching every request in "Would you please do me a favor?" He was unerringly silent around her, an absence of boss, a veritable Gandhi of corporate wonks. He bankrolled an ongoing lunch hour yoga class for Ivy League Ivy, who, Val suspected, just took the dough and bought stuff off eBay. Peter Hathaway really liked to be loved by people whose names he couldn't remember.

In the Camp Sajo kitchen she let the water run out of the ice pack into the gleaming industrial sink, and set the empty bag down on the counter. With a wet paper towel she dabbed at the nachos stain on her top, then gave up and cream-cheesed two halves of a bagel she didn't want to take the time to toast and poured a chipped mug of coffee from a pretty decent little Krups coffeemaker.

Tucking the briefcase up under her arm, she managed everything else and figured the shortest way to the camp office was through the dining room—where four young men were sitting together at one of the long plank tables, shoulders hunched over that final cup of coffee. One guy had vine tattoos snaking their way up his bare arms, and another sported a neo-mullet shaved high around his ears. Maintenance boys? Leftover counselors?

She winced a smile at them as she passed, and all four of them nodded gravely and went back to musically discussing the NHL. Her beached jellyfish look was nothing new for this group, who were apparently equal opportunity brawlers. Whoever Luke was, out there loose on the campgrounds with a gassed-up chainsaw, he was doing the heavy lifting at Caroline Selkirk's camp.

Val let herself into the lodge, which in the daylight had the kind of cool, weighty stillness of an empty church. Somehow last night she had overlooked the real chair of the meeting, a lugubrious moose head mounted over the stone fireplace, presiding over the madness. And here, closer to the entrance, were a couple of sizeable area rugs—nice Turkish flatweaves, from what she could tell. The rest of the camp buildings, at least the ones she had seen, had electric power, including the attached office, if it included a fax machine, but not the great room of the lodge. A propane nod to yesteryear.

She made a quick tour of the display cabinets, where she found memorabilia from the establishment of Sajo first as a fishing camp back in the late twenties. Those days were noted with some framed pictures of trophy fish being measured and weighed, and men in collarless shirts and narrow suspenders smoking languidly in rockers on the porch of the lodge. The times changed, the way times do, and interests began to collide. There were framed newspaper clippings of protests against the mining and lumbering ventures. In one, the beautiful blond, Leslie Selkirk, and a man leaning wildly off an ore crusher that had been toppled. The other protestors were crowded around them. "BIG WIND?" was the headline, and the caption read: *Leslie Selkirk and Charles Cable claim big wind damaged Regent Mining equipment.*

Another framed photo showed Leslie Selkirk and Charles Cable surrounded by followers on the steps of the Houses of Parliament in Ottawa. *Selkirk and Cable after historic vote to halt clearcutting.* A leaner Charlie Cable had an arm around her in a clinch, the other arm thrust high toward the camera, his fingers splayed in V for Victory. He looked strong through his shoulders and chest, his eyes glittering, a man whose picture was snapped at the height of his powers, the day he had everything he ever wanted. And that was even before he started writing space junk thrillers.

Ivy League Ivy deigned to pick up the office line after eight rings. "Ivy, this is Val Cameron."

"Oh."

"I need you to fax me another contract for Charles Cable."

"What happened to the first one?"

She's challenging me?

The girl was like roadwork: nobody likes it, it slows you down, it's possibly unnecessary, and you must proceed with caution. "It was damaged in a brawl." Let her wonder. If Peter had asked Ivy League Ivy for a new contract, she would have written one out with a nib and her own blood.

"Oh."

Val gave her the number and asked for Peter, who apparently hadn't arrived yet. She called his cell, and reached him at his place, where he sounded like he was dreaming, his words just an incoherent rumble. It was the first time they had spoken since the mattress histrionics of two nights ago.

"Peter, I need more time."

He was aghast. "You didn't get the contract signed yet?"

"No, it got destroyed in a fight."

"A fight? Are you sure you're in the right place?" There was a sound of splashing.

"What's going on? Are you in the tub?" By her watch, 9:16. "Aren't you going in today?"

"Daria's giving me a peppermint foot bath. And then I'm going in." In the background, Daria recited something from her own canon about *words, words licking the sap of fevered treeworks, a rind of love phloem combing through—*

Val felt like she was suffocating. "In pursuit of Charles Cable— and I do mean pursuit, Peter—I got knocked out—"

"Knocked out? What the hell's going on up there?"

"Your fishing buddies appear to be having a disagreement. And by the time I—"

"So you missed Cable. Is that what you're telling me?"

Her head started to hurt. "He's not a train, Peter."

"But you missed him."

All he had heard of what she was telling him was that the contract was still blank, not that she was injured. She set a hand lightly over the right side of her face. "Unconsciousness slowed me down."

"If I wanted a screw-up, I could have sent what's her name, the yoga girl—"

Some things even a peppermint foot bath can't help. "You didn't *send* me, Peter. You damn near begged me." Through the open window she could see Caroline heading her way. There was silence on the other end of the line, either while Daria Flottner got to a particularly sensitive zone on the man's fallen arches, or Val's boss, colleague, supersonically escaped lover was toiling through possibilities, looking for an appropriate reply.

"So what's the plan, Val? You're up there on the company dime." The tone improved, but not the message. He should have toiled a little longer.

Val's eyes felt like slits, her sight pinpointing a tree on the far shore, there at the top of the low ridge across from Selkirk Peninsula, and not a rind of love phloem anywhere around it.

"Val?"

The plan?

At thirty-four, did she really have to account for herself? Caroline Selkirk came into the office, shot Val a smile, and started rummaging through the small drawers in her rolltop desk. Val resisted the urge to hand the phone over to Caroline and let her fill Peter in herself on the feud. Instead, she realized she was speechless, without even baldheaded lunatic poetry of any kind.

The silence stretched.

Peter Hathaway finally plucked an appropriate remark out of the peppermint splash in his sterile epicurean condo. "So," he ventured, "are you—" Why was it so hard? Was he worried she could possibly mistake it for a marriage proposal? "—all right?"

Val pursed her lips tight. She could take his opening for a few moments of description—gaveled into oblivion, waking up the poster girl for a new line of cubist cosmetics—followed by something frank and sad about finding herself dropped into other people's battles when she couldn't even identify her own. But then the protective inner voice she had heard now for plenty of years, the one who felt like a dear friend, said *don't tell, don't ever tell, not him, not any of them.* It seemed driven by the sound of little drawers slamming—Caroline at her desk—and Val found that very practiced, lying voice no one could say wasn't her own. "I'm fine," she said, and quietly hung up.

Val stood staring at the utterly silent fax machine as she waited for Ivy League Ivy to do her job a thousand miles away. Caroline, pushing back a wet forelock, was boxing up some separate piles of folders, old mail, staplers, papers, rolled up maps, power cords, and coffee mugs. When one carton was full, she ran a quick line of strapping tape over the opening, then scrawled CHARLIE in thick black marker on the top. She was finally getting around to organizing this camp office, she told Val, what with all her beloved "migrant workers" moving onto their own places.

Wade Decker had called the camp office his "uptown" location while Leslie was alive, when they spent so much time here at the camp that he needed to telecommute. Peter Hathaway had holed up here with his laptop, catching up on work, a few years ago. A cottager friend of Hope Selkirk, Caroline's mother, had a start-up cottage-decorating business while Hope was alive and she could use all the camp office equipment for free. A mining company had the run of the place for a while, when Trey was looking into leasing the mineral rights to Selkirk Peninsula.

Caroline strapped and marked another carton WADE. Over the sound of the chainsaw another noise drew closer, the steady drone of a motorboat. Caroline leaned toward the windows, squinting, then set down the tape gun. "Looks like Martin's coming to call. Come on, Val." She opened a locker in the corner, eyeballed Val's feet, and pulled out an old pair of tennis shoes, and then, from behind a long jacket, a rifle.

"We'll see what Martin wants, and then, if you like," she shut the locker door and handed Val the shoes, "I'll show you the scene of the crime."

"Where...your sister died?"

"Different crime," she said, snorting softly. "An illegal access road. I check it once a week for as long as I'm here, just to make sure work isn't," she made a wry face, "progressing." Caroline detached her keyring where it was looped to her cargo pants, and from the locked bottom drawer of the locker she pulled out an ammo box.

"And the rifle?"

Caroline smiled and rippled an eyebrow. "Well," she said, widening her eyes, "maybe work's progressing." The idea of bushwhacking with an armed stranger through the wilderness was making the prospect of whiling away the day waiting for Ivy League Ivy to fax a new contract look pretty appealing. "Just protection, Val," Caroline said softly. "If I were a dangerous woman, I'd be dead," she loaded a round, "or rich," she loaded another round, then looked up, "or married."

Val pushed her feet into the tennis shoes and wiggled her toes. They'd do. She laced up. While Caroline locked the ammo box and returned it to the drawer, the fax machine whined into service. Val waited for the pages, watching Caroline go through an open wire bin—"The camp Lost and Found," she explained—and pull out a navy blue long-sleeved t-shirt, which she tossed to Val. "Here. Compliments of the house. These things hardly ever get claimed. We'll put your own shirt in with the wash Kay's doing today."

When the last of the contract came through, Val stacked the pages and set them inside her briefcase. She was just about to slip out of her soiled shirt when Caroline called out, "Morning, Martin, what brings you back to the Rumble in the Jungle?" Val saw a man step up to the outside of the office window, backlit by the soft morning sun.

"Need help?" He straightened his arms against the window frame. Val sprang up the step, back into the cool and shadowy silence of the great room, where she traded tops in ten seconds flat.

"All taken care of," Caroline announced in a high, competent way.

"Are you coming outside or shall I come in?"

A man accustomed to talking the talk on his own terms.

"Out," Caroline called back at him, steering Val with one hand and toting the rifle with the other like an off-duty drum majorette—a little casually, considering it was loaded. So much for Caroline's definition of dangerous.

7

They rounded the corner of the lodge, where Martin Kelleher met them, shaking Val's hand. It would take more than high winds to move this man, whose every cell seemed crammed with confidence. Late fifties, maybe? He had the square, solid feel of a guy who used to be an amateur boxer and was still light on his feet, wearing a snug white polo shirt with a green Sierra Club logo over the breast pocket, khaki shorts, and Topsiders. Altogether a one-percenter, Northwoods-style.

"Quite a scene last night, Caroline," he said, flattening out his mouth in the slightly disgusted way of a boss who's just pointed out an underling's goof and waits for an explanation. Certainly less hysterical than Peter Hathaway, who would have been filing police reports, nattering on about too much Pitta, and pouring them all some nasty dishwater tea she suspected didn't do him half as much good as his Zoloft. But, then, she was angry.

"Was that my fault?" Her voice was light.

Martin Kelleher widened his very blue eyes. "It was everybody's fault," he said, folding his arms, "except yours."

"Thank you." Caroline stood like a Minuteman, gently working at the dirt on the path with her rifle butt. The two of them nodded at each other for a few moments while the invisible Luke ripped and growled, felling another small scraggly tree.

"You took the brunt." He eyed Val.

"I was trying to get to Charles Cable."

Caroline leaned into him. "Val works with Peter Hathaway."

He scrutinized Val, nodding. "And Hathaway wants to sign him, is that it?"

"That's it."

Martin Kelleher crossed his arms. "Well, you would have been better off waiting outside for him, since Charlie Cable takes off at the first sign of trouble."

Caroline seemed restless. "Oh, not the first."

He gave her a wry look. "Actually, you're right. He's usually long gone before the first sign of trouble."

"He never used to be that way. The fight went out of him. He's the most radical of all the—the—"

"Environmental bloc?" His brow shot up.

"The most radical, and the least—"

"Visible."

"You can still count on him, Martin."

"If you're a loon."

Caroline looked out over the water, her eyes narrow. "He'd say the loons deserve the help—and people don't."

"So he has the loon chick project. I've told him the change in loon breeding is just one of the effects of pollution and habitat destruction. All the more reason he should stick around for the fight." Martin tipped his head toward Val. "Especially now that the fight comes with punches."

"Violence is nothing new," Caroline said wearily. "Not for any of us, Martin."

His eyes narrowed. "You're talking about Leslie."

She was surprised. "No. No, I mean the graffiti, the vandalism at the boat landing near town. The sneaky things." With a frown, she added, "Leslie surprised a robber. Or else she got in somebody's way."

"You would think that's hard to do in the wilderness."

"She died in her apartment in the boathouse, Martin. Not quite wilderness enough."

He changed the subject. "Remember, dinner tonight, our place. It's time we get organized." With a quick shift of his jaw, he went on to say the only way to save the lake is for the environmentalists to form a special interest group.

Caroline blinked. "To do what?"

"To raise money, to market the cause, to run for municipal office, to hire legal help—"

Caroline scratched her head. "Martin, half the cottagers are Americans, like you. You can't run for office."

"The other half can. And I damn well expect them to."

Her voice dropped. "This is a bad idea. A special interest group is just going to antagonize people."

"Well, if that's what worries you, learn to like casinos and Sea-doos, and *E. coli* levels that'll make Lake Erie stand up and salute."

"These are good people, Martin. They won't let the lake go down."

He looked at her shrewdly. "Caroblind."

A sharp intake of breath. "Where did you hear that?"

"It's what Leslie used to call you."

"It doesn't mean she was correct. My big environmentalist sister Leslie is dead. I'm still here, Selkirk Peninsula is my property, and Camp Sajo is still open."

"Caroline, wake up and smell the cesspool. Camp Sajo is water sports and wilderness fun. If kids start going home with mysterious rashes and say their night hikes took them right by some nice neon signs for high limit slots, those parents in Toronto are suddenly going to start thinking horseback riding camp in Virginia is a damn nice alternative."

Caroline suddenly burst out laughing, then turned to Val. "This is what Martin and I do. We wrangle. We're each other's best whetstone, eh? We try out all our best arguments before taking them on the road." Val thought Martin looked doubtful, but on that face, it was no more than an amused flicker. "Ask Diane what I can bring tonight," she said, hugging him with one arm.

"She'll say 'nothing.' She likes to cook."

Caroline patted his granite cheek. "She does it well, Martin, that's not the same thing as liking it. I'll bring artichoke squares."

Martin looked at Val. "Dixon Foote got you." He knobbed at his nose with a fist. "He was aiming for me."

"He wasn't aiming for you, Martin," said Caroline impatiently. "You always think someone is aiming for you. Val just got in the way."

Like Leslie Decker? All Val herself had done was intercept a punch. But in Leslie's case, there must have been so much more at stake. Exactly what did Decker's wife get in the way of? She had been beaten up and hurled through a glass window two stories to her death on the rocks below. There was some kind of rage at work that made Val shiver.

Martin Kelleher gave Caroline an inscrutable look. "Seven tonight. And tell Wade." Then he started down to his boat. "Oh, and Val," he said, half turning, "if you get an audience with Charlie Cable, ask him about his new book."

"*The Asteroid Mandate?*"

Martin snorted and kept walking. "No, the other new one. The one where he lays all of us out in a row like a shore lunch. Ask him about that one."

"Martin hasn't read it," explained Caroline, as she slung a black backpack over her bronzed and bony shoulder, and he only happened to hear about it from one of the barge operators on the lake who was transporting the new kiln his wife Diane had ordered for her studio. Apparently he had just come down the lake from delivering supplies to Charlie Cable—well, as close as he could get them, before the moose muck portage, where Cable had to meet him.

While they transferred the supplies off the barge into the flat-bottomed steel boat, Charlie Cable had been railing about how all the subterfuge and dirty tricks the lake and town people had been up to were getting exposed in his new book like goddamn crayfish in the moonlight. *Man hasn't been right in the head for a couple of years now*, Tippy the barge operator had commented. To Caroline,

Martin added that surely Charlie Cable wasn't right in the head long before that.

Val's shoulders slumped. *Wasn't right in the head* was not the sort of considered opinion she needed to hear about the elusive author she was enduring night terrors—followed by day terrors—to find and sign. Her mind naturally landed back then on the *Downy* incident. Was Fir Na Tine's desperate near-miss with the sex offender down the street really—as Peter Hathaway lost no opportunity in suggesting—a failure of Val's own due diligence? What if Martin Kelleher was right, and Charlie Cable was...off? Where was Val Cameron's due diligence on this one?

"There are gaps," Caroline said over her shoulder to Val, "in all our personal histories." Cable hadn't lived on the lake full-time until the wilderness cabin went up two years ago, so maybe his life down in Georgian Shores, where he worked as a stringer for the local paper—"Oldest stringer in the history of the Western World," Martin had scoffed—included a family. As Caroline spoke, they bushwhacked their way farther into the wilderness of Selkirk Peninsula.

"What does Martin Kelleher's company do?" asked Val.

"Cintorix?" Caroline shrugged. "Couldn't tell you. And where did Dixon Foote's wife go, considering no one has seen her for four years now, and he's got the kids?" Caroline came to a stop at a place where the forest seemed dense. "And Leslie," she said softly. "Oh, yes, Leslie."

Val looked around uneasily. "How she died—"

"What the hell she was doing back here at Camp Sajo in the first place."

"So, she—"

"She told Wade she was visiting me in Peterborough. She wasn't. On October 6, she came back to camp."

"And you don't know why."

"We'll never know why." Caroline stood still, her arms hanging loosely at her sides, as if the full realization of that mystery had finally sunk in. Then: "Just another gap." They had reached a place dense with birch and maple trees and more undergrowth, including wood violets and red toadstools. Caroline pushed on, and there was nothing for Val to do but follow her because she sure as hell didn't want to be left behind and alone. As she crunched twigs underfoot, she found herself wondering why Leslie Decker made a sudden trip up to the lake from Toronto that weekend in October two years ago, well after the season was over, without telling Wade—or Caroline— where she was going.

The two of them pushed aside branches from a couple of spruce saplings and stepped into a clearing that'd had a lot of help, depending on how you looked at it, from man. On the north side of the clearing was a small cliff just one story high. And coming around it, having chewed through the wilderness of the Selkirk Peninsula, was a dirt road wide enough for a small truck, easy, and enough passing room if one traveler pulls way over. The only sounds were birds rustling in the undergrowth, flapping lightly across small branches, searching for food.

Val and Caroline were alone.

Caroline strode to the dirt road and looked around, kicking at some stones, her fingers restless on the rifle. Val picked burrs off her pants, jumping at a sound that turned out to be a red squirrel skittering its way up a red pine. She felt her guts lurch, and she looked around wildly. It was probably a bad time to get straight on the subject of bear strategies—were you less likely to be mauled if you banged pots or played dead? Climbing a tree even Val knew was a mistake, because then you could pretty much count on being mauled *and* falling out of a tree.

Caroline indicated the access road. "I hired a backhoe operator—someone who works for Dixon Foote, actually—to block the way. I don't know who's behind this, but I figured I'd make it more of a challenge." She leaned against the rock wall, where the cliff began to slope upwards from the unfinished road.

"How did you get a backhoe in here?"

Caroline laughed, her red waves falling back from her face, then watched a couple of noisy crows hop heavily in the treetops. "I used their own road. About ten kilometers out of town there's a turnoff for a legal road—an old logging road called the Timberline Trail. These guys," Caroline swept a hand at the road, "whoever they are, came 2K down Timberline with their heavy equipment and started working their way down Selkirk Peninsula from there. That's where I had my own people put up 'No Trespassing' signs, for all the good it's done."

"But it made you feel better?"

"Surprisingly, no."

Val looked around at the wilderness, which still seemed dense, and at the crudely plowed road that was causing so much trouble. "It seems like a lot of bother, doesn't it? Why would these guys—"

"Hunters, fishermen—"

"—not just drive on down to the landing and then get where they're going by water?" It made no sense to Val.

"The expense, I suppose. Marina fees, dockage fees. And the time. If they're hunters, this road—" she kicked up some dust and stones, "—opens up a whole new range for them. If they're fishermen, a little four-wheel drive brings a ten-horse motor down the road which they can then clamp to the boat they've left turned over in the bushes down by the water, and they're off."

"Only they can't get to the water yet."

"No, not quite." She smiled, curling a hand over the barrel of the rifle. Then she stood up quickly and set the rifle upright in the cracks of the rock wall. Val watched Caroline Selkirk unzip the small backpack she had brought and pull out what looked like a rod of solid gray rock, maybe a foot and a half. She held it up like a wand. "This is a core sample. Survey geologists drill down and bring up core samples, which tells them what the minerals are, and whether it's worth mining. This one," she moved it in the palm of hand, as though weighing it, "was my sister's paperweight."

"Where would you even get something like that?" Not a common household object.

Caroline shrugged. "Behind the camp there's a footpath that goes straight to an old mining camp. Selkirks have owned the

Peninsula for about a hundred years, and we've prospected a few times." She held the core sample up to the sunlight and scrutinized it. "I guess we can never quite believe we get more minerals in a multivitamin than we do from a total of forty-two acres of land." She grinned. "Last time was when I was a teenager, and my father was hoping for some windfall as a hedge against hard times. Leasing the mineral rights would have done nicely. It was the closest any Selkirk had ever come to mining near Camp Sajo itself."

"Still nothing?"

"Nothing. In a crazy kind of way, I think my father was relieved. When none of these damn things—" she held up the core sample, "—yielded enough copper to make a full-scale mining operation worthwhile, he polished off half a bottle of Jack Daniels and said, 'Well, I guess at least I don't have to destroy the camp to save the camp.'"

The sunlight brightened the clearing just two steps away from where Val was standing, and without a word the two of them moved into it, turning their faces upward. Caroline went on: "It was the only time I'd ever seen my father drunk."

"How did he save the camp?"

"In the end, I'm not sure he did." Bending, Caroline pinched off a hard, waxy green leaf. "Leslie kept this core sample as some kind of reminder. She told me it helped her focus." Caroline lifted her shoulders. "On what exactly, I couldn't say." She scored the leaf with her fingernail and then held it up to Val's nose.

Val sniffed. "Wintergreen?"

Caroline let the leaf drop. "My dad took a second mortgage on our house back in Peterborough and then there were some difficulties with campers, bad PR—"

"Like what?"

"Twenty years ago a kid named Marcus Cadotte died on one of our canoe trips, drowned, which led to months of questions about supervision—" her voice was tightening up, "—which had been just fine, of course, but it was a terrible accident. Hard for us to come back from." Caroline drifted to some place in the Selkirk past where damage control measures were kicked around at a somber dinner table. "When money got tight my father decided to up the ante on the publicity coming from his own exploits. But by then he was pushing seventy and just got caught in an avalanche when he damn well knew what the weather conditions were. Finally," her chest heaved, "he just couldn't swim up."

"Swim up?"

"Avalanche training. You're taught to swim up through the snow. Dad was done swimming up—through anything, I think. Snow, financial uncertainty, life. My sister Leslie said he died doing what he loved. I said no, he died doing what he used to love—what he never would have found himself doing at the age of seventy if it hadn't been for the final bust at copper prospecting. Or the bad PR over that camper's death all those years ago. Sajo had never recovered. Leslie went crazy, and we could never talk about it again."

"So there's been no more prospecting."

Shaking her head, Caroline explained that all that's left of those days are rows of dilapidated shelves holding trays of core samples, where the old mining camp used to be. Everything rotted over the last thirty years. Rotted and scattered.

As Caroline pushed back her hair, Val noticed how brown and weather-beaten her hands were. Like the walls of the Sajo cabins. "The old mining camp is like a monument to human failure," said Caroline quietly.

So is Camp Sajo, thought Val. And so is the woman standing in front of her with only a rifle set awkwardly against the years of bad luck. "I'm sorry." She didn't know what else to say.

"Don't be." Caroline Selkirk leaned close and wrinkled her nose. "To tell you the truth, I like it. And as long as I own Selkirk Peninsula, there will be no more prospecting, no more logging, and no—" she raised her voice, and pumped the rifle for good measure, "—access roads for hunters too cheap and lazy to go the goddamn long way around."

"You can't protect it forever," Val pointed out.

Caroline let out a bleat. "You're right. I can't. In fact, I can only protect it another two years."

"What do you mean?"

The stately redhead tugged reflectively at her long tanned neck. "The ninety-nine-year lease expires."

"Lease? All this Selkirk land is just leased?"

"Five generations of my family have been on this land," she told Val, her jaw set. "It's ours. Ask anyone."

Val tried to keep the disbelief from showing on her face. "What happens when the lease expires, Caroline? Do you lose the camp?" From what Val was hearing, Camp Sajo was vulnerable to more than one way to disappear forever.

"Remember, the camp is a separate parcel. In two years, the rest of Selkirk Peninsula reverts to Crown land." Then Caroline left her at the base of the cliff and headed toward the wilderness still untouched by any trail from the camp or illegal access road made by trespassers. Away from the place where someone was just waiting to clear the next meter or two in the inexorable shortcut to the lake.

"Which means?" Val called after her.

"Which means the Queen can pitch a tent on it or clearcut it. It's hers."

Val watched as the embattled owner of Selkirk Peninsula stepped nimbly over fallen logs and sidestepped undergrowth until her bright green top disappeared into the forest.

At this point in the season, Val thought, while Caroline Selkirk stood watch at Camp Sajo—Caroline with her loyal cook and industrious handyman and hockey-loving goldbricks—the road was blocked, the clandestine work postponed. But...why? Why hadn't the secret road crew cleared Caroline's rocks? Why the delay? They've got heavy equipment bigger and tougher than anything Caroline Selkirk could muster. Surely her little roadblock must seem like a fly on a lion to those folks, whoever they are. All it would take is a swat. So why hadn't it happened?

What was Caroblind missing?

Despite her roadblocks and rifles, Caroline Selkirk couldn't stand watch forever as the days shortened, the temperature dropped, and the few remaining lake dwellers drifted home for the long winter. For a moment there was complete silence, even the crows content, and suddenly Val heard the sound of leaves tearing, twigs breaking. Then nothing. In a little while, a glimpse of a green shirt pushed toward her in the clearing, and Caroline emerged.

The core sample was gone.

8

When they got back to the camp office, and her bear issue was happily unresolved, Val realized just how hard her heart had been pounding. She looked around as she followed Caroline Selkirk into the camp office. At least on the grounds of Camp Sajo there were enough wide open areas she'd be able to see seven hundred pounds of danger coming at her, perhaps with enough advance warning that the playing dead issue would resolve itself.

Noting the chainsaw and rough-looking work gloves that had been set on the porch, Val stepped inside the office where a man was leaning against the desk, in a narrow slant of sunlight, downing a can of Coke. Dressed in a faded red t-shirt, jeans, and tan work boots, he had brown hair pulled back in a ponytail and the kind of face that looked good with permanent windburn. Val put him in his late thirties.

Caroline headed straight for the locker. "Val," she tossed back, "this is Luke Croy, friend and camp handyman."

Luke set down the Coke and straightened himself away from the desk. He was slender and tall, and for someone who hauled and hammered and stacked, his handshake was surprisingly gentle. "Kay tells me you're here for Charlie Cable."

At least he had the tact not to mention her shiner or swollen face. Val nodded. "I didn't know it was going to be a blood sport," she said with a little laugh, catching sight of Kay just outside on the path heading down to the boathouse, a white laundry basket tucked under her arm.

Setting the rifle in the locker, Caroline slammed the door shut and spun the combination lock. "I'll make some calls, Val. We'll track him down. He's probably having eggs and hash browns in town."

At which Luke Croy shook his head. "Well, if he had his eggs and hash browns, he had them pretty early this morning," he said. "Lake grapevine says he hired Portage Airlines to fly him home."

Val felt herself sag.

Caroline shot her a sympathetic look.

Luke went on, "Caroline, you've got some decisions to make about those black spruces down at the waterfront. Want to take a look?" He spread his arms wide. "I'm a man in full chainsaw mode right now."

Caroline gave him a smile. "You win. Let's go," she said, jerking her head toward the office door. As the two of them left, wrangling about whether it was better to thin out the cedars or the spruces, Val slipped out of the office and headed to the boathouse where she caught up with Kay Stanley.

"Morning, Kay."

The woman jumped, nearly dropping the laundry basket. "You surprised me," she said with a hearty laugh. Val watched her reach behind a black shutter for a key. "How's the swelling this morning, Val?" she asked, giving her a quick look, then unlocking the bright yellow front door. Someone had painted it over with swirling green vines and blue flowers.

"A little better, I think," said Val, not at all sure, her fingers patting softly at the cheek that stood farther out from her face than it should.

Kay stashed the key behind the shutter. "Come on in," she said, and swung the door wide. Inside the boathouse Leslie Decker had renovated and called her home, Val let her eyes get accustomed to the low light. Right near the front door, a set of narrow wooden steps led up to the second floor, where that day in October two years ago Leslie had met her killer. Val eyed the staircase, wondering how she could get invited to see the upstairs room, and giving it up for now.

Kay was all business, setting herself up in front of a short row of commercial washers and dryers. What looked like two of each. Giving Val an apologetic look, she waved a jug of detergent, saying, "After Leslie died this place worked out good for camp stuff like laundry. Storage." Her thick, competent hands started stuffing thin, well-used white towels into one of the washers.

Val scanned the room. The interior walls had been left unfinished, and it was clear the boathouse hadn't been winterized. But here, too, a few of the vertical studs had been painted with green vines and blue flowers. Leslie? Some were left undone. Maybe just a small thing cut off by her murder. But Val warmed to the look, like living in an illustrated fairy tale, and wondered what it said about Decker's dead wife. Slashes of sunlight slipped through the horizontal spaces between the boards, falling on the broad plank flooring that Leslie had installed.

Just then Kay flicked on a switch and two rails of overhead track lighting sprang into life. Against the near wall was a sleek, built-in kitchenette in stainless steel and high-gloss maple. But stacked against Leslie's high-end workspace were rusting bed springs, three-legged chairs, unglued table tops, and stained mattresses.

Along the long wall overlooking the rocks where Leslie had landed in a torrent of shattered window glass, broken masts for camp sailboats were piled in front of three overturned old canvas canoes with cracked and faded yellow paint. Life jackets that had seen better days were tossed on the heap. And then there were baskets storing what looked like chipped crockery, hurricane lamps without chimneys, camping skillets without handles—junk. And lots of it.

A broken Leslie in a place of broken things.

But then Val noticed the far end of this downstairs room where the beautiful new line of casement windows looked out over the lake, and saw what was left of Leslie Decker's home. A gleaming black wood-burning stove of a modern circular design. A daybed with thick off-white throw pillows set in an expensive, dark hardwood frame. A matching glass coffee table. A Persian rug. In caches built into the studs in the wall overlooking the water, Leslie had set a collection of natural crystal lamps that must've been beautiful when lighted. More fairy tale.

Val shot Kay a glance. "Leslie had some very nice things. What's it like upstairs?"

Kay kept shaking her head. "I haven't been up there since it happened," she said breathlessly. "It was Leslie's bedroom before she got married, and also her office. I don't think Caroline cleaned it out at all after the police finished up." Then she added with a little shrug, "Neither has Wade."

"Why not?" Why enshrine a murder scene?

When Kay lifted her arms helplessly, Val could tell it was something that bothered her. "Oh, I wanted to clean it up real good. At first she let me mop the floor—" here Kay's head drooped, "—but no more. I threw out a couple of broken things, a lamp, a flower pot, that sort of thing, and I put the furniture back." At that Kay Stanley looked Val in the eye. "A couple of chairs got knocked over in the fight before, well..." And her mouth went grim.

Before Leslie was thrown out the window.

"Can I see the upstairs?"

"Oh." Kay looked shocked. "I thought you understood. Caroline doesn't want people going up there." Just one more rule at Camp Sajo...

Val leaned across the broken masts that blocked the side windows, craning to see the rocks below. "Who found Leslie that day?" she called over to Kay, who suddenly stood still.

Turning slowly to Val, she said, "I did." As the washers churned away at threadbare camp towels and the distant rip of Luke's chainsaw indicated some decisions had been made about spruces and cedars, Val listened to Kay Stanley describe the day Leslie was murdered.

Kay lived alone in the town of Wendaban, just behind the train station, no family left, not since her Pa up and died on her just a few years ago. But before the lake freezes and winter weather hits, she runs her little boat out to Camp Sajo once a week just to check on things. There's no permanent caretaker anymore—too expensive, and Caroline just can't swing it. Kay likes her mornings at the empty camp. When nobody at all is there, she can still think it's a proud place, a successful place, a place with a fine history. And all the ghosts are just the high, remembered voices of healthy young folks over the decades.

But that day in October...Kay shook her dark head sadly, looking down at nothing. That day in October was really the end for Camp Sajo, after all the lean years even the charming, hardworking Trey Selkirk couldn't help. The morning was cool but the wind was still, and she was glad to be out on the lake on just that fine day. It was almost enough to make her believe that things would turn around for Caroline and Leslie's beloved Camp Sajo, that campers as numerous as the stars in the Big Dipper would swarm the property next summer. As she headed into the West Arm, she could almost hear the ghost voices rising above the treetops, carried out to her from the best past years of Camp Sajo.

But as she got close, Kay Stanley knew right away something was wrong: a second-story window in the boathouse was open. No, not open, gone. But how? And through the gaping hole that had been the window, the sheer curtains were dangling against the outside wall.

And then she saw the rocks.

And she couldn't make sense of what was on them.

Clothing?

With shaking hands, she managed to dock with a thud and nearly fell out of the boat onto the warm wooden boards. As she struggled to her feet, she glanced quickly out over the lake. Flying east, well out of range of her yells, was a black and silver speedboat she didn't recognize.

Kay Stanley ran toward the boathouse where something was terribly wrong. Only she slowed as she got close enough to see what was on the rocks, too close to tell herself a moment longer that there had to be a reasonable explanation. Someone had dumped clothes out of the second floor window. Someone was sleeping on the warm rocks. Someone, someone. Finally, not just someone.

Leslie Selkirk Decker.

Kay walked the last twenty feet on legs she didn't recognize, legs that must belong to somebody else, smaller, slighter, less in need of support. She felt white-blind from the sight of the bloody, broken body, the kind of blind where the world goes clean, scrubbed white on you. She stumbled those last few feet to the body of the girl she had known from infancy, willing Leslie to stand up and shake herself off away from the glass and blood and broken bones. With her white-blind eyes fixed on the dead girl's back, Kay howled at a morning that changed everything forever. Somehow Leslie Selkirk Decker had fallen out the window to her death.

Finally, with a long, sad look at Val, Kay said, "And there she was, and I—" She stopped talking suddenly, tipping her head. Her eyes narrowed as though she was trying to make sense of a sudden recollection.

"What?" said Val softly, standing with her arms folded.

Kay shrugged, laughing just a little. "Funny I only just remembered..." She grabbed a rag and wiped down the lid of the washing machine. "Rounding the tip of Selkirk Peninsula, almost out of sight. If only he'd heard me, he could have helped." She bit her lip, knowing there hadn't been enough help anywhere on the planet that day for Leslie. Leslie in her high-end storybook apartment painted with blue morning glories forever open. "Charlie." She gave Val a fond little smile.

Val felt a chill. "Charlie Cable?"

It was the stern of the boat Charlie keeps at the municipal dock in town. Definitely, nodded Kay. "It's a Stanley all-aluminum boat," she said proudly, "and it's got two little flags, port and starboard, he flies off the stern—the Maple Leaf and the Jolly Roger. Well, that's Charlie for you."

So Charlie Cable was on the lake the morning Leslie was murdered. As his future publisher, assuming she could wrestle him to the ground and get his signature on the contract, Val felt disturbed, her heart pounding. How could she get more information about what he was doing in his silly Jolly Roger boat that morning? Had he gone to the cops once he heard about the murder? If he had, wouldn't Kay Stanley have heard about it somehow? And if he hadn't...why not?

Suddenly she knew due diligence when it stared her in the face. In the case of the problem with the author of *Downy*, all along the way, due diligence had failed horribly. The agent, the publicist, the cops, Val, Peter, Ivy League Ivy, CEO Henry Schlesinger himself—any one of them could have discovered the truth about the author, but it was Val who took on the responsibility. Now here in this wilderness called Wendaban, where the author of *The Asteroid Mandate*—who was thought to be "not right in the head"—was spotted near the scene of the murder, due diligence fell like an anvil across the trembling shoulders of senior editor Val Cameron, and no one else. All hers. All.

The door swung open and a brawny blond man in a Roots t-shirt stood leaning in the doorway in a bright square of sudden sunlight. Kay kept sorting the laundry, her face tight with the memory of the murder. "I figure I can make it up to you," he called over to Val.

Then she recognized him. "Ah," she said. "Dixon Foote." Backlit by the sun, even the veins on his biceps stood out. Which may have been part of the problem when his fist had hurtled toward her face. Long in the waist, he wore loose-fitting work jeans and Teva sandals. A bit of a belly pushed at his waistband.

"There's been a Cable sighting." Now he had her interest.

Val approached him. "Where?"

"Putting up cranky signs at the landing, near Portage Airlines."

How was that going to help her, the ultimate landlubber? "And?"

"Come on." He waved her over like he was organizing his kids for a ride in the car. "I'll take you, but it's got to be now. My way of saying sorry for the KO last night." He rubbed at his nose.

She gave him a wan smile. "How can I refuse?" Although the

prospect of getting into a boat—at least she hoped it was a boat—with the man who had decked her but good was pretty tepid. Still, the chance to catch Cable had fallen into her lap and, while she permitted herself some good brooding time over the murder of Leslie Decker, some altogether new company—even Dixon Foote—seemed appealing.

Kay pushed a hand at her. "Go," she said, "go. I'll set your top back in the office when it's dry, okay?"

With a quick shout goodbye to Caroline, who was walking toward her on a path along the waterfront, Val followed Dixon Foote as he headed down to the docks, noting he was a bit bowlegged. He had a jerky vitality, the sort of guy who waits impatiently for the next task to shimmer at him in the wings of his life. His shoulder blades tucked back so far they were nearly touching, he led with his chest, like a street fighter.

Tied up at the first dock was one boat, maybe forty feet long, the pontoons keeping it level with the surface of the dock. In just a few long steps Dixon Foote was ducking inside a tiny wheelhouse of weather-beaten wood, and then an outboard motor the size of a doghouse rumbled into life. Painted in beige and covering most of the side of the wheelhouse was a disembodied foot outlined in black. It had a rough heel and curling toes and bore a strong resemblance to the kind of appendage she'd seen in illustrated editions of "Jack and the Beanstalk." The foot hovered over bright blue ripples and a single word in big glossy letters, CONSTRUCTION.

Dixon Foote waved her aboard, which was when Val saw that the "logo" decorated the front of the wheelhouse too. She was guessing the other two sides hadn't escaped the gigantic foot. With her arms floating at her sides to steady herself, she walked straight onto the deck, which sported thin, wet old indoor-outdoor carpet worn clean through to the fiberglass in some places.

Suddenly Dixon Foote charged out of the wheelhouse, cast off the lines, and ducked back inside, yelling something to Val she couldn't hear over the motor. As they started to pull away from the

Camp Sajo dock, she stumbled closer to the open side of Foote's commercial barge and longed to be back where her favorite form of dangerous transportation was a Yellow Cab.

9

Val clung to the frame of the wheelhouse and stepped inside next to the skipper. After a few minutes of no conversation, which Foote passed by whistling "Bad, Bad Leroy Brown" through his teeth, Val realized that chasing down Charlie Cable on the Foote Construction barge was like joining a high-speed car chase on a scooter. A river cruise on the Rhone could putter along at that speed and seem incredibly romantic, when maybe the only thing you wanted to catch was a good night's sleep and not the elusive bestselling writer of the kind of crap professional editing careers depended on. Off one side of the barge, she could swear a cruising duck passed them.

"Can you let it out all the way?" she asked Foote, not even sure that was quite the way to suggest anything at all about speed, barges, and desperation. Still, she tried to sound optimistic.

He gave her a serene look. "She's running full throttle," he explained, which Val took to mean this was as fast as it got. "Fastest barge on Lake Wendaban," he added proudly.

Eventually they oozed around the islands closer to the beginning of the West Arm of the lake, and Val took a long look at Charlie Cable's old place, where a small shingled cottage had been boarded up and the rubble of the boathouse he had dismantled was heaped behind his TAX THIS! sign. The work of a madman? Someone with the kind of anger that gets him turfed to a court-ordered anger management class? Did it signal the kind of rage that leads to murder? Maybe writing space junk thrillers was this guy's occupational therapy. The rest of the property was overrun with late-flowering purple weeds. Maybe, given enough time, the weeds would hide the rubble, hide the crazy sign.

"Kind of an eyesore," she put out there to see Dixon Foote's reaction. After all, her personal ferryman, a lifer on this remote lake, was no natural ally of an eco-warrior like Charlie Cable.

Dixon Foote snorted. "Agreed," he blurted. "But I got to feel a little sorry for the bugger. Poor old Charlie can't get his messages sorted out. Municipal taxes keep us strong, you know," he flicked her a quick look, "and strong means less likely to go after the prospecting and timbering he's been fighting for decades," he said slowly, negotiating some shoals peeping out over the surface of the water. "But he went kind of wrong in the head after that Decker woman died."

Or maybe just a minute before, thought Val.

No, *wrong in the head* was definitely not going to play well under the author photo on the back cover of *The Asteroid Mandate*. She started to feel the kind of queasy that had nothing to do with seasickness. All she could do was listen while Dixon Foote spoke up over the rumble of the motor.

"That place is cursed, that Camp Sajo, all the way back, back even before the blond went out the window. Back before the dad, that mountain man Selkirk himself—" here Dixon Foote flung up a hand in a futile kind of a gesture, "—back before the old man fell off some mountain and the family didn't know which end was up anymore. They lost campers when those things happened. Who'd want to go to a camp where the black flies eat you alive, and it can rain like hell for weeks, if now the famous guy was dead?" Foote looked around, trying to find just the right idea to make his point. "It'd be like going to a Stones concert after Mick Jagger's in the ground, see what I mean? And the killing of the blond, well, that's the sort of thing that makes people nervous, you can understand."

Val thought she could.

"But the curse on that Selkirk camp started all those years ago—" Dixon Foote punctuated the idea by pushing the air and years away from himself, "—when that Cadotte kid died on one of their wilderness canoe trips." Dixon himself was twenty-seven at the time, but his cousin Max Foote, who was nineteen, was one of the counselors on that trip and was there when it happened. "His life was hell for months after that, what with cops and media and so on—and the old guy himself, Trey Selkirk, fired him right away. He called it a blot on Sajo's perfect safety record." Selkirk was trying for some damage control, everyone on the lake thought, giving interviews about what a fine lad the fourteen-year-old Marcus had been. Terrible accident. A scholarship kid. "Selkirk kept emphasizing that," Dixon Foote glanced at Val, "making it sound like scholarship kids were a dime a dozen at his precious fancy camp."

"Weren't they?" asked Val, interested.

He snorted at her. "Are you kidding? Far as I know, the Cadotte kid was the first ever, with nothing special to recommend him, from what Max told me. Barely passing in school. Living all the way off in Newfoundland with adoptive parents. How did a kid like that suddenly get on the radar of a place like Camp Sajo?"

It was a good question.

"Poor Max and the other counselor, Belinda Conroy, wanted to send the parents a condolence card—pretty stand-up, I thought, considering," he said, eying Val, "but when they went through the camper files, they couldn't find the usual paperwork on the dead Marcus Cadotte. Even Selkirk's own kid—that blond who went out the window—she'd been assistant counselor or whatever they call them on that trip, she couldn't get any address. Which—" Dixon Foote said quietly, narrowing his eyes against the sun as the lake opened up and he headed for the landing, "—was enough to make me believe that something else had to explain the only scholarship kid Camp Sajo had ever taken."

Squinting at the landing, where already she could tell there was no soft-in-the-head old Charlie Cable tacking up cranky signs, Val felt distracted.

"What are you saying?" she slid a look at Dixon Foote, who shrugged.

"I always thought there had to be some kind of personal connection between that kid Marcus Cadotte and the only person who could ship the kid in from Newfoundland, write off all the expenses, and waive the paperwork."

Val waited.

"Trey Selkirk," said Dixon Foote, downshifting. "Besides, the kid's death broke the guy. They lost the kid, they lost Selkirk, and they lost the camp."

While Dixon loaded an order of two by twelve boards he'd ordered from the local lumberyard onto the Foote barge, Val scuffed through the gravel at the landing with her hands on her hips. The only other people in sight were a couple of what she could only call strapping young men unloading eight green canoes from a rack trailered behind a pickup truck with WENDABAN OUTFITTING CO. painted on the side. Their hair was clean, their teeth the bright white of sheer youth and no cigarettes, their bodies naturally lean. They were swinging canoes around as easily as if they were grabbing a box of cookies from a cupboard.

A small yellow school bus thundered into sight, kids' hands waving madly out the windows at the busy outfitters, voices high. Val figured them for the canoes' intendeds, and when the bus braked and the door groaned open, she gave them a wide berth and headed for the community bulletin board. Charlie Cable wasn't on the bus, or in the pickup, or hiding behind the bulletin board. How does the guy come and go so slickly? She scanned the notices. Some were handwritten scrawls seeking the return of a lost iPod, mutt that answers to Sheldon, and dock that had floated away in the ice breakup last spring.

The better signs flogged the community for contributions to lake-related charities, and one announced the annual benefit gala, a square dance in support of the Wendaban Youth Alliance. *August 16th, 7 p.m., Lake Wendaban Community Center, Municipal Dock. World famous caller Shelley Timms. Music by Finger Pickin' Pea*

Pickers. Quilt Auction! Come support our kids!

Only in this outpost of minimal civilization would a square dance be considered a gala. Val sighed, turning back to the teens pushing each other playfully and hauling their backpacks off the bus, loping over to the canoes that were riding lightly at the water's edge. Overhead, towering white clouds were bunching and rising in the very blue sky. A sky she'd love to see at home, but not here. At that moment she heard a shrill whistle and saw Dixon Foote waving her back, his hands on his hips, all the lumber aboard the barge. Then he pointed to a boat idling fifty feet out, *Camp Sajo* peeling on the side.

Caroline Selkirk stood at the wheel, Kay Stanley sitting beside her. Val hurried onto the Foote barge and went to the back, the closest she could get. Caroline cupped her hands around her mouth. "Wade called. Charlie got taken out by plane from the landing."

"Taken out?"

Caroline smiled. "Taken back to his place in the wilderness," she hollered. "Wade called the pilot."

She didn't get it. "Okay..."

"Told him to let Charlie know you two are coming."

"Oh!" So they were going to corner the fox in his den. It was finally going to happen. A signed contract. Or an exposed killer. Either way, the trip home. Standing there in the August heat, she got a chill. No, more like a thrill.

"He'll pick you up at four."

"Today?"

Caroline gave a tight shake of her head. "Tomorrow. He's got work to do, and tomorrow's the earliest he can do it," she called. "He'll fly you."

Well, there had to be a downside. In this case, two downsides. A day's wait—Peter will be so thrilled—and a small plane.

At that, Caroline Selkirk ran a hand through the thicket of her red hair, then jerked her head toward Kay Stanley. "We're going into town to pick up mail and buy provisions..." *Provisions.* The kind of word that sounds like wilderness adventures. The teens at the landing, heading out with packs and canoes, they had provisions. Caroline Selkirk had words. But Val found it oddly touching. "You'll come with Kay and me to the Kellehers' tonight," Caroline threw back at Val. A smiling Kay lifted a beefy hand as Caroline shifted and the Camp Sajo boat cut through the water. Once she cleared the No Wake zone, the motor roared and the boat zoomed around a bend in the shoreline, disappearing white in the persistent summer sunlight.

And there she was, Valjean Cameron, left behind on the slow boat to China. She spent a useless few moments wondering—as Dixon Foote settled himself happily back in his little weather-beaten wheelhouse—if the barge had been faster, would she have caught Charlie Cable there at the landing before he got spirited away by some local flyer? Would she have been spared a return trip set upwards of twelve thousand feet in the company of a man whose wife had met such a spectacular and mysterious end?

Behind her the outfitters were shouting instructions to the teens who huddled, smoking, and weren't too cool to squeal as they loaded their packs into canoes. It struck Val that Caroline Selkirk and her sidekick Kay would probably be away from Camp Sajo for a few hours, what with just getting all the way to town, picking up mail, food shopping, and whatever other stops they had in mind for "provisions." Unless Val was mistaken, what had just fallen into her lap was an opportunity.

The barge might move at the speed of the last Ice Age, but Val had to give it points for stealth. When Dixon Foote sidled the forty-footer up to the Camp Sajo dock, Val shook his hand, thanked him for the effort, and saw him on his way. From what she could tell, her arrival hadn't drawn anyone's attention. No hockey-loving goldbricks. And, more importantly, no handyman Luke Croy. She had no desire to antagonize anybody with a power tool. But maybe he was off in the brush with noise-canceling headphones somewhere. Still, he wasn't checking out the Camp Sajo dock to see who'd arrived.

Val scanned the perimeter for movement and sound. No distant voices. No doors lightly shutting in the still morning. Nothing but a couple of noisy crows cawing high up in the treetops. Then she hurried to the camp office, where she slipped noiselessly inside and grabbed her briefcase. Stepping back outside, Val stood on the low porch and glanced around. Still no Luke in sight.

She could justify hanging out around the camp office if she came across the handyman, but not what she was about to do in pursuit of information on Charlie Cable. Her first true act of due diligence. If Cable was just a little wrong in the head, Fir Na Tine could deal with it. The same could be said for half their authors, anyway. There were days when she suspected it was a prerequisite to a book deal. But murder? If Charles Cable had anything at all to do with the death of Leslie Decker, any talk of a contract was over. There were plenty of things she would take a chance on in this life—for instance, coming up to this godforsaken place to placate her boss—but just assuming the cockeyed best about Charles Cable in hopes of swelling Fir Na Tine's bottom line was not one of them. In a matter of seconds, she found herself in front of the shutter next to the door of the old boathouse. With one last quick glance behind her, Val eyed the sad old empty camp, then slid her fingers behind the loose shutter and drew out the key.

10

A quick turn in the lock and she had let herself into the Camp Sajo junk room and laundromat, then slipped the key back into place behind the shutter. Once inside, she turned the lock on the doorknob, pressed the door shut, and moved soundlessly up the stairs to Leslie Decker's private space. The murder scene. With any luck at all, she'd discover some overlooked piece of evidence that would pluck Charlie Cable right out of her suspicious mind, where he was starting to loom like a homicidal backwoods coot in *Deliverance*. Something. Something the cops might've missed two years ago because they were already looking at the crime a certain way. A robber. A husband pushed a little too far—

No. Put that possibility right out of her head. Because to let it marinate there meant she was either being flown by a killer or to a killer, and nothing she had endured in the last years with Peter Hathaway could even prepare her for either of those truths. She looked around, a tougher thing than it had been on the first floor. The plywood board nailed over the window pretty effectively cut off any light from that direction.

Leslie Decker's private space, a room placed off limits by Caroline, was pretty much the way Kay Stanley had described it: untouched. Kay may have swept and straightened up after the cops were finished with it, but dust had settled over every surface like a thin, dry snowfall. It reminded Val of an attic where nothing ever changes in a limbo of disuse. In this space devoid of life, where the remaining windows were shut up tight and the sun heated the semi-darkness, the only scent was what the unfinished pine boards of the walls gave off.

Val crossed the large room to the window that looked south, toward the far tip of Selkirk Peninsula. She was surprised to see a fire escape just outside the window, rusting metal steps leading down to the narrow boardwalk that ran around three sides of the building. Next to the bottom step were two large, cylindrical propane tanks. Out the other window, the western exposure, all Val saw was forest. Somewhere in that direction was the illegal access road that Caroline was monitoring. The morning of her murder, had Leslie Decker seen trouble coming?

Val stood in the center of the room and did a slow 360, taking in what the murdered Leslie had left behind. Then she moved methodically around the space. Near the top of the stairs was a small but functional bathroom that would have been right at home in an Airstream. The toilet paper roll was almost at an end, one half-torn sheet still hanging, forever hanging. A mink-colored plush towel, shoved hastily onto a towel bar, had long since dried. A plastic bottle of Alba Botanica body wash was nearly empty. A bottle of Alpha Keratin shampoo, nearly full. Val unscrewed both tops and sniffed. She didn't know what she was looking for, but the bathroom seemed disappointingly normal...right down to the two blond, desiccated hairs trapped forever in the shower drain. Suddenly the dead woman seemed disturbingly close, and Val was struck by how the merest things of life outlast the flesh and blood— the dried, cramped towel, the shed hair, the toilet paper torn by fingers long gone.

Suspended from the ceiling next to the john was a rack holding a few clothes Val forced herself to riffle through as minimally as possible. A dusty Lily Pulitzer dress. A couple of Banana Republic shirts, one yellow, one melon. Two pairs of slim Ann Taylor pants. In a large, square canvas bin on wheels was a jumble of colorful lacy camisoles, Reef sandals, thongs, a floral bikini. On the outside of the canvas bin was a small wash of spattered blood. Duly noted? Overlooked?

The most imposing piece of furniture, in a tidy kind of way, was a large cabinet of some kind of expensive hardwood on the wall between the two windows. Tugging at a handle, Val peeked inside at a Murphy bed. No blankets, but fine Egyptian cotton sheets in sage green. Was the bed up or down, in or out, at the time of the murder? Why had Leslie Decker lied to her husband, telling him she was visiting her sister? What was behind the lie—an affair? In which case, maybe the bed was down and deployed and Leslie had fought for her life with a crazed lover. Val always hated crazed lover scenarios, whether she found them in the lives of her friends or in fiction. They always seemed like the easiest, tawdriest explanations for anything. Like Daria Flottner.

What else could be behind Leslie's great lie the final weekend of her life? A secret meeting of some other sort? Did the woman have that kind of life? A Persian rug stood rolled and vertical in a dark corner behind the S-shaped glass and chrome desk that dominated the other half of Leslie's upstairs room. Attached to it by a stiff wire was a cleaning tag. So it had been sent out for cleaning after the crime—blood?—but nobody had the heart to put it back down on the floor. Or take it out forever.

An Aeron desk chair stood at an angle away from the desk, as if Leslie Decker had just pushed herself back to greet somebody coming up the stairs. Stacks of papers ranged over the desk, hastily tidied, probably by Kay Stanley in that moment in time when Caroline needed something to be done at the scene, to reassert some normalcy over the grief and awfulness, before she closed it off for good. Thumbing through the stacks, Val found the papers to be the same stuff in anyone's life, murder victim or not. Printed receipts for books ordered online. Empty new manila envelopes. Post-it notes. Scratch pads—nothing incriminating, just doodles.

Brochures from Save the Children and Heifer International. Old flyers from Lake Wendaban events—including the annual fundraising square dance "gala" for the Wendaban Youth Alliance from two summers ago. A couple of two-year-old *People* magazines. Alumni directories from Trent University and Humber College.

Nothing had any bookmarks or dog-eared pages to point Val to a useful clue. Somewhat in frustration, she took the Trent alumni directory and shook it open. Two slips of paper fluttered to the floor.

Deposit slips for an account at Toronto Dominion Bank. Was it the Camp Sajo account? Did Leslie Decker do the bookkeeping up here in her upscale renovated boathouse? Thirty grand, forty grand, dated a month apart. Leslie had to keep better records than this. But where? Any computer equipment had been removed. At any rate, the camp must have been doing better than Caroline was letting on—at least as of a couple of years ago. Val set aside the deposit slips.

Then she tackled the final dark corner on the same wall as the boarded-up window, where one large covered basket and two metal boxes were lined up alongside each other—stored upstairs, Val noted, and not downstairs at Leslie's. Interesting. The tightly woven basket had a hard shape with straps and ties and a flat side. On the hinged lid, CAMP SAJO was stenciled in brown. Above it, in sunny yellow, TREY. Val opened the lid and pulled the basket away from the wall to shed more light on the contents. It turned out to be a trove of random things, a catch-all of little things valued by the embattled owner of Camp Sajo. Val crouched by the basket, which was not even half full, and grabbed a handful of items she set out on the floor.

Homemade Valentines addressed to Trey.

A wind-up sailor toy.

A wind-up Yeti.

A wind-up Superman.

Some unopened packs of Smarties.

Unopened bars of Cadbury chocolates, years old.

Framed photos of Trey with different campers. Some with heart stickers glued all around the borders.

Unframed photos—even some old Polaroids—of Trey with different campers.

A pair of crudely knitted wool gloves.

A pair of more crudely knitted wool socks.

Postcards from far-flung campers after they returned home.

Crocheted neck gaiters in blue. In brown. In green.

Val could tell she was digging into a stockpile of all the little love tokens starry-eyed campers had presented to Trey Selkirk over many years of operation. She wondered if the drowned boy, Marcus Cadotte, had given him anything. Probably not, considering it was his first time at camp and he had never returned home. Never missed Sajo, never missed Trey. But over the last twenty years, missed everything else.

Val dug out a bunch of old photos rubber-banded together, slipped off the band, and thumbed through them. For the most part, small group shots, the handsome, craggy, buff Trey Selkirk at the center of every grouping, his hair graying over time. But in the earlier shots, before the gray, before the shoulders seemed a little more fragile, he was a compelling figure, a bright smile and crinkled eyes deathless in the summer sun. These pictures were all anyone would ever need to understand the concept of charisma.

He was gorgeous.

She quickly separated out a few shots of Trey Selkirk with family—a young Caroline, a younger Leslie, what could only be a windblown wife, Hope, looking ever so stalwart in a buffalo plaid jacket—and then shots of others Val recognized. A younger Martin Kelleher in his safari jacket, still a powerhouse of concentrated will, his arms folded, his stare seeing four moves down the road in the chess game, Trey's arm chummily around his shoulder. A much younger Trey Selkirk, Hope, and Kay Stanley with shoulder-length hair and bangs framing a slightly worried face—and off to the side, carrying canoe paddles, that face Val recognized across time from the back jacket of *The Nebula Covenant*: Charlie Cable. A Charlie Cable in an era when he still apparently cared to shave daily, caught mid-sentence, clearly ribbing the photographer about something. Taller even than the magnetic Trey, more powerfully built even than Martin Kelleher. Val re-banded this little stack of old photos and slipped them into her briefcase for a closer look later on.

Then she held up the old gaily painted kaleidoscope from Trey Selkirk's basket of treasures and saw—nothing. Pressing the eyepiece against her eye, she rotated the tube. Still nothing. Puzzled, Val tapped it lightly against the basket, her breath catching when it came apart in her hands. Inside the old tube was a roll of papers. She knew she was onto something, and her fingertips separated the papers enough to see that they looked like old letters, maybe a couple of camp forms. For this discovery, she wanted time and a whole lot more privacy than she could get trespassing at Leslie Decker's. Val tightened the roll of papers, slipped the tube back into place, and set Trey Selkirk's kaleidoscope into her briefcase, where it bulged at the bottom, but not too suspiciously, she thought.

She pushed the basket back into its place against the wall and checked out the two identical metal boxes. Old Army green, big enough to hold file folders and records of all sorts if you didn't mind ugly. Stenciled in white on the dusty metal lid of one was HOPE. Etched neatly with a knife on the front of the other was CAROLINE DUNGANNON SELKIRK. Neither had a lock. Val took a quick look inside Hope's storage box and discovered old knitting pattern books, straight and circular needles, stitch holders, and a skein of rainbow-colored acrylic. It was nothing more interesting than Hope Selkirk's knitting bag, camp-style.

Caroline's held a spiral-bound notebook filled with decent fashion sketches done in colored pencil, signed CDS. In the margins were funny little notes to herself: *Chiffon, Selkirk, really?* and *See if L. will model this when I run it up.* And next to a diaphanous blue nightie she had penned, *Too sexy for W.D.?* In another notebook, labeled THE LIVING HISTORY OF CAMP SAJO, WENDABAN, ONTARIO, CANADA, NORTHERN HEMISPHERE, THE WORLD, were the first few chapters of a book begun by Caroline, who saw herself as the camp chronicler. A quick look yielded nothing more scandalous than the camp's original building, back in 1899, as a Jesuit mission. The earnest little historian was careful to include footnotes everywhere. No photos, no hidden roll of secret letters.

No knitting, even. Nothing to shed light, all those years later, on the murder of her sister.

Val pushed the metal boxes back into place next to Trey's basket of collected presents, which was when it struck her. The whole Selkirk family had a box or a basket—except for Leslie. Val crouched closer to the floor and saw, next to Caroline's rectangular metal box, an empty space in exactly the same dimensions, where the dust had been disturbed. Leslie Selkirk had a metal box too. And not all that long ago, it had disappeared. In the stifling space upstairs at the boathouse, Val felt a chill.

Had it been the killer who found what he was looking for after all? With the room torn apart in the fight, with Leslie hurled through the glass window to the rocks below, did the killer then take his time, his very sweet time, and go through the things on her desk the way Val herself had done—finding, finally, two years later, just what he sought in an old green metal storage container that looked like it had been picked up for a song at an Army surplus store?

What was inside the box that must have been labeled Leslie?

Where was it now?

And who had such easy access to the murder scene to keep hunting for whatever it contained?

Had Caroline simply not noticed the box's disappearance?

At that moment, Val heard an unmistakable sound: below her, the door to the boathouse had been opened and someone stepped inside. Val sat utterly still, her heart thudding, wondering how in hell she'd account for herself if the newcomer headed upstairs. It couldn't be Caroline or Kay—too far off in town, too many errands. Luke? She wouldn't have thought the slender guy she had met in the camp office would be so heavy-footed. But maybe. Dixon, looking for her? If the eastern window hadn't been boarded up, she could stretch herself up just enough to see whether the barge had slipped back into camp.

Directly below her feet moved around, what sounded like boots rasping against the floor, then Val heard metal banging against metal. With any luck at all, whoever was moving around downstairs was looking for something among all the cast-off bedsprings—or adding something to the junk pile. The boots then moved back toward the door—Val sucked in a breath, willing him to go out, go out—and then came a footfall on the lowest step heading up to the second floor.

In that moment, two things became clear: there was no place to hide and Val, confronted, was going to tell the truth, because it was more excusable than any lie she could possibly concoct that would get exposed for exactly what it was in less time than it would take Dixon Foote's barge to move two feet away from the dock.

Discovered in Leslie Decker's off-limits space, Val figured anybody would understand that, as his publisher, she was looking around for evidence that either cleared or condemned Charles Cable of Leslie's murder.

Unless, it struck her suddenly, the man at the bottom of the staircase was Charlie Cable himself.

The heart-sinking truth of that possibility lasted only a couple of seconds, because then she heard the downstairs door open and the heavy, clomping feet leave the building. Val counted to ten, then counted to ten a few more times until she was sure the visitor wasn't coming back. And even then she didn't trust herself. Finally, tucking her briefcase under her arm, she gave Leslie Decker's upstairs room one last look around, wondering what she was missing, then slipped down the maddeningly creaky old stairs where she peeked out the front window. Not far from where she was hiding she glimpsed a figure disappearing down the path to the camper cabins. Red shirt. Jeans. Had to be Luke Croy, off to fell more intrusive trees.

Val quickly checked the pile of old bedsprings leaning up against the long wall under the windows. Here it wasn't so stuffy and still, unlike the upstairs, because people came and went all the time, tracking in wet, decaying leaves or brown, fragrant pine needles or their own sweat.

Tucked behind the first twin-sized bedspring was what looked like a rusty metal stovetop, missing its burners. Had to be Luke's new contribution to the pile.

She briefly wondered why Caroline Selkirk didn't just hire Dixon Foote to haul away all this unusable trash on his barge. Who was ever going to clean and repair all this worn-out old stuff? And who, then, would ever use it? Val ran her hands along the metal rail of a bedspring that would never again hold a sleeping camper. Something leftover from the days of Trey Selkirk, she was betting, and so, in the absence of Hope and Leslie and good luck and success, Caroline stored the things that had furnished the dying camp in those earlier times. Things that Trey had moved, things that Hope had cooked on, things that Leslie had sailed. Maybe, for Caroline, getting rid of all this trash was no different than tumbling her own personal history into a landfill.

Val poked behind a few small, three-legged tables. No missing metal box with Leslie's name stenciled on. She'd keep her eyes open for it. After all, what would the great activist daughter, whose crusading face hit the newspapers along with Charlie Cable's, keep in a fireproof box? Val felt a hopeless twinge that the hands that had carried it off from its place upstairs on that day in October had murdered Leslie in pursuit of the box's secrets. In that respect, she herself had something in common with Leslie Decker's killer.

At that moment, as she let herself out of the old boathouse, the chainsaw rumbled nearby, and Val listened to the unmistakable sound of its steady, merciless cutting through wood.

11

In the summer sunlight that seemed to be dodging heaps of clouds, there was still a good deal of heat, although also a good deal of loneliness. Voices floated distant, the unhurried shouts of workmen. Val wanted to take a quick nap and then clean up before going with Caroline and Kay to the Kellehers', but there was no way she was going to let herself drift off in this strange, ponderously quiet ghost camp. And a change of clothes she'd wear back in her professional life was not making any sort of miraculous appearance.

Alone in the camp kitchen, Val slathered herself a peanut butter sandwich, which she slid on a dingy Melmac plate pulled from the dish rack. Then she made her way along the path, slipped up the step to the porch of her sleep cabin, and let herself inside. She would wait out the return of Caroline and Kay and deal somehow with the uneasiness that never left her in this wilderness place people actually paid to experience.

At a small unfinished table by the crude window propped open with what looked like a free paint stir from Sherwin Williams, Val set her plate and her briefcase which, she was hugely pleased to note, looked like its fine New York self. While she munched the sandwich with one hand, the other clutched her briefcase to her chest the way she did on the subway, not at all suspiciously.

Grabbing the stack of photos she had found in Trey Selkirk's funny old strapped basket, Val spread them out on the table, halfheartedly arranging them in some sort of chronological order according to how old the Selkirk girls looked. She didn't know what she was looking for. And even if she found something important, how would she know? Aside from a very few faces—Trey, Hope, Caroline, Leslie, Wade, Luke, Kay, Charles Cable, Martin Kelleher, and Dixon Foote—who else would she recognize? To know a clue when it slapped her silly would depend on a familiarity with these lives that she didn't have. For a few deflated minutes, she sat there, letting her fingertips drum gently against the photo spread.

Little by little, things jumped out at her.

Wade Decker in one shot, maybe around eighteen, his arm slung around a Selkirk girl—only it was Caroline tucked in against him, her head thrown back, laughing. Off to the side, crouching, was a teenaged Leslie, loading "provisions" into a basket a lot like Trey's, her eyes inscrutably on her sister and Decker.

A snowy shot of Trey Selkirk on skis, smiling and relaxed, captioned *Whistler 1991.* He had pulled his goggles down for the photo, and Val thought those eyes probably looked best—and saw best—what was either in the far distance or no distance away at all.

There was a shot of Hope Selkirk and Kay Stanley at a quilt show, dated 1989, arms loosely on each other's shoulders. Behind them, in front of wooden display racks holding handmade quilts, was the quilter, standing with a tense expression and her arms folded, probably wondering if she had made a sale.

Then there was the shot of Leslie and Charlie, clearly jazzed by the public attention, on Parliament Hill on what seemed to be the same day as the picture that ran in the paper.

A scallop-edged black and white photo from the fifties, showing Hope Selkirk in her early twenties, standing proudly with what Val guessed were her parents and an older brother in front of a new '57 Chevy. No Trey. No Camp Sajo.

A Polaroid shot of Trey Selkirk and Kay Stanley, his hand clamped on her shoulder. A felt-tip scrawl had labeled it *Iqaluit, June 1981.* Val spent a moment wondering why they weren't in Wendaban, Ontario at Camp Sajo during a summer month. More than thirty years younger, Kay's face was thinner, her features caught in a time before they started to sink into the soft folds of age.

Her black bangs were cut thick and straight across her forehead.

The landscape in the place called Iqaluit was sparse, dotted with a few modular homes indistinguishable from one another. Trey Selkirk was standing companionably next to her, a man used to smiling into the sun that nearly cast them both into whiteness. He had one leg out, the way athletic people do, Val noticed, like he was ready to spring into action. There was a windburned handsomeness to the man, the kind of looks rough use only enhances. Val was just about ready to move onto the next photo when one final detail of the Iqaluit shot flooded her consciousness.

In June of 1981, Kay Stanley was clearly pregnant.

Val's fingers pushed through the photos, pulling out the one marked *Xmas 1981, The Gang,* and setting it next to the Iqaluit photo. Caroline and Leslie as roughhousing girls, Trey with a Santa hat rakishly on his head, Hope pointing down to her new boots, Kay holding a turkey baster, a balder version of Hope's brother, Charlie Cable with his head turned, caught mid-yell to someone off camera—all of them standing in front of a tall, full tree decorated in a happy, slapdash fashion. But no infant in sight. Given how pregnant Kay Stanley had looked in June, she should have had a baby in September.

Val's fingers nabbed any photo labeled winter and spring of 1982 that had Kay in it. No baby anywhere. Factoring in off-camera naptimes and hours in the company of possible babysitters, babies had a tendency to show up in photos. But not this one. And, jiggling the Selkirk Christmas photo between her fingers, Val suddenly remembered what Caroline had said offhandedly about Kay's never talking about her family, if she had any. Interesting footnote, thought Val, to her poking into the circumstances of Leslie Decker's death, but she couldn't see how Kay's mysterious pregnancy was relevant.

The sound of a motorboat closing in on the dock alerted Val. Standing quickly, she craned her neck to see if she could catch a clear view of the waterfront. Not happening. But she could make out Caroline's musical voice sailing out to someone—Luke? Val had to work fast, before Caroline came hunting for her. One thing for sure, she did not want to be caught thumbing through ill-gotten Selkirk memorabilia. Her hands surprisingly steady, she gently pulled apart the kaleidoscope she had taken from Trey Selkirk's basket, then lifted out the roll of papers.

She was right: letters. Every single one of them.

Short, handwritten letters.

From Kay Stanley. To Trey Selkirk.

Val let out a soft whistle, expecting a revelation of smoldering passions or an offer of a peppermint foot bath. But they were grateful and practical and even just a little bit poetic. *Dear Trey,* began one. *Here I am at Great Auntie LeFay's place just below the Arctic Circle. Thank you for the money and the promise of more if I need it. It's hard to say if I will. I am cooking for her at home. She's seventy-two now and tired of kitchen work, she tells me, and I will cook at her restaurant until the baby comes. The doctor just flies in once a month for everybody who needs him and he tells me what I'm feeling is called quickening. The baby is growing big enough for me to feel it. In some way I have to confess it all feels more like deadening than quickening, but I try to stay cheerful and think about your loving goodness, always.* She had signed it *Yours, K.*

Another, two months later, was more telling. *Dear Trey,* it began. *I am missing my life with you in Wendaban. Everything feels dark and far away, even the moon, and I am rubbed raw like this earth up here. Auntie LeFay, my only living relation, now tells me she has the cancer growing inside her in the same place I have the baby, but she is too busy right now to fly down to Ottawa for it. What will come out first, I wonder, this baby or that tumor? Thank you for helping me to do this my way. I confess I am ashamed, and I could not face Hope and the girls, but in this place where nothing is fake, I can do this. Can you come to visit? Will you have to tell Hope?* And again it was signed, *Yours, K.*

Val figured the photo of Trey and Kay, standing in that sparse, northern place where nothing is fake, came next chronologically.

There were two more letters dated that summer of 1981, with more talk about money, characters at Auntie LeFay's restaurant, and a growing belly. In one, she thanked Trey Selkirk again for his visit, and if he ever wanted to know the plans she has made for the baby, all he has to do is ask. She thinks while she passes children tearing around on their little bikes, dressed in her big, loose dress that sways when she walks, although the baby does not, that love leads to people. *But it doesn't always go the other way,* she writes. *People don't always lead to love, and doesn't it seem a shame? Perfect circles are only for bike wheels.*

The final letter was dated mid-September. *Dear Trey,* wrote Kay Stanley, *tonight I heard the wolves. They are out there in the night, close. Dodie Slocum, who cleans at the restaurant, brought her little dog inside. The wolves are telling me the baby is coming, and I am telling them this baby, this baby will be as invisible to me as the howlers themselves. We have quite a conversation, me and the wolves. When I leave Iqaluit, I want to remember the wolves. And I want to remember the baby. Although it will never remember me. And I cry a little because wolves and babies and tumors and Kay Stanley really ought to make sense—but only the wolves do. Yours, K.*

Val carefully folded the letters and set them back inside the kaleidoscope where Trey Selkirk had kept them. Hidden. She looked out the window and saw Kay Stanley, more than thirty years after she dated that last letter, lumber up the path to the camp kitchen, lugging bags of provisions. Even hard work didn't keep off the little fat rolls around her elbows. *People don't always lead to love, and isn't it a shame?* Even if—as Val was now wondering— golden man-child Trey Selkirk was the baby's father, that particular circle had been unclosed. The baby was gone. Interrupted lives were resumed. Secrets were kept from those they would hurt. And Kay Stanley had ended up as far from love as she had been from the Arctic wolves calling in the night.

Without thinking about them a minute longer, Val rubber-banded the photos and set them and Trey Selkirk's broken kaleidoscope back inside her briefcase. Somehow, later, she'd figure out how to return them to the murder room in Leslie Decker's boathouse. Val didn't like having secrets. She especially didn't like having other people's secrets, not when they didn't entrust her with them in the first place. The truth about Trey Selkirk and Kay Stanley and the baby that became someone else's was like finding a ten-dollar bill on a sidewalk while you're on your merry way somewhere the hell else. There's no way to return it. If you leave it there, it could go to waste. But if you take it, and you do, the lunch it buys is never quite worth ten dollars.

At dusk Val was standing in a clutch of bemused dinner guests on the Kellehers' multi-level cedar deck that wrapped around the sprawling cottage. Outdoor electric lighting came on automatically at the same moment someone named Clem Corcoran was extolling solar as the environmentally responsible choice. Some of the guests Val recognized from the brawl at Camp Sajo the night she arrived on the lake.

For dinner at the Kellehers', the men had slipped fishing vests over their Canoe Head t-shirts, and the women had changed from pants with thick elastic waistbands to skirts with thick elastic waistbands. Several had dolled up with stonewashed baseball caps with The Wendaban Moment machine-embroidered across the front, the back, or the bill.

"Ah," sighed a portly woman, pointing west with her green insulated stein full of lager, "there's a true Wendaban Moment, if you ask me." Everyone else spun to face the sun sinking as a great fuzzy pink blot in the sky over the distant mainland. They gasped. Another woman clapped her hands to her heart to keep it from leaping clear out of her chest. The sunset duly noted—"Number Three on The Best Wendaban Moments List!" Clem cried—the others fell into a competition that seemed to have more at stake than Val could understand.

"Best Wendaban Moment?" claimed a short woman with

shocked eyes and a floating raft of gray hair. "Millions of mayflies falling spent into the lake after their single day of life." With that, she turned to the others with a challenge in her eyes. *Top that, if you can.* This was followed by murmurs.

"Good," cried a tall man in nylon hiking pants and a white mesh hat with its brim snapped up on the sides, "but I go with the great blue heron fishing in the shallows. So elegant, so patient." Nods of agreement.

"Skinny dipping when the water's fifty-seven degrees."

"Loon chick riding on the mom's back."

"Foggy dawns."

"The Aurora borealis," breathed a woman with a frank, friendly face, trailing her fingers through the air over her head.

"Cindy Wilson," said Caroline with a laugh, "I swear you're the only one who calls it that." Martin Kelleher raised his glass. "Say Northern lights, Northern lights—"

Cindy knocked back a margarita. "It's my Wendaban Moment," she said with a frank smile, "and I can call it whatever I damn well please."

Sipping a Chilean Malbec, Val watched Martin Kelleher circulate with a platter of beluga caviar toasts. He approached his guests with a stern intensity that looked like he was giving them their choice of dueling pistols. Across the water, the light shifted and shadows lengthened. All that was left in the western sky was a vermilion cusp of a sun.

"Mine is that thunderhead with all those lightning bolts that time."

"What's yours, Caroline?"

Val glanced at the owner of Camp Sajo, where she stood in a loose yellow sleeveless shift, her silver bangles glinting in someone else's Wendaban Moment, and she smiled into her single malt on the rocks. "Mine?" She looked up at the cottagers who drew closer, curious and protective, wondering if it had been a thoughtless question, what with one Selkirk tragedy after another. Caroline's thicket of red hair was held off her face tonight with a wide gathered headband of teal and rose. "I have so many," she said finally.

"One, just one."

"No, two or three," someone coaxed.

Caroline's gaze passed them all. "Night fishing with my father," she said with a beautiful smile. Someone clapped. "Dancing at eighteen in the Sajo lodge—" she lifted her cocktail glass, "—with Wade."

At a flurry of "naughty, naughty" sounds and cautionary finger waggling, Martin floated behind her and whispered, just loud enough to be heard, "Keep it clean, Selkirk."

Everyone roared in a lively, bawling way that told Val they were waiting for something choice to go on about, and Caroline Selkirk had supplied it. Foggy dawns and dead mayflies just weren't going to do it.

Cindy of the Aurora borealis took that moment to jump in again, saying baldly, "And then that sister snagged him." *That sister.* The chorus of horrified gasps that followed might very well have qualified as Val's own perfect Wendaban Moment. Maybe she should buy a hat. "Well, what?" responded Cindy, splashing her drink. "She did!"

"And then look what happened to her," someone in the back actually muttered. As though snagging Wade Decker and getting hurled through a second story window were cause and effect somehow. The cottagers fell quite silent, their poor faces stricken. At the truth. At Caroline, who deserved better. At their indiscretion. A series of old lined lips hung open, waiting for something, something to make it all right again. Just a nice evening at Martin and Diane Kelleher's cottage, where the food was splendid and the drink was plentiful and the devotion to the preservation of the lake was shared.

Caroline stepped forward and grabbed Cindy in a hug. It was a fond and deliberate move, and Val felt impressed. "You're so right, Cindy. Leslie just up and snagged him. She was a quick one, that sister of mine. Do you remember the camp races every summer?"

Nothing quite like an appeal to the communal memory.

Spirits lifted. "No one could beat her!"

"Wade and I were just kids," she went on to explain with a dismissive little laugh. "I went on to other things, and Leslie Selkirk and Wade Decker teamed up for the long run."

"Those things happen," said a wise old head, nodding. And so does murder, thought Val, and sometimes those long runs aren't so very long, after all. She sipped her wine, noting that Caroline had defused a tense moment among Wendaban Moments without really explaining much of anything at all. Not what happened to her and Wade, not what led to Leslie and Wade, not what other things she went on to, unless it involved keeping a failing family business alive. And certainly not what happened to her murdered sister.

Val folded her arms as the little crowd fell back to blurting their favorite moments. A man with a buzz cut and a tidy little paunch suddenly blared, "That eight-pound pickerel I caught three years ago, that's my Wendaban Moment."

"Oh, Stan, you and that pickerel, enough already."

Others laughed nervously. But the gaffe with Caroline had made them all edgy and quantities of alcohol kept them there. Just as Diane Kelleher appeared in a black camisole and elegant white palazzo pants to announce dinner, Martin planted his legs like a captain on a quarter deck. Passing the tray of caviar toasts to Clem Corcoran, who seemed honored, Martin folded his meaty arms.

"With the acid rain levels on this lake," he said in a commanding way—never very far from a board room—"you won't be catching any more eight-pound pickerel, Stan," he shook his head at him, then kept going around the circle of guests, "and you won't be getting your mayflies, or you your great blue heron, or you your loon chicks, or you—" touching Caroline's perfect shoulder briefly, "or you your camp, Caroline."

Diane lifted her chin with a thin smile. "Martin." She cued him with a small gesture.

His eyes merely rippled at her. "Step inside, my dearest pals on this beautiful lake, and over whatever Diane has in store for us,

I'll share the latest environmental studies with you." They were definitely in for it, Val could tell. As the guests stepped haltingly past him, gabbling their alarm that now had nothing to do with Caroline Selkirk's family history, Martin threw in conversation killers like blueberry blight and eyelid palsy. At that point, Val expected a band to launch into a number about seventy-six trombones.

Val was just close enough to Caroline to hear her say quietly, as she passed him and leaned in, "Really, Martin. Any day now you'll equate tailings from mining ore with erectile dysfunction."

They gave each other a complicated look. "I don't have those figures," he told her with a tight smile.

"Not interested?"

"I stick to what's relevant."

Caroline's eyes widened, only slightly. "Lucky Diane," she quipped, and for some reason, Val thought there was something wicked afoot that had nothing to do with Leslie Decker's murder. As Diane lighted the tapers and fourteen dinner guests struggled with place cards and chairs, Val could hear in their chatter there was some generalized hysteria about declining property values.

Martin Kelleher was masterful.

If only he could mobilize the cottagers, property values would remain high and properties would stay off the market. But these berry-picking cottagers were in their sixties and seventies and maybe they were weighing the relative merits of working themselves silly, with no guarantees, for laws to protect The Wendaban Moment against selling out and buying some Disney timeshares. Martin Kelleher's master plan might well backfire.

Could Leslie Decker have made a difference?

Had she not been murdered, would she have been the perfect poster child for preserving the worsening Lake Wendaban environment that, to listen to Martin Kelleher tell it, would soon be held responsible for flatulence and ugly hats? Val ended the evening scrutinizing the dinner guests, trying to penetrate any hypocrisies that might have wanted someone to keep beautiful, blond Leslie Decker from the work she was born to do.

No obvious suspects jumped out at her.

All of them seemed perfectly appalled and sincere.

With possibly one exception: Diane Kelleher. When Leslie's name came up during dinner, in much the same way as people talk reverently about the miracle at Lourdes, only Diane stayed silent, swirling her wine. And Val suddenly remembered what Wade Decker had said about his murdered wife after the mêlée at Camp Sajo when they were cleaning up the messy aftermath. *One of these people killed her.* Caroline had scoffed, but Decker was very clear on that point.

But Charlie Cable had been at the meeting in the Camp Sajo lodge, however briefly, and hadn't been invited to dinner. Despite his being an environmental activist of long standing. Or had he been invited and declined? Was that life so utterly behind him? Or did he just try to minimize his contact with the sister of the woman he had beaten up and thrown out a second-story window?

Diane knew the signs.

She knew the signs before they even became signs. For instance, Diane knew her father was running around on her mother two months before her mother figured it out. He started wearing an ascot—of all the damn things—and Brut, the cologne choice of twenty-somethings, back when. Once, when they had gone to the Jersey shore without her, Diane poked around and found Grecian Formula for Men and gold chains so her Mayflower daddy could look like a goombah.

And there, lying in a dish on his dresser, any of them to see, was a phony New Jersey driver's license. Harlen March was now someone called Arnaldo Marchione. Apparently Mr. Marchione, who looked like a darker-haired version of her father the classics professor, lived on a nonexistent street in the next town. At eighteen, she was old enough to know he wasn't a spy. And she was young enough to feel the world she knew rumble beneath her feet.

So she had known Martin Francis Kelleher, Boston College distinguished alum, Wharton M.B.A., CEO of Cintorix Corporation, was sticking it where he shouldn't. Again. On the days she worked at her potter's wheel, her mind roamed over things. There was something about the rhythmic spin of the wheel, the feel of the wet clay under her thumbs, that led to strange moments of insight.

With Martin the signs did not include Grecian Formula or tacky jewelry. No, with him it was philanthropy. The more serious the fuck, the greater his contributions. The Arts League, the Children's Hospital, Our Lady of Perpetual Help Catholic Church. A year ago he was singlehandedly responsible for the new choir loft. Diane had come to think of it as Martin's guilt tax. She kept an eye on his contributions the summer he was boning a Continental Express flight attendant, and he only sweetened his annual membership to public radio by just a few dollars, which Diane took to mean the flight attendant was hardly worth the price of a room.

But these days Diane didn't know where Martin was stripping off his monogrammed silk boxers. Her best guess was at Stacy's, the robo-blonde Cintorix hired to head up inside sales, all the while making some inside sales of her own that were not included in the job description. There is always a woman, somewhere, eager to sleep with your husband. That much Diane knew. And Martin still had a kind of Irish streetwise charm that played well in airport lounges, boxing matches, casinos—all the places that poor kid from south Philly still inside him liked to prowl when he stepped outside the boardroom of Cintorix Corporation.

The money had just given him added luster. *I'm a halfway laddie*, he had told her when they were dating, which was just his way of telling her something about his background. He had grown up with two half-brothers in half a house with a driveway shared by another family and a father he saw only every other week. The yard, already small, had been divided by the landlord with an ugly vinyl and chain-link fence so each half of the duplex was clear on what's what. Diane knew his childhood had something to do with his hunger for land.

There was certainly nothing halfway left in Martin Kelleher, when some casual acquaintance brought him and another Wharton guy to the dance at Bryn Mawr. He was different from everything Diane March hated in those days, which was everything from fake goombahs to pathetic intellectual classics professors. *I'm going places*, he told her, and she knew it was true. And since she wanted to see how he worked it out, and the natural smell of him was greater than anything Brut could bottle, she found herself tearing at his pants in the back of his half-brother's borrowed Mustang just three weeks later.

Two weeks after graduation, they got married—Martin insisted on a full Catholic Mass at a Mainline Catholic Church—and as she sat there composed and slightly bored behind her white veil while the priest raised the Eucharist, she knew it had less to do with Martin's faith than it did with his certainty that this was the first influential club he could join in his bid for wealth.

The sun slipped behind the trees as Diane watched Martin oversee the activity on the dock. One gal started up her engine, which burbled loudly in the first slip, and shouted her anxiety about illegal access roads. Martin said something brief and cast off her line. Caroline stood talking with the woman from New York who had the angular brightness of that beautiful city, not to mention a shiner.

Two of the dinner guests settled into their tandem kayak and adjusted the straps on their Australian outback hats. The others spread out over the deck of a pontoon boat, topping each other with questions for Martin. One kept wanting to hire a lawyer, as if yelling it over and over again would make it either happen or worth doing. Another departing guest insisted a petition campaign was the way to go.

To Diane it had the sound of all the same old impotencies in the face of a dreary inevitability. Martin seemed unfazed, which meant he had something up his sleeve. Diane wondered if it had something to do with the calls she'd overheard during the last few months, the couriered papers, the closed doors, which, when she asked, he dismissed with something about diversifying. Was Cintorix starting up a mining subsidiary? A distinctly interesting possibility, but only because he wasn't sharing it tonight at dinner with his cottager coalition.

Caroline Selkirk shook hands with Martin and climbed into the Camp Sajo skiff, a lovely old boat that needed some work—like everything else at the camp, according to Martin. The gal from New York was huddled in her life jacket as Caroline, at the helm, waited for the pontoon boat to clear the dock. There was something in the way she waved at Martin, who nodded, that made Diane wonder whether the statuesque Caroline was Martin's reason for the choir loft. Diane narrowed her eyes at the first interesting idea she had come in contact with that whole night. Yes, Caroline Selkirk might definitely explain a big ticket, guilt-tax item like a choir loft.

Diane looked around at the first dab of nightfall, when the wind settles down. *Goodbye, Diane,* people were calling, the voices lovely, and they were all of them caught poised in a golden story about happy times among the rich. Diane waved to no one in particular while Martin stood stock still at the end of the dock, arms crossed, legs apart, like he was reffing a game, which was in a way always the truth.

And what, Diane wondered, did Leslie Decker have to do with whatever secret expansion Cintorix Corporation, a software company, was now experiencing? There was no one Diane could talk to about how very much she had disliked Leslie Selkirk Decker because, quite simply, everyone on this lake was either her family, her father's former employee, her gobsmacked fan, or her lover. Martin wasn't related, he had never worked for Trey Selkirk, and he didn't always agree with Leslie, even in public.

But Diane knew her to be what hardly anyone ever says about a woman anymore, that she had been dangerous, and it really had very little to do with the fact that in the year or two before Leslie's death, Martin began to mention how he was talking to the Arts League about starting an endowment for scholarships to young, disadvantaged artists. And there was that weekend itself, that weekend Leslie Decker went out a second-story window, when the Kellehers were home in Philadelphia, and Martin told Diane he was sailing the schooner down off the eastern shore of Maryland, where he could do some fishing and work on a big presentation. Alone.

She wondered whatever became of the Arts League endowment.

She knew what became of Leslie Decker.

But not entirely.

12

The hands set the dull green metal box on the table. It was a tall box, and wide, and deep enough for file folders, if that's what it ever held. Fireproof, Army surplus, old, any of which could be true—or not. Like its owner, about whom anything at all could be true—or not. It was thin metal, two small dents in front. The hands rotated the box: one dent in back, some rust. It had a lid that closed over the top, hinged at the back, and where a padlock would slip through the latch, someone had driven a thin and bent piece of metal. Probably the owner, right after she scratched her initials into the front, just above the latch: *LDS.*

Leslie Dungannon Selkirk.

Each line was scratched several times, either to thicken each initial, or make it more artistic, or make it clear once and for all that the box was her very own property. None of it had happened. The letters weren't any thicker, they certainly weren't artistic, and the box had only been Leslie Selkirk's property for just as long as she was alive. It was pure Leslie, after all. Nothing ever turned out quite the way she expected, but she was self-absorbed enough not to notice. It was an attitude that led to—trouble.

For a moment, the hands were still, resting alongside the box that had been stood up on the table. Then they slid out the piece of bent metal and opened it all up. The box was tilted backwards, and the contents slid out. A camera, a few photos, loose papers, clippings, a wallet, piece of jewelry, notebooks, little dollhouse toys, a jump drive wrapped and rubber-banded with a scrap of paper labeled MY FOOLPROOF PLAN TO SAVE OUR PRECIOUS CAMP.

Something on the level of bake sales, no doubt.

It was all old, old stuff. Nothing that would get the authorities any closer to figuring out what had happened to her that day in October—unless her theft of her friend Janie's Weebles Treehouse when she was ten finally caught up with her. The treehouse, according to the ratty spiral notebook used as a proto-diary by the girl Leslie, never found its way back to Janie's.

Janie has like twenty-seven Weebles, can you believe it? What a pig. And Janie has two, TWO! Weebles treehouses, went the rationale, *and can hardly use them both, who could? And besides, after I play with it just for tonight I will donate it to the giving tree at school, wrapped up of course so Janie doesn't see it, and some poor kid will get it and really really like it. BUT WHAT IF THE POOR KID WHO GETS IT DOESN'T HAVE ANY WEEBLES FOR THE WEEBLES TREEHOUSE??*

This was indeed a fair question, and gave the little thief some pause. In pencil, after she had given the matter some thought, she later wrote, *She will just have to save up her allowances and buy her own Weebles. Gina the circus Weeble is far out!* The possibility that the "poor kid" who got to unwrap the secondhand gift of the treehouse might never even get an allowance to begin to save up for Weebles Who Wobble But They Don't Fall Down was never addressed in Leslie's notebook. Nor was the possibility that the other child might have had more use out of winter gloves and a hat.

But a casual mention was scribbled a few days later: *Janie came to school all red-eyed from crying saying her mother wanted to know what happened to the Weebles treehouse her Uncle Lloyd bought her, and Janie didn't know at all and said it must have gotten lost, and her mother said her uncle was out of work and saved up for that toy, maybe she should know that before being so careless and because she could use a sense of how money doesn't just grow on trees she wasn't getting any allowance for two whole months. Poor Janie!! She'll never be able to buy "We Are the World" like she wants to, and two whole months without Yipes Stripes gum or Dr. Pepper Lip Smackers is really heavy. Janie's mom is not cool when it comes to people losing things.*

Val spent the night at the Hathaway cottage, listening for noises that could portend god-awful death. Snuffling, growling, clawing, heavy footfalls, buzzing chainsaws, that sort of thing. When nothing materialized, Val realized she'd been condemned to another day in somebody else's paradise.

Val still had no answers she could live with, and the nonstop flight to Cable's hermit hut in the wilderness was now just hours away. She decided she'd get the contract signed and, if proof of his guilt surfaced, Fir Na Tine would just have to break it. Maybe after the signing she could talk Decker into flying her to the nearest airport, where she'd happily wait on a hard, molded plastic seat to fly standby...exactly anywhere. Anywhere south of Lake Wendaban. As the dawn crept in between the blinds, Val could press her eyes shut and smell the hot dogs and sauerkraut from the Sabrett's truck at Columbus Circle. No more delays, no more missed opportunities.

She was that close to going home.

Downing the last of Muffy and Lana's eggs, which she scrambled up with a handful of diced up summer sausage and what was left of a mild, unmarked cheese, she systematically went back through Trey Selkirk's photos, rearranging, grouping, and finally lining them up in the best chronological order she could determine. When she was satisfied, she lightly numbered the backs. She debated whether to leave them behind at Peter's when Decker came for her later, and decided against it. She wanted to stay as streamlined as possible—if Decker could get her out of Wendaban that very day, she'd have to unload the snitched photos on him to get them back to his former father-in-law's memorabilia basket. No point in having to stop back here for anything at all.

What any of the photos told her for sure about Leslie Decker's murder was uncertain. Maybe she and Caroline had vied for Decker when they were younger, but as recently as two years ago? Not likely. Besides, Leslie had married him. Was it possible he and Caroline had been fooling around? Had Leslie found out and threatened something terrible? As distasteful as any of those possibilities sounded to Val, they might be worthy alternatives to the frightening possibility that the bestselling author she was trying to sign may have committed murder. And what Kay Stanley's baby with the charismatic Trey Selkirk could possibly have to do, over thirty years later, with Leslie's murder was completely unclear. Could there be an inheritance issue? But what inheritance issue would include Leslie and not Caroline? And, if it did include Caroline, was she in danger as well? On this score, Decker himself might be a good source, if she handled it lightly. She'd try to draw him out on their flight to Cable's.

All Val knew was that her eyes kept returning to the photo on Parliament Hill. Leslie Selkirk and Charlie Cable, victorious. But victories were fueled by personalities, it seemed to Val, and maybe there was a falling out between the two eco-warrior pals, the two firebrands. Had Charlie Cable grown tired of the fight? To hear Martin Kelleher describe it, Cable had lost the taste for the struggle, had walked away. No, had run. Had Leslie Decker badgered him until he snapped two years ago in this lonesome place?

Or was something else at work between those two?

She pushed the photos down into her briefcase for safekeeping. Then she washed her dishes and dressed for the day. At least, thanks to Kay Stanley, her own brown top was clean and dry and paired back up with her drawstring pants. She slicked on some blush and lipstick and called herself ready to meet and greet authorial dragons. Better a possibly murderous Charles Cable than a rogue black bear any day. Cable had nothing against Val, but she was pretty sure bears didn't need a reason.

By the time the sun was high and the heat was thick, Val, barefoot, dragged an Adirondack chair down to the dock. Then she strolled back, grabbed a white tennis visor from a peg, and scanned the Hathaway bookshelf for something to read. She spotted an uncorrected page proof of *Cling!*, one of Fir Na Tine's less stellar books by a shrink calling himself just Belaziel, who believed half the world's problems came from an individual's misguided desire for too much independence. Since she hadn't read the book all the way through when it had come out, Val slid it off the shelf and clutched it, along with the hidden letters from Kay Stanley, and plopped herself down in the chair she had set on the dock.

But she felt unsettled and looked around. More frightening silence. More silence the likes of which, if it's in a movie, erupts in terrifying close-up violence. But everywhere she turned in the thick heat, there was just secretive and unmoving rocky islands and forest, and secretive lake waters that rippled first in one direction and then in another. In the distance, a boat sped by, glimmering in the sun, nearly too far off to hear. Val fought a strange doziness by turning first to the uncorrected page proof of *Cling!*, opening it to a place held by a bookmark that turned out to be a receipt from a Husky gas station, and read a paragraph that was explaining the Civil War as a prime example of failure to cling. When she almost dozed off and felt the book slip from her hands, she startled awake, set aside the book and started again through Trey Selkirk's set of letters from Kay.

What she knew in a distant and indifferent way as her head dropped back to the chair and her hair slid gently away from her cheeks was that she was falling asleep, and anything could happen to her there in the smothering silence. But at least she wouldn't be awake to see it coming. Her fingers settled like claws on the stack of letters and *Cling!* and, as she drifted off, Val hoped it was enough to keep it all on her lap.

The thrum that woke her up was the propeller on Decker's Cessna as it cut across the water toward the Hathaway dock. Val jumped up, fighting off how spacey she felt, aware of Decker's grin from the cockpit as she clutched at the stuff in her lap. "I'll be right there," she managed to yell, making a quick stack of Kay's letter and the Fir Na Tine book, and took off at a sluggish lope back up to the cottage.

In record time, she slung the visor back on the peg, packed up her suitcase, wondered if she needed to brush her teeth but didn't want to take the time, and stashed the roll of letters back into the kaleidoscope, which she rammed into her poor briefcase. Her eyes still half shut, she locked the door of the cottage behind her and hauled her overnight bag, briefcase, and purse down the hill, nearly stumbling on her shaky legs, and out onto the dock of a place she was certain she would never see again. Even if she and Peter Hathaway came to their respective senses and headed toward some kind of life together, she wasn't sure Lake Wendaban would ever figure in her vacation plans.

When thoughts of Peter stalled her in her steps, right there as she couldn't make sense of her personal and professional lives, Decker came up the dock to grab the bag. Leaning into her, he looked her over quickly and smiled. She noticed he had applied a new coat of Nosekote that was disappearing into his ruddy olive skin, and he had shaved. In that moment the world felt like a fine and orderly place, and her heart lifted.

"This time you're going to do it," he told her. But first he had to make a stop in town to pick up Charlie Cable's canoe that had been left for Kevlar repairs at Lakeland Canoe Company. They'd lash it to the floats and fly it back to Charlie.

She shook the last of the sleep from her brain, climbed into the Cessna, and slid a look at the pilot. How long would she have to wait before she could tell him about Kay Stanley and Trey Selkirk? How long before she could ask him just how likely it seemed to him that the man they were flying to see had killed Leslie, his wife?

13

Half an hour into the flight they changed course, heading northeast, and she saw the weather change. What was clear and easy dropped away, and stringy white clouds dashed at the windshield, twisting away into the reduced light all around them.

She could feel Decker's body tense, which didn't do her own a whole lot of good, and they flew on for another ten minutes. "Sometimes it's just a patch," he said softly, only this time it wasn't. Breathing felt experimental, and all she had left was fear when she realized fog has a smell because now it was inside the cabin, and she could no longer see the islands or the sky.

As he took them down to six thousand feet, she kept her mouth shut and waited to slam into the side of a pine-covered island. "I'm landing." As black water approached, Val gripped the sides of her seat and wondered whether anybody back in the office would water her ficus. Decker set the plane down and they sputtered slowly along, the fog rolling over them.

She covered her face with her hands, pressing back tears. "Where are we?"

Decker took the map from her, refolded it open to a different place, and looked silently out the window for about five minutes. He stared at the water, at the nearness of either shore when the fog moved aside, and then twisted around to look at what was behind them. "I think we're here," he said, pointing to a place on the map that meant nothing to her. "But I'm not entirely sure." He hit the map with the backs of his fingers. "If I'm right, then I did this as a canoe trip maybe eight years ago." He looked straight ahead. "Here are the choices. I've got a backpacking tent in the back and two days' worth of emergency supplies."

She turned to face him. "How far are we from Cable's?"

Decker gave her a frank look. When he said, "A two days' paddle," Val shielded her eyes with her hand. It wasn't what she wanted to hear. "Or," he said reasonably, "we can head for home."

"How far?" Anything less than two days was a winner.

"I'd say four days."

Why did all the choices seem to be no better than waste your time or work your ass off? No, waste your time in a scary place or work your ass off in a scary place? In that moment Val knew there was absolutely nothing Peter Hathaway could do to make this week up to her.

"We could stay put for an hour," Decker suggested. "Maybe the weather will break."

"And if it doesn't?"

"Then we're an hour closer to nightfall—"

"And no closer either to Charlie Cable—"

"Or home." Decker went on: "Your call."

Wasting time had no appeal.

"Won't somebody come looking for us?" Val asked with a little surge of spirit.

"Who? Even Charlie Cable doesn't know exactly when we're coming."

Charlie Cable. The loon chick man. She didn't care if his new book left Jeffrey Archer in the dust, right now all she knew was that she was risking her life in this godforsaken place for ten minutes with the loon chick man. Her happiness depended on so little, really, and none of it had anything to do with being lost in the fog in the near dark in the Canadian wilderness, with black bears the size of pickup trucks waiting to hook her out of the tent.

Val sat up straight and stared out into the enveloping whiteness. "I say we go find the loon chick man." She sounded to herself like an announcer for The End of Days.

"All right," he responded with the sort of brisk bonhomie she hated in a man.

The wind and waves were rocking the helpless plane while Decker dug around in a box in the rear. Val watched dispassionately as he pulled out a flashlight, a length of rope, a First Aid kit, a stiff pair of tennis shoes, a pair of old khakis, two cans of SpaghettiOs, three boxes of kitchen matches...and a worn copy of *Kama Sutra*.

She held it up. "What every well-stocked emergency kit should have."

"Hey," he said with a tight grin, "we've got to pass the time somehow."

"Just get us the hell out of here." She turned away.

Decker clapped a hand on the top of her head like he was unscrewing a pickle jar and turned her to face him. "Listen to me. Nothing bad is going to happen to you out there."

For a moment they looked at each other and she very nearly believed him. "I'm sorry."

Decker said nothing, just unhooked the clips of the dry bag and unrolled the top. "Why would you agree to some silly errand in a place where everything terrifies you?" He stuffed in her briefcase, a roll of toilet paper, a thin bath towel, and what looked like a travel kit.

"You're about to tell me, aren't you?"

His eyes flashed. "You're afraid of either losing your job—" he threw in a handful of crumpled packets of Cup o' Soup and a crushed box of kitchen matches, "or—" he gritted his teeth, "—your boss."

Val's breath caught in her throat. "Well, with insight like that," she said, before she could stop herself, "you must know what happened to your wife."

He gave her a long look, then turned back to the dry bag. He muttered something that sounded like, "My wife happened to my wife," then rolled the top down once, squeezed out trapped air, and rolled it back down all the way. After checking the map, Decker sputtered the plane slowly along the water until he found a decrepit dock on Val's side of the plane. "It's the best we're going to find," he said.

Val slid out of the plane onto the pontoon, holding onto a wing strut, and flung herself at the dock. Decker killed the engine, and when the props sliced to a stop, Val grabbed the nose rope and held on. He climbed down beside her long enough to secure the plane to the dock, and she saw he had changed into the old khakis and tennis shoes. Then he pulled himself back inside and wordlessly handed down the dry bag, a blue nylon tent bag, a small black leather day pack, the two paddles, and a rucksack stenciled with RCAF. She set each of them down on the strongest part of the dock and went back to help.

Decker locked up, inched his way to the back of the pontoon, straddled it, and began to untie the canoe. Cold and scared, Val crouched on the dock and watched him in the failing light, because it sure beat the hell out of staring into the forest. A ripple of wind snapped the back of Decker's shirt and his hair flopped forward as he half stood, bearing the weight of the canoe as he eased it slowly down to the water. "Can you bring it around?"

She clambered over the rotten wood to the far side of the dock and laid herself out flat. Grabbing for a half-submerged cedar that had fallen over from the rocky shore, she cracked off a skinny branch sticking up out of the water to use as a tool to bring the canoe around. But as it started to fall out of her hand, she clutched it harder, ramming splinters the size of toothpicks into her palm. On the whole, pain was a damn sight better than fear.

As she shifted her weight to get better control for one long, last pull, her right leg stumped through a rotten board, and the blast of frigid lake water numbed her all the way to the hip. She swallowed her shriek. "I think I'm caught on something."

Decker grabbed her from behind in a hold that would have been swell if she'd been either amorous or choking and freed her in a single tug. Then he flung the branch into the lake and managed to pull the canoe over to the dock. Swaying, Val steadied herself, looking balefully at her pants leg that hung open in a torn flap, a thin line of blood trailing down her calf.

Kneeling, Decker tied up the line, turned, and looked up at her. "Let's see." She gave him her left hand, palm up. He took it in his hand and raised his eyebrows. The canoe thunked softly against the pilings as she lowered herself beside him on the boards. He pulled a penknife out of his pocket, flicked it open, and set to work with the blade, gingerly picking at the splinters.

Val felt Decker's breath on the skin of her hand.

The only source of heat.

When the bags were loaded, Val lowered herself into the bow, running her hand over the blood caked on her sore leg. Grabbing the paddle he held out to her, she felt Decker get into the stern and settle himself, sending the canoe into a rough couple of tips that made her clutch the sides. Shuddering so hard it must have looked like a seizure, she turned to see what he was doing.

He held the Tiparillo between his teeth, flicked a lighter and touched it to the end of the cigar, sheltered by his cupped hands. As he sucked in smoke, he looked at her and slipped the lighter back into his pocket.

Then they set off.

The fog brought everything unknown closer to her. Including Decker. It felt like what she imagined madness to be, a warm, wet shapelessness that prickles the skin, enters the nostrils, and comes between whatever goes on in the skull—and what really *is*. They glided through the dark, their paddles scraping the hull in some sloppy human way they couldn't help.

Val had just run them up on a barely submerged boulder she told herself she had no way of seeing, listening to the long damn scrape measure every inch of her mistake, and sat there defeated, her paddle loose in her hand.

Decker eased them off the boulder without a word and gracefully nosed the canoe ahead. Squaring her shoulders, she pitched in, paddling like a doomed galley slave. He started humming in time with each stroke, then sang out how *near, far, wherever we are, I believe that the heart does go on.* She was too tired even to roll her eyes.

She realized after a while that they had left the shoreline, blown by a gentle crosswind, and finally there was nothing familiar at her side. Nothing at all. The canoe rocked sideways. She looked around at the crushing darkness and pulled her paddle in, acutely aware of her own body. It was all she had left—a sense of where she began and ended. Breathless and scared, she jerked around.

"I'm here," Decker said. His voice was disembodied, but close.

In the dark, the world was suddenly a small and intimate place and they were discovering it by canoe, finally finding a good-sized island with a campsite. She held the flashlight while he unloaded the canoe. They didn't speak. Decker pulled the canoe up out of the water while she unpacked two sleeping bags compacted to the size of small watermelons, and because they were too tired to set up the tent, she agreed to sleep out. She realized with a kind of distant interest that she didn't care what happened.

They found a tent site with pine needles an inch thick, and while Decker disappeared into the bushes to pee, she laid out the bags about three feet apart. Let the forest do its worst, at least she was off the water. The wind was soft and high in the treetops. She heard him coming back, his footfalls ranging over leaves and twigs. Then in a moment of new anxiety she pulled the bags closer together by a foot, close enough for grabbing if the night terrors got the better of her, crawled inside one and hunkered down.

He grunted as he squatted beside her, ran the zipper partway down the bag, and lay down inside. She didn't hear him zip back up, but didn't ask. They wished each other a polite good night like strangers leaving the theater, hailing separate cabs.

14

In the morning, what she wanted was a nice half-melon dotted with blueberries, French toast sprinkled with confectioner's sugar, fresh-squeezed orange juice, and a mug of Starbucks coffee, any flavor. What she got was a can of succotash. Not even a whole can, since she had to share it with Decker. She eyed the rucksack. At least he hadn't pulled out the SpaghettiOs.

And he had given her a spoon of her own. A plain metal camping utensil that stood between her and starvation. When she was done, she rinsed the spoon in the lake, dried it on her torn pants, and stuck it in her pocket. She might have to trust Decker with her life, but she damn well wasn't about to hand over her spoon.

Down at the water's edge, Decker dropped to one knee, scooped up water in his cupped hands, and drank. Then he moved out of the way so she could do the same. Visibility was better, but not by much. The water was cold, gently back blown into half curls. The early morning air was cool. Decker stood next to her, tucking in his shirttails while she drank. It had no taste at all, which made her realize how pure it was.

Decker raked his hair back with both hands. "They say once you drink the waters of Lake Wendaban, you'll always return."

Not likely. Even if she decided Charles Cable was no killer and he became their next front-list wonder, before she'd come back here she'd buy him a fax machine herself and pay Decker to install it. Her contact with nature consisted of a daily glance at the geraniums in a window box on the brownstone in the middle of her block, and that was plenty.

Return? She didn't think so.

They followed the left shore to an angular bay where the pine forest retreated behind a rocky outcrop. Snaking through the shallows, they wedged the canoe between boulders rising out of the water by the shore, unloaded the gear, and carried the canoe up out of the water. Val climbed over the boulders for a better look at the portage: boulders so big you could damn near stage the next final Rolling Stones tour on them.

Decker passed her with the canoe overturned on his shoulders, finding footholds in crevices. His shirt dangled behind him, where he'd tied it to a thwart, but he was still wearing a lightweight capilene tee. "So it's a thousand meters, Val," he said as he went by, "which is about half a mile to you." His foot started to slip, but he caught himself, readjusting the canoe with a grunt. "And we'll each have to double back for another pack, eh?"

She nearly dislocated her shoulder getting into the straps of the dry bag and settling it on her back, but it seemed to be the heaviest bag and if Decker could carry the canoe she could jolly well handle the worst bag. She had her pride. So she started out, realizing quickly that when she leaned to the left, the bag leaned farther. The damn thing threw her off balance.

At least the morning was gray and cool.

To the far right the rock sloped off in the forest, banked by a couple of thirty-foot white pines, where a mound of tangled roots and pine debris offered a softer way over the rock. Steep, she thought, but a nice change from rock hopping. She was practically to the top when she discovered there was nothing in sight to hang onto and both feet started to slide out from under her.

The weight of the dry bag pressed her face into the dirt as she slid all the way back down, her chest slamming against roots spaced like ladder rungs. She jerked herself onto her back, wheezing noisily for air, thinking she must be the first woman in the history of the world to get beaten up by her own breasts.

She swatted pine dirt off her lips and dragged her hands over her face, her heart still pounding. It all came, of course, from not being willing to wait out the fog a day ago. No, it all came from being willing to do Peter Hathaway's damned errand in the first place.

By the time she got to the other side of the portage, she was winded and shaky, but rather than admit it, she headed back for her second load on legs that looked like a pair she saw on late-night TV in a flick about the undead. Once the gear had all been moved to the end of the portage, she sat on a rock with her hands hanging limply over her knees, and watched Decker load the canoe. When he told her she should get in, all she could muster was the kind of stiff dignity that any cop with a Breathalyzer could see through in a minute.

They were crossing a small lake, he said, that had no name. *What kind of country,* she wondered, looking narrowly around, *has so damn many lakes it doesn't even have to name all of them?*

They paddled for nearly an hour at a pace designed to incorporate some rest. When they were close enough to the far shore—and the next portage—to see what was ahead of them, she heard Decker go "hm" in a way that suggested he'd met his first challenge. She squinted. The water was getting very shallow and the far shore seemed brown and reedy. She could see bottom. A few more strokes and the canoe was effectively beached.

Only they were still a hundred yards from the shore.

"Damn," said Decker. *"Moose muck."* She heard him sigh, and before she knew what was happening, he eased himself over the side of the canoe and sank up to his thighs in mud.

With his arms high, he pushed his way past her to the bow, where he grabbed the rope and started to pull, heading slowly for the shore. She felt like a prima donna. Or Hepburn on *The African Queen.*

"I'm getting out," she said, laying aside her paddle, rolling up her sleeves, and giving Decker plenty of time to say something gallant like he wouldn't hear of it. Only he didn't.

"Thanks," he said, steadying the right side of the bow while Val climbed out the left, the sensation of cold thick mud hitting her all the way up to her crotch. She moved to the stern, where she gripped and pushed the canoe as Decker pulled from the bow.

Every step was an extraordinary effort, heaving each leg out of a paralysis of mud. It found its way between her toes, it filled the space under her arches, it plastered her pants to her legs. There was something about the suction that was horrifying. She kept herself from getting sick to her stomach by clenching her toes to keep her tennis shoes from being pulled off her feet.

Finally, after her leg muscles felt like they were hanging in tatters, the rivulet they were following deepened near the shore and they were able to float the canoe well enough to ride the remaining ten yards. Val, letting out a cry that seemed to carry an accumulation of agony from the last twenty years, heaved herself into the canoe, nearly tipping it. She sprawled over the seat and the packs.

"Oh, God," she said half a dozen times. The canoe stopped moving.

Decker stood next to her. "Are you all right?"

She looked at him and shook her head, speechless, flinging her arm toward the mud in what she hoped was conveying something. He smiled at her, his eyes narrow, and then said something about how the wind would dry out their pants pretty quickly, but she really didn't care.

The canoe stopped and before long she felt Decker tugging the rucksack out from under her, heard him sloshing nearby, and then nothing. After a while she rolled to her side and saw that he'd tied up the canoe to a couple of aspen saplings growing out of a beaver dam, where he sat firing up the camp stove. Lunchtime. Lunch. A hot lunch. Never had the prospect of food filled her with such mindless joy. He looked so wonderful half-covered with mud, sitting on the sturdy beaver dam making food for her, that she wished she liked him better than she did.

Decker looked up. "How's SpaghettiOs?"

*   *   *

Val sat in her underwear at the end of the moose muck portage washing her pants, bunching up the parts where the mud had caked the worst and scrubbing them against each other. By the end of the portage—which featured three-quarters of a mile of more mud and a plague of mosquitoes—her pants felt like they'd been dipped in plaster of Paris.

Decker's solution for himself was to drop his last pack on the ground and dive clothed into the water. She watched the mud swirl up brown from his clothes and disappear into the lake. When her turn came, she made Decker paddle out far enough into the lake that she'd have some privacy—he muttered something about a Victorian novel, but he went—then she stripped down to her underwear, burped up SpaghettiOs, and set about washing her clothes.

At a sudden sound from behind, she whirled around, and a strapping, blue-eyed young lad singing "Alouette" swung a camp canoe off his head and into the water. He flashed her a dimpled grin and said there were ten fourteen-year-old boys right behind him.

It was a headwind.

Her teeth must have stopped chattering about an hour ago, although the noise inside her head was the only sure sign she was still alive since every part of her below the waist had dropped off long ago, and any last reserves of pride had been extinguished at the last portage in a clutch of pubescent boys.

Clouds like lead had overtaken the sky. Behind them at the horizon there were slashes of bright blue, so maybe people elsewhere on the lake were going about their business in the sunshine. Nowhere looked as bad as it did directly overhead, but the headwind was so strong she couldn't believe it wouldn't propel the storm clouds clear into another region. She watched three columns of thunderheads gather and churn.

Decker was rustling around in the rucksack. "Here, Val," he said, handing her a red plastic rain poncho. Around them the lake was a dull, silver gray that seemed deeper than ever. He pulled a purple poncho over his head and quickly smoothed the plastic over his legs. He looked like a Druid.

She slipped on the poncho as they paddled along the shore to a campsite. With a quick look at the sky, Decker moved fast, unloading the canoe, then pulling it up out of the water with her help, and turning it over.

She felt lobotomized.

Behind her by about forty feet Decker was shaking the two-man tent and the poles out of the bag. She watched him for a while with a kind of utter detachment, as if what the man was doing had absolutely nothing to do with her, then lost interest and looked away. Finally, she heard a long zip. "Are you coming in?" he asked just as she felt the first raindrop.

She shook her head slowly, not even knowing what she meant. Only she thought it had something to do with how small and futile and ridiculous she had been feeling all day. What was left of her was just the exquisite solitude of every forgotten thing from the beginning of time. The mote that fell from Adam's perfect hip. The flake of cerulean blue from under Michelangelo's nail. She heard Decker toss a bag into the tent and then zip himself inside as he whistled "Waltzing Mathilda."

Thunder came toward her in a slow tumble but she didn't move, not even when the rain was falling straight and hard. She pulled her knees up under the poncho and watched the rain soak the sleeves of her shirt as the temperature dropped. Ten feet away was the overturned canoe, the rain drumming its hull. Maybe she could tuck herself under it, along with the packs and paddles.

"You could crawl under the canoe," Decker called. "You'll stay dry," she cursed him because now she couldn't do it or it would look like his idea, "but you won't be warm." Val twisted around and could see his shadow in the lantern light of the tent. "Now, I happen to have a change of clothes, a dry sleeping bag, and a Cliff

Bar I'll give you whenever you decide to stop acting like an idiot."

Her bangs were so wet they were mixed up with her eyelashes, but it wasn't until she realized her pants were soaked through to her underwear that she knew she hated Canada, hated Decker and damn near herself for being there. She rushed the tent, unzipped the flap like she was slashing it with a knife, and fell inside at his feet, grunting, inching every last wet bit of her out of the rain. Then she lay there dripping and panting and not giving a damn.

Decker leaned over her and calmly zipped the flap. Her hands were shaking while she tried to sit up and pull off the plastic poncho. Only the tent was so low even a schnauzer couldn't stand up in it. "Need some help?" he asked.

"No."

He ignored her. "Put out your arms," he said. "Go on."

She figured it was better to get it over with. She crunched, stuck out her arms, and Decker grabbed the plastic in four different places and worked the poncho over her head. "Hands across the border, and all that."

"Just try," was what she said instead of thank you.

"The rest is up to you." He balled up the wet poncho and stuffed it in a corner of the tent.

Val leaned out of his way, shivering, as he lay back on his side, propped up on an elbow. "Where's the change of clothes?" She looked around. Lifting himself up slightly, Decker pulled out what he'd been using as a pillow at the head of the sleeping bag. It was his capilene tee and boxers, folded into a neat square. He handed it to her. "This is it?" she said, looking him over, taking in the unbuttoned plaid shirt and the jeans that were slung so low around his hips she should have seen some jockeys if there'd been any. "This is your underwear."

Decker looked up from laying out a hand of solitaire. "I said a change of clothes," he said with a quick smile. "I never said they were clean."

Val glared at him. "Turn around."

He muttered something.

She shoved him. "Turn around."

"Suit yourself." In one easy motion Decker turned his back to her, tossing a small towel over his shoulder. "You'll need this."

Val undressed, her teeth chattering, and sank her face gratefully into his towel, needing it more for comfort than anything else. She slithered into the legs of Decker's boxers, then the shirt, smoothing the front down over her chest with stiff fingers. They felt warm and used and comfortably baggy. She was just about to take the towel to her hair when she stopped and looked around. He had opened up one summer-weight down bag and spread it out on the tent floor, laying over it a second bag like a coverlet. The Coleman lantern was set down near Decker's head. The light it cast on the back of his neck was puny and greenish and wonderful.

His shoulder, her arm, the glint of his hair the color of old coins, in the reduced light from the lantern, these were the known world. Down at the dark end of the tent she could barely make out his feet. But it was the sound all around her that was beautiful, the rainwater hitting the nylon like the rustle of a blue taffeta party dress she had worn when she was thirteen. Val heard herself sob and hoped Decker took it for something outside the tent.

He didn't. "What's the matter?"

So she sobbed again, and without answering, crawled under the top down bag. When she felt him turn back over to face her, Val flung her forearm over her eyes, hoping to hell he'd let it go. "I don't know why we don't just annex this goddamn country and be done with it," she blurted, then had to listen to Decker laugh, like she hadn't meant it.

She felt him moving around, and she shifted her arm enough to see him set out all her clothing at the bottom of the tent, like they had a chance of being dry by morning. If there was one thing she liked in a man, it was hopeless gestures. Then he settled back next to her and Val lay very still. She could feel him looking her over, his breath on her jaw. "You should dry your hair."

Then she heard herself say an extraordinary thing. "You." She wondered if he could hear her since she could hardly hear herself.

"You, Decker," she said, groggy, turning her face away from him. "Please." And as she listened to the rain with her eyes closed, she felt him take handfuls of her wet hair in his hands and rub them dry in the towel in time to words she heard over and over, words about a jolly swagman camped by a billabong. And Val could tell before she gave herself over to the sound of the rain that Wade Decker was singing her to sleep.

15

Breakfast was B&B Baked Beans, "avec jambon," the label said, and camp coffee that went down as smooth as sand. While she sat moodily on a rough log with a sleeping bag over her shoulders, Val chewed her coffee and listened to Decker prime the stove for the second time, which flamed with a whoosh when he set a match to the ring.

Crouching, Decker held the can of beans over the flame with a camping handle and stirred with thoughtful, slow strokes. Val watched him and felt useless, only neither of them seemed to mind. He needed a shave, she thought, his day-old growth of beard just a pleasant sort of dirtiness on his face. She felt bad about yesterday, knew she must have looked like a spoiled American baby, and it bothered her. "Sleep well?" She jerked the bag over her shoulder.

His eyebrows shot up and he nodded. "You?"

"Pretty well." She remembered waking up warm and blissful at about five a.m., when light was just seeping into the tent, only to find she was lying up against Decker, who was sleeping on his back, with her head in the crook of his left shoulder, her arm flung over his chest. His arm was curled over her, his fingertips in her hair. She jerked away, jabbed the top sleeping bag down around her, and fell back asleep.

"This is just about ready. Hungry?"

Nodding, she staggered to her feet and set aside the sleeping bag. While she was still asleep, Decker had spread out her clothes to dry on the hull of the canoe. She felt them all—still damp—and thought he probably wouldn't mind if she paddled for a while in his underwear. The lake was so still it looked like a hard, polished surface.

"Sun'll burn off that mist," Decker said. "And when it does," he tapped a spoon against a metal bowl, "we're going to have a hot day." She went over to Decker and sat down cross-legged with the camp stove between them. He stirred her share of the baked beans avec jambon and handed her the bowl. "We'll be at Charlie Cable's by dinnertime," he said, dipping his own spoon into what was left in the can, "and from there we can call Portage Airlines to pick us up."

Val felt stunned. "Does it have to be tonight?" What was the matter with her?

He was silent. "No," he said, chewing reflectively. "It doesn't." He looked at her as he settled back on the ground, hooking an arm around his bent knee. "I just thought you'd want to get back to town pretty quickly."

"I do," she said as she straightened up, "but we've come all this way—"

"And Charlie's good company."

"Well, I don't know about that, but I can't think a few hours will make any difference." Besides, she could poke around for some incriminating evidence.

"Neither can I."

She tried to be serious. "And we could always contribute the other can of SpaghettiOs."

"You can't wait to get rid of them, can you?"

They both laughed. Then she took a heaping spoonful of beans, her fingers pushing in a couple that were about to get away. They ate quietly, watching two ravens who swooped overhead and settled in separate treetops. They made their hoarse call, inching on spindly legs along the fragile branches. One of them lifted a shiny wing and picked at himself. The other turned to face the lake. Still they seemed aware of each other. Val wondered if they were mates. "Thanks for setting out my things," she said.

He raised a hand dismissively, his eyes still on the ravens.

"Tell me about Leslie." She didn't know she was going to say it and knew it was a mistake as soon as it was out. His face changed as fast as the weather. She watched his features draw together, completely losing the good-natured openness she had only ever seen. He looked older. He looked eternal. Then he shook his head. It was a small movement, tight and slow, one that left no room for another opinion. His eyes never left her face.

She edged closer to him. "What if," her voice dropped, "what if Charles Cable..." If she voiced it, she was giving it a kind of credibility that scared her.

Decker waited. Then: "What?"

"What if Cable killed Leslie?"

He practically fell over. "Charlie Cable? Is that what you're thinking?"

He seemed so incredulous Val felt insulted. "He was on the lake that day, and Kay said—"

"I told you I'm not talking about it."

"You damn well have to talk about it—"

"Oh, really?"

"—because I can't sign a killer!"

He looked at the sky. "Ah, that explains it."

"Can you imagine the publicity if it got out?"

"Maybe you'll sell more books," he said softly.

Val heaved a sigh, watching him scrape his leftover beans into the fire. "You know that's not what I mean. If Cable's anywhere on the edges of a murder case, I have to figure out just how close to the heart of it he really comes. If there's any suspicion about him and we signed him anyway," she opened her hands helplessly, "we've had it." Then she added, "And I've had it."

"Clear him or nail him, is that it?"

"It's due diligence."

"Peter on the same page?"

A beat. "Yes." Of course he would be. She'd clear it with him later. Sometime between signing and countersigning.

Wade gave her a hard look. "Charlie Cable was the only one around here who actually liked Leslie," and then he seemed to hear what he'd said and pulled back, "so you'd have to be—"

"How could that possibly be true? There's Caroline, there's you—"

"You heard me," said Decker softly, reaching for her bowl.

He was diverting her from the strong possibility that Charles Cable had killed Leslie Decker. *Why?*

He went on, "You're leaving out the cops' favorite suspect."

"Martin Kelleher?"

His eyes slid to her. "Me." Without another word, Wade Decker grabbed the pot, the bowls, and the spoons and headed down to the water to wash them.

She followed him, crouching alongside as he dipped water into the pot and started to scour it with a sprig of pine needles. "Tell me what you think happened that day, tell me what she—"

"Sorry, Val." He scrubbed harder.

That was it. They looked at each other silently for what seemed like a long time, then Val looked away. She thought she understood. "We share a tent, some underwear, and a few bad moments," she said, "but it doesn't make us close."

"It doesn't even make us friends."

She looked down, folding her arms across her chest. "Right," she said quietly, feeling unbearably sad.

"Look," he said, grabbing their spoons from the ground, "you had one hell of a day yesterday and a good night's sleep, and you woke up in the arms of a man you don't know—and don't even particularly like—and it felt just great." He widened his eyes at her. "But, no, I won't tell you about Leslie." His voice dropped. "Leave it alone."

"I can't."

"Then you're on your own." Wade Decker opened his hand and let the spoons clatter against the inside of the can, like dropping a gun after a shooting.

*   *   *

The trail continued uphill into the forest, where it was suddenly cooler, but then she could feel her own sweat and the mosquitoes started to check her out. She thanked God for DEET and figured she'd find Decker sooner or later. The climb was just starting to make her cranky when she finally heard the waterfall. The trail split, one half angling off to the right to some vacant tent sites scattered over the rock, the other continuing upward over a footbridge.

Val heard a thunderous splash and a whoop that echoed all around her. Heading toward the sound, she passed the canoe, where Decker had lodged it upright in the crotch of a fir tree. Then she saw the waterfall, the white, plumed water churning down over the high rock wall and ripping away downstream over shallow rocks.

Just as she noticed Decker's clothes in a heap on the dry rocks, she heard him call her name, and she caught sight of him standing behind the waterfall in a shallow crevasse, a wedge-shaped grotto formed by the overhanging rock. The water crashed fierce and thick in front of him, the white spume like a curtain pushed upward by air and might.

It was beautiful.

"Val," he yelled, his arm jutting through the falls, beckoning. "Come on in. Just swim out hard," he was yelling over the noise of the falls, "swim out hard and I'll catch you and pull you in." The day was hot, and her shirt clung in patches. All she had to do was strip, drop herself into the pool and swim out to Decker.

"Val!"

She looked away downstream, then back at Decker. If she stripped, she'd have to swim, if she swam, she'd have to swim to Decker, if she swam to Decker—she'd never get a foothold in such a small, close place, not even for a second. "I can't," she yelled back, her voice lurching with a feeling she didn't understand.

"Come on, I'll catch you," he called from behind the waterfall, naked and laughing, taking the force of the water, expanding into all the corners of life that she left unlit. Through the years she had placed so many pieces of herself in reserve that she no longer knew where to find them.

"It's all right," she yelled, when it wasn't at all. "I'll wait for you."

"We may never get another chance."

That she knew.

She was counting on it.

16

At the end of the trail above the falls, Decker and Val studied the channel. They had stayed long enough at the falls to set Val's clothes out to dry on hot, clean rock face while she watched the clouds, and Decker bathed and shampooed his hair with an old plastic bottle of CampSudz he found in the rucksack.

The sky burned blue, the clouds hardened into alabaster, and Val felt herself tempered by the force of sunlight. They had a lunch of Slim Jims that tasted better than she'd imagined. She changed back into her own shirt and torn pants and handed him his underwear. Decker decided to go shirtless, then stashed everything except the jeans he was wearing into the dry bag.

It was what lay just below the waterline that made the channel almost unnavigable. Enormous, submerged boulders of varying shapes and sizes, some mossy, some not, all slippery. As clear as the water was, when the sun and clouds shifted it was impossible to tell where to put the next foot—except by feel.

Val pulled off her shoes and tossed them into the canoe. They tried what turned out to be false passages, where the spaces between boulders weren't wide or deep enough for the canoe to pass, and backed up to try others. Her bare feet slid into deep underwater crevices she could only let happen, keeping her ankles soft as they twisted. Val's shirt, unbuttoned below her heart, floated up around her chest.

Once they were past the rocks they traded places in the shallows and climbed back into the canoe. "That was good," Decker said, smiling, and she nodded. They stretched themselves toward the middle of the canoe and studied the map he spread out over the dry bag, then paddled to where the channel forked. To the right was the way to Charlie Cable's.

After they had paddled slowly down that right fork for about an hour, well ahead of them on the near shore was a dock that appeared as a bold outline in the sunlight. They paddled through a field of water lilies, which parted as they came, and pulled up to the dock. It was in good repair.

Decker unlashed the packs, landed them on the dock, then hoisted himself up and steadied the canoe for Val. "Getting out?" he asked as he tied the canoe to a cleat. Lifting herself onto the dock, she sat beside him. He unrolled the top of the dry bag and pulled out his shirt.

Val said, "I'd like to wash up first."

They looked at each other. "I put the CampSudz in the side pocket of the rucksack," he said with a smile. "I'll meet you up at Charlie's." He left the dock pulling his arms into the shirt and she lost sight of him on the path into the woods. She found the CampSudz and set it on the dock. Then she stood, slipped out of her clothes, and dropped them beside her.

Crossing her arms over her chest, Val looked down at her tired feet. In that moment she believed that all around her was silence and goodness, and nothing else. She let her suspicions of Charlie Cable just float on away from her like a random leaf in a tiny breeze. Curling her toes over the front edge of the dock, she pulled her hands quickly overhead and did a shallow dive.

It was cold. But somehow not as cold without her clothes. She surfaced, driving hundreds of white bubbles before her, and swam to the lily pads. Treading water, she touched the thin, round pads that floated in green perfection, the pure white flowers open to the sunlight that swelled everything. Back at the dock she climbed out long enough to lather up, running suds over the goosebumps, squeezing suds on her hair, working them through with the kind of zeal only a wet body on a warm day can feel.

Val dived again, rubbing her head clean, and felt the soap leaving her body. Swimming to the surface, she turned smiling and crying to squint into the sun. Then she headed back to the water lilies, swimming underwater with her eyes open, threading her way among the slender, waving stalks.

She looked at her rippling white body, her legs hanging like stems, without clothing, without transportation, without shelter—with literally nothing between her and whatever could befall her—and felt exquisitely human. Downright epic, even. She had survived moose muck, teenage boys, headwinds, SpaghettiOs, Wade Decker, and the platoon of bogeymen inside her head, and she had prevailed. She, Valjean Cameron. She came up for air.

Standing at the edge of the dock, not three feet away from her, his arms crossed and his shoulders jerking around like he must be carrying ferrets inside his shirt, was Charles Cable. "You can't have the book," was what he said.

While she struggled into her poor pants, she was angry. The problem—she thought, banging her shoes against Cable's dock—the problem with epics is that you never quite kill all the monsters. No matter what you do, there will always be something that steps out in front of the next guy, the next foolhardy schnook with enough hubris to inflate a damn blimp. When it came right down to it, she had flashed a bunch of camper boys—she had to tell herself their laughter was the nervous virginal sort—gagged on succotash so bad that botulism could only improve the flavor, and left some of her sanity back there slurped down, down, down into the moose muck.

Now here she was and that baffling, bestselling, possibly homicidal proto-coot Charles Cable was telling her Fir Na Tine couldn't bring out his book? This went way beyond Peter Hathaway. This went way beyond Peter Hathaway and Daria Flottner. This was Cameron and Cable, mano a mano. Finally, she would do it for herself. Maybe, she thought as she squinched her feet back into the stiff shoes, maybe this was what being a professional really meant. Forget the skills, forget the taste, the judgment, the sheer grit of getting through editorial meetings, handling textbook neurotic authors. Being a pro was finally just a matter of acting like one.

She'd hear what the man had to say.

And she'd damn well try to change his mind.

Through the screen door she saw Decker, with a beer in his hand, running a finger across the spines of the books lining one of Cable's shelves. Cable himself was tending a pot on the two-burner stove. "Well, are you coming in?" he bellowed at her.

She stepped inside, ruffling at her wet hair. Decker gave her a cool, inscrutable look, then winked. She took it for encouragement about Cable. "I'm Valjean Cameron, Mr. Cable—"

"I damn well know who you damn well are."

"—and I work for Peter Hathaway."

He glowered at her. "What took you so long?"

"Weather." Then she added, "And my inexperience."

"Peter a good boss?"

She felt off-balance. "Good enough to stay out of my way. Mostly."

Val watched Decker pull a bottle from the small fridge, flip off the cap with a wall-mounted opener, and bring it over to her. Decker eased over to the photos and pictures and mail strung from cord tacked up on the wall. She took a long swig and tried a discreet burp.

At length, Charles Cable announced, "You'll stay for supper." He rapped the spoon against the side of the pot. "It's stew."

"That will make a nice change."

"Good year for loons," he announced like a town crier.

"Lake must be healthy," she commented, assuming he wasn't referring to anything actually *in* the stew.

Cable flattened the flyaway hair with his forearm, and slipped her a quick look. "Quite a shiner."

"That it is."

"Foote?"

She blinked, wondering. Another swig. "No," she said. "Fist."

"Dixon Foote," Cable bellowed.

She jumped. "It was accidental. He apologized."

Cable grunted. His shoulders started rippling again, this time in the direction of plates and bowls, set on an open shelf over the porcelain sink. She took it as a directive to set the table. Only the table, which had a hurricane lamp and a typewriter on it, didn't include any chairs. No laptop, even, she thought, looking around.

So the great writer stands and bangs it all out, like Hemingway. Only she'd bet Hemingway never came up with phrases like *harrowing heliotropic iron ovoids hurtling toward the mother ship.* There was a simple staircase up to a sleeping loft, a change of clothes on a couple of crude pegs, and a double futon mattress against the side wall, which was practically all window. Next to it stood a small table that held a marine radio, and what looked like a golf cart battery that must be storing solar power.

"You like *Nebula,* Cameron? Get yourself a bowl. You too, Wade. Step up."

"I didn't read it." No way around it. One look at the *harrowing heliotropic iron ovoids* line was enough for her. And now here, with the acclaimed author of this space drivel, she could only be exposed as a liar if she pretended otherwise.

Decker widened his eyes at her. "After you," he murmured, handing her a bowl. Together they stepped up to Charles Cable, who stood poised to ladle out steaming stew, them in their ragged tripping clothes like workhouse beggars. Cable's eyes were big and china blue, like his wall-sized shadeless window that can't keep anything out.

"Neither did I," said Cable, digging around for a few potatoes for Val's bowl, "read it, that is. Not the final version. Pounded out the revision, sent it off, and the rest—" he daintily dropped a sixth potato into her bowl, "is crass commercial history. Ha!" She couldn't tell whether he was bleating at how many potatoes he'd managed to shovel into her bowl or how very well he'd hoodwinked a major publisher and the general reading public.

Decker moved in closer, she felt him up against her back, and the prospect of some home-cooked stew made her feel surprisingly weak in the knees.

"Bloody bore," Cable barked. "The things I love can't earn enough for a postage stamp." He ladled stew into Decker's bowl. "The things I hate could buy a whole floor of offices on Bay Street and start a goddamn foundation."

Val headed over to the futon and sat cross-legged with her bowl. Decker joined her, leaving more room between them than they had been able to spare anytime over the last couple of days. "Which is why," Cable said, pulling what looked like a couple of reams of paper out of a wooden basket next to his wood stove and slamming it onto the table—Val thought she saw the typewriter jump—"which is why you can't have *Asteroid* unless—" Val watched him over a spoon topped with parsnips and beans; with the word *unless*, she was back in the game "—unless you publish this one first." He divided the stack of papers into two unequal piles of typescript, then whacked the smaller manuscript with the back of his hand.

She could hardly catch her breath. Suddenly it was all hers, a publishing coup that would evaporate all strangeness between her and Peter Hathaway, his harrowing heliotropic ovoids hurtling toward her mother ship in final committed abandon, and her hands started to shake as she came to terms with how damn much that was exactly what she had wanted all along, all along. "What is it?" she managed to croak as Decker took the bowl from her and she tried to get to her feet. They were hers—*Asteroid*, Hathaway, and the slim unknown.

Charles Cable tugged at his waistband in a confrontational kind of way. "My memoirs," he bellowed.

17

Stall him.

It was the only thing that made sense once she abandoned the idea of pummeling him senseless with the ladle. It was a tumble of decision-making in the space of less than ten seconds while she chewed and swallowed a parsnip and controlled her expression. She then said the one thing no author in her experience could ever resist, which would buy her time to figure out her next move. "Tell me about your memoirs, Charlie."

If Cable had known Val Cameron, he would have instantly been suspicious of her motives. *Tell me about your memoirs,* for Val, was something along the lines of encouraging him to describe his most disgusting personal habits, naked and with full sound effects. But it worked. He launched into some proto-PR spiel about the time being right to expose something or other, presumably not himself, and Val's brain went into overdrive.

If she told him she couldn't make such a deal, that Fir Na Tine couldn't be pressured into publishing a book it hadn't even vetted just to get *The Asteroid Mandate,* then she'd lose the contract. Also Peter. And probably her job. Her whole body felt scalded with an anger she had to hide. If she agreed to his absurd demand, this snaggletoothed, thunderbolt-hurling weird-ass writer of space junk, then where in the hell were her professional standards? And how on earth could she equivocate without his seeing right through her? Which of the following reasonable replies would buy her some time?

I'll have to talk to Peter, Charlie.

I'd like to read the memoirs first, Charlie, before committing.

Let's do one deal at a time, Charlie. First The Asteroid Mandate, *then we'll talk memoirs.*

Nothing would fly, and she knew it. For all his bellowing and bluster, he'd see right through her, take whatever she said for reluctance—worse, criticism—and they'd lose him. Since he set this ridiculous condition in the first place, he was not in a reasonable frame of mind. But if she didn't say something along those lines, then he'd clap his hands, ask for the contract she'd brought, sign it, and she, Val Cameron, would have to go home to her apartment and turn all her mirrors to face the wall so she wouldn't have to face herself. Ever.

No, she'd have to stall, and stall so sublimely Charles Cable would never see it. "Excuse me, Charlie," she said, dabbing her lips with her shredded napkin just as he was launching into the year he covered city council meetings as a stringer for a newspaper. "Bathroom?" She ignored Decker's quizzical look as Cable directed her to the outhouse in the woods behind the cabin.

She walked out in an unhurried way, drew the front door shut, and dove into the rucksack Decker had blessedly left there on the porch. She pulled out the contract Ivy League Ivy had faxed and slipped it out of sight under the waistband of her sorry-looking pants. As she turned to head into the woods to find the john, she saw Decker standing inside at the window, a beer in his hand, watching her with a slight smile.

He had seen it all.

She flashed him a look of wide-eyed desperation, something she thought might convey *what the hell am I supposed to do?*—the same look he'd seen plenty of times over the past two days—and clutching the contract against her skin, she loped off into the woods.

Charlie Cable's outhouse was maybe half the size of Bob's Bait Shop and had a stack of old magazines, a pyramid of toilet paper rolls, posters stapled to the inside walls about the virtues of sunscreen, and—unbelievably—a seashell pink toilet seat in the built-in bench over the pit. What it didn't have was a door. The man can't tolerate human society enough to live in town like a decent person, but when he does his business, anyone's welcome. Fortunately, the outhouse faced away from the cabin. *Where's that contract, Cameron, huh? Just hand me a pen and I'll hand you two manuscripts!*

Val pushed back the lid. For some reason, she thought as she breathed through her mouth, she just couldn't lie and say she didn't bring a contract with her, not in front of Wade Decker. Maybe she couldn't swim naked in the waterfall, but she could at least tell the truth. So she watched in a disembodied sort of way as her hands tore the contract in half, then quarters, and let the pieces flutter down into the pit.

From deep inside the sleeping bag, Val shined the flashlight on her wrist. 2:47 a.m. She flicked off the light and lay there, the weight of the manuscript on her stomach. She was wide awake. And all she was aware of was the sick pounding of her heart. At the end of the evening all three of them had gone to bed, Cable climbing the ladder to his loft, his baggy jeans slipping to a point below his butt crack.

She shook her head.

He was going to be some all-new circle of Hell for the Publicity Department. Decker clipped off a smile at her as he turned on his side away from her in his sleeping bag, some four feet away. Val waited until Cable's snores burbled out from the loft, and Decker's steady breathing told her he was asleep, then she crawled out of her bag and felt her way to the table where Cable had left his memoirs.

She had palmed Decker's LED flashlight while they stayed up swapping stories, then she dug deep into her sleeping bag, turned on the light and started to read the mem-WAHRS that were holding *The Asteroid Mandate* hostage. Four hours later she turned off the light, half sick. "Actually, Charlie, I don't have a contract," she had explained earlier when he brought it up. "I just thought it would be nice to meet, spend some time..." She waggled her head in a loosey-goosey way that had nothing to do with who in the world she really was.

A stellar move, it turned out. He seemed to buy it. And for the rest of the evening she strove for enough bonhomie to prove her point. She was gay just short of manic, charming just short of sociopathic. She discovered a tilt of her head she never knew she had, an arch of her eyebrow that could house Boy Scouts in a storm. She laughed musically. She imparted confidences of no substance whatsoever.

The closest she came to flirting with the coot was to touch his arm once, when she asked whether brawn *and* brains ran in his family. She was a full set of underwear short of shameless. Then she remembered an old boyfriend had once told her that whenever she thought she was being winsome the average male still needed a secret decoder ring. Even Decker seemed to like the show, which really depressed her. By bedtime they were singing Welsh drinking songs and everybody forgot about contracts and memoirs.

Val eased out of the sleeping bag and tiptoed over to the table, where she replaced the manuscript. She was strangely devoid of feeling. And strangely devoid of a plan. She climbed back into the bag, her eyes wide and inconsolable in the dark. There was a rustle, and a hand drew back the flap. Decker's whisper came close to her ear. "How bad are they?"

"Oh, God, Wade," she moaned softly, happy he was awake and she could disgorge some of the horror. "They're self-indulgent and actionable."

"Oh," he whispered. "I see."

"They're disorganized, petty, and boring." She sniffed. "You come off okay," she added with a little roll of her hand he couldn't see because it was inside her sleeping bag.

"Good to know."

Val started to feel giddy. "Although why the resplendent Leslie chose you is a matter of some mystery, apparently."

"I can understand why."

"He devotes a sentence and a half to you."

"True love."

"Half a dozen others don't get off so lucky."

Silence. Then: "Can you edit them?"

"No one can edit them. Where they're not actually incoherent, they're rant, cant, and bile in Courier twelve point." And, although she wasn't about to mention it to the man who wouldn't talk about his dead wife, Charles Cable's mem-WAHRS contained some disturbing passages about Leslie Decker that were dated two and a half years ago. All of which added up, in Val's mind, to a possible motive for murder. *She's all I have, my beautiful brave Leslie, all I have in the noble fight against everything wicked that seeks to destroy our lake paradise. Without her fine mind and passionate heart, everything we've worked for is lost. If something happens and Leslie walks away from this life and death struggle where we've been comrades in arms all this time, I'll just have to wring her faithless neck.*

This sort of revelation was baffling.

If Charlie Cable had killed Leslie, why would he draw such attention to himself?

If Charlie Cable hadn't killed Leslie, why would he draw such attention to himself?

And how had a writer that bad topped the *New York Times* bestseller list for thirty-two weeks?

Decker curled an arm under his head. "The show tonight was very entertaining."

"I'm glad you liked it."

"A side of you I've never seen."

She shot him a hangdog look. "In our very long acquaintance."

He grunted. "What are you going to do?"

"Cry. Chew off a fingernail. Stall."

"And then what?"

Her lip trembled. "Call my unindicted co-conspirator and appeal to his better nature."

"That would be Hathaway?"

"Of course," she hissed. "Who else is there?" It was such a sorry truth of her life, such an elephantine truth about her heart, that she started to cry. Her shoulders were too tired to shrug. "He's got to walk away from everything with Charlie's name on it."

"If you can appeal to sex, money, or vanity, it just might work."

Val kicked at the interior of the bag in a fit of sudden sweatiness. "You don't know him," she whispered fiercely.

"Actually," said Decker lightly, "I know him very well." He started to move away. "I just haven't slept with him."

The next morning, while Decker took a quick dip in the glassy lake, Val shoveled in some stale cornflakes and watched Charlie Cable hook up his marine radio just long enough to call Portage Airlines for a pickup. An hour and a half later she cast a mournful eye at the manuscript for *The Asteroid Mandate*, where Charlie had tossed it on his breadbox until Fir Na Tine met his demands, and felt that leaving it behind was some kind of heart-wrenching war story about separated lovers. All she could bring away from her two days in wilderness hell were Charlie Cable's memoirs, which she clutched under her wing. She found herself wishing it was a can of SpaghettiOs.

Cable had made it clear while he soaked his eggs in ketchup that Val was his editor. "Cameron," he said, "you're a stand-up kind of gal. I trust you with my memoirs. Nobody else. You, Cameron, you hear me? Part of the deal. Least I can do, you come all this way for me." His uncombed hair was vertical. On him it looked like an experiment in static electricity. And all she could say was, "Oh, Charlie," wondering balefully just how fast she could circulate her c.v. She felt like a 1983 Dodge Dart in a wrecking yard, compacted down to the size of a suitcase.

Decker beamed.

She loped to the float plane and turned. Because Cable was watching her intently, she gave him a look like she knew she was holding a lost book of the Bible. Many waves, a few blown kisses, and Val found herself airborne with Decker and a burly guy named Luther. She sat behind them, past caring about altitude. The two men speculated happily about the cause of engine malfunction all the way back to the Hathaway cottage. After a perfect landing at Peter's dock, Decker absentmindedly helped her out of the plane, arguing the fine points of pistons with Luther, gave Val's back a brotherly pat, and climbed back inside.

She stood there watching as Luther backed the plane away from the dock, feeling strangely disappointed. *We shared SpaghettiOs and underwear and moose muck and that's the best you can do, Decker?* Her baldheaded, gay accountant had patted her in the same way after he told her she owed the government over a thousand dollars. Just then Wade Decker looked right at her through the windshield, mimed a telephone with his right hand, and pointed at her.

She gave him a tight smile that would have put a toothless moonshiner to shame, and then tried a casual wave that came across like she was casting out demons. What on earth was her problem? Maybe she'd used up all her charm the night before. While Luther kept jawing away, turning the plane in an easy float, Decker smiled and gave her a two-fingered salute.

Inside the Hathaway cottage, she set Charlie Cable's manuscript on the table by the phone, then went into the L.L. Bean bedroom and stripped off the torn pants that dried mud had hardened into a papier mâché sculpture. She shuddered as she pulled off the top that smelled like either bog or sweat and allowed herself a naked sixty seconds collapsed on the down comforter before showering and getting into the change of clothes she had brought. As she brushed her teeth and hair and slid some lipstick over her mouth, she felt a ripple of her professional self. Good. She found a bottle of Perrier in the fridge—Muffy and Lana weren't completely useless—and filled a glass. Time to make the call, but first she needed to settle into her game head.

But instead of dredging up useful memories of publishing contracts where she had bested Peter Hathaway, she pictured toting the rucksack and paddles and life jackets through mosquito-infested woods. She pictured paddling so hard she could no longer feel her arms. She pictured dragging the canoe through the deep mud until her legs were shaking uncontrollably. Not only had she, Valjean Cameron, done these things, she had done them well.

Game head, achieved.

She picked up the phone and dialed the private line.

"Hathaway." No peppermint foot bath today, apparently.

"Peter," she said in her most business-like way. "Val."

"Where the hell are you?" His voice had rocketed up an octave. He actually sounded worried.

"At your place."

"I had to call Caroline Selkirk, finally, when I didn't hear from you." The way he said Caroline's name made her sound like some especially difficult department at AT&T. "She didn't know where you were either. Just that Wade Decker was flying you to Cable's and that's the last she heard."

"The weather was bad, so we did the rest of the trip by canoe."

"Canoe?" He was incredulous. As if she had said jet pack.

"Yes. Listen." This was her one clear shot at getting him to understand the problem and work with her to figure out a solution to Cable's extortion. "Charles Cable won't sign off on *The Asteroid Mandate*—"

"What!"

"—Listen. He won't sign off on *Mandate* unless Fir Na Tine first comes out with his memoirs."

"Are you kidding me?"

It was delicious to hear his disbelief. The Peter Hathaway of yore. "No."

"What did you tell him?"

"Without Cable's knowing, I read the memoirs last night."

"And?" He sounded like she couldn't possibly get the words out fast enough.

And this, Val told herself with quiet satisfaction, was why she was Peter Hathaway's senior editor, for just these matters of taste and experience. "They're unpublishable." It was a word the two of them saved for only the most craven and despicable works, because each of them believed there was nothing so problematic they couldn't bring it into line with some Olympian editing.

There was silence on the other end. A thousand miles away, she could still see his face, that narrow-eyed look he'd get when he was calculating how to get the author he wanted at a price he could tolerate. But in the case of Charlie Cable's demand, professional pride would bubble to the top of the bile in Peter Hathaway's throat.

Fir Na Tine stood for something, damn it, in that amazing shrinking world of book publishing. Without standards of excellence, pretty soon what everyone called literature would be shaped by writer wannabes with a credit card and the link to CreateSpace. Saying no to Charlie Cable's demand drew an indelible line in the sand, and Val and Peter stood unbowed on the other side.

Finally, he spoke. "Sign him."

Her heart did a tumble. "What?"

"You heard me. Sign him."

"Sign him."

"We're editors, Valjean," Peter barked into the phone, cutting her off while she sputtered. "Whatever's amiss with Charlie's memoirs, we'll fix it."

"Amiss?" She yelled into the phone. "He calls Dixon Foote a womanizing hammer monkey who doesn't pay his taxes and has a secret taste for little boys."

"It's a joke. He's joking."

"It's libel."

"I can finesse that kind of thing."

"But you won't have to, Peter." She took a deep breath. "There's condition number two of Charlie Cable's handing us his space junk thriller—"

"Namely?"

"I have to edit the piece of crap memoirs. Me. Not you, not

yoga girl, Peter, not some schizo bad poet you rescue. *Me.*"

He was silent for a long moment. "Fir Na Tine needs *The Asteroid Mandate,* Val." His voice dropped. "And I'm not entirely sure even Charlie Cable can keep us afloat."

She got a little chill. And as all the spaces between his words got filled in, she saw she was left with a strange choice. Refuse to meet Charlie Cable's demands for the thriller and leave her job at Fir Na Tine, or meet Charlie Cable's demands and possibly lose her job anyway.

"Please," said Peter Hathaway softly and let it hang there.

With a sigh, she finally said, "I'll try to change his mind."

"About the memoirs?"

"About my editing them." She knew there was no chance Charlie Cable would give up on the memoirs altogether—he was too irrationally attached to them.

A beat. "And if you can't?"

"I don't want my name anywhere near the book."

"Fine. Fine. You got it. You'll see, Val, it won't be so bad." Val stared unblinking at the raised pattern on the duvet cover until it was all she could see, while the maddening man she loved was nattering on about how squeaky clean Charlie Cable is—

Squeaky clean? There was that little bothersome matter of his threats against Leslie Decker. Should she mention it now? Why wasn't she mentioning it?

"—which," Peter was saying, "would certainly go far in terms of establishing Charlie's creds as a memoirist. It'll give the libel lawyers fits."

And then what suddenly came to her was the sort of bargain she had never before struck. She piped up, "Then I want *The Asteroid Mandate.*"

He didn't understand. Libel, yes. Business in the toilet, yes. Peppermint foot baths, yes. This, no. "What do you mean?"

"I want to edit *The Asteroid Mandate.*" Not really, but it would look good on her c.v. if she either left her job at Fir Na Tine...or Fir Na Tine collapsed right out from under her. "Be the publisher,

Peter," Val went on, reasonably, noting how plain it all sounded. "You don't need to edit it too." When he didn't say anything, she went on, "That's my price."

While she listened to him huff and sigh a few times, she rolled her eyes, counting just how many fingernails she had broken—five—on the canoe trip from Hell. And without her even trying particularly hard, a plan appeared before her like the opening credits of a movie. Try to get Cable to change his mind about the editing of his mem-WAHRS without drawing his suspicion about how much she hated them. And dig into the murder of Leslie Decker, despite Wade Decker's stonewalling, because all bets were off if she could lay the deed at Charlie Cable's feet. Finally, update her c.v.

Peter Hathaway's voice came over the line. "Deal." And just as Val's heart lifted the way it had when she and Decker had reached Charlie Cable's wilderness cabin and she thought her hardships were at an end, Peter Hathaway attached a condition to the deal. She had until the end of the day to fax him a signed contract with Charles Cable, or he would come up to Lake Wendaban and damn well get the job done himself—and, if that happened, Valjean Cameron would be out of a job. Fir Na Tine needed team players. "And, for your information," he ended prissily, "Daria Flottner is not a schizo poet, she's a schizo performance artist."

As he hung up on her, Val's first cold, outraged response was to get yet another copy of the contract faxed from the office, hire the Portage Airlines guy to fly it up to Charlie Cable, get his signature, and fax it back to the office. She could get the repellent job done without having a hand in it. Everybody happy. She'd hang onto her job and find ways of keeping Peter Hathaway out of her line of vision. Off her radar. Out of her office. And most definitely her pants. Val could just head home. But not until she could clear or condemn Charlie Cable for the murder of Leslie Decker. Like stumbling across boulders shouldering a stuffed, sixty-pound dry bag in order to hold her head up while Decker carried the canoe, it was finally maybe just a matter of crazy-headed pride. Getting at the truth of Charlie Cable's involvement in Leslie Decker's murder was just one more sixty-pound dry bag. And the boulders were somewhere up ahead.

18

Her Aunt Greta Bistritz always told her, "Where you begin is where you end." Because she lavishly admired this aunt who raised her, Val tended to put this observation right up there at the top of the pithiness scale with Sartre's "Hell is other people." And because Val really never understood what the hell Greta meant, she kept waiting for an experience of her own to clarify it. She was still waiting. Greta's other rules for living included things like "It's just as easy to fall in love with a rich man as a poor man." Greta had hip fifties hair all her life, like a load of medium-length, elegant ash blond commas had been unloaded over her head. She had almond-shaped hazel eyes, a wide, wry mouth, and an acute angle of a nose that was really too large for her face, but nobody cared, least of all Greta.

A Manhattan office job with the Department of Commerce had somehow brought her, at age forty, Ben Biderman, a bioethicist at Columbia. Val suspected she must have got him drunk, grilled him about his finances, and signed on. Or maybe she didn't, maybe she ignored all her own advice and just fell in love. For eleven years, he and Greta climbed ruins together, carved turkeys together, and shared each other's bed every Friday night like clockwork, only they never made a commitment.

In many ways it suited Greta, who at midlife came to think of inaction as a kind of rest. "Our relationship," she told Val as they walked into a Zabar's on Lexington Avenue so she could buy the Baci chocolates she served Ben for dessert every Friday night, "is like treading water. We're not getting anywhere, but we'll sink to the bottom if we stop."

Maybe from the Bistritz side of the family Val inherited a taste for inertia, riding on her chromosomes like attached earlobes or male pattern baldness. Maybe this inertia genome was what explained her relationship with Peter Hathaway. So she looked to Greta's life for a clue to her own. And Greta was now sixty-four and alone ever since the day thirteen years ago that Ben Biderman collapsed on the platform of the number six train, effectively ending their decade-long discussion about whether marriage made any sense for two people who didn't plan on having children—a problem that had long since become moot.

Where you begin is where you end.

As Val folded the one spare top she brought with her to this Northwoods gig, she knew she felt shot through with inaction. And—she thought as she jammed the top mercilessly into her laptop case—nothing would change, nothing at all, until the next time her boss turns his countenance upon her...the next time she takes on his most unreasonable demands as her holy mission.

She heard a boat pull up at the dock. Maybe she'd get lucky and it was a team of waterborne Jehovah's Witnesses. She could smile politely and tell them no, she hasn't given much thought to the End of Days. Then they'd leave her a copy of *The Watchtower* and go. Anybody else meant more trouble than she could handle for however long she remained on Lake Wendaban. She stood inside the screen door. It was a woman she had never seen, tying up two boats, the one she'd come in and the one she had apparently towed.

Already Val didn't like it.

The newcomer looked early twenties, tops, and had loose black curls held back with a twisted pink bandana. The white cami looked great against her tan and she had a denim skirt that sat low around her hips. Maybe it was just another poet babe who stopped by to see if Peter was around. The Daria Flottner of the Northwoods.

Val stepped outside.

"You must be Val," said the newcomer.

"Hi."

She came across the dock in her negligible little rubber thongs. "I'm Josie Blanton. I'm just coming from Wade's. He says you need a boat." She started untying the tow rope.

The fact that this tanned and slender lovely was coming from Wade Decker's place at nine thirty in the morning made Val stop in her tracks. "Did he happen to mention why?"

Josie Blanton looked skyward. "He said to tell you he was betting against your boss's better nature and that you'd need the little runabout to find Charlie."

So now she was totally on her own. "Did he also send along a bloodhound?"

"You don't need one." Josie hooked her thumbs into the beltless loops of her skirt. "Charlie's coming to town today."

"Do tell." Would the pilot, if she hired him to fly in to get the signature, miss Charlie Cable? Would Val be out of a couple hundred bucks? Was it still tax-deductible?

"He called Wade late last night on the marine radio—well, it took two relays to get him the message. The MNR's going to be on the lake a week ahead of schedule and Charlie is meeting with them to go over the loon data."

"What's the MNR?"

"Ministry of Natural Resources."

Val nodded, longing to be back in the place where no one, but no one, ever uttered expressions like *loon data*. She sauntered over to the boats gently bumping up against the dock. "What do you do for Decker?"

Josie's eyebrows shot up. "This here's the one you can borrow." She parried Val's question, then gently pushed her toward the red and white Lund. "Twenty-five horse." Then her thumbs ran sort of experimentally around the inside of her denim waistband. "As for Wade, I clean, I help with the books, sometimes I shop, cook, garden." Her brown eyes were serene. "Whatever he needs done."

"So, you're an employee?" Val turned quickly to the other

woman as though she was trying to trip her up on the witness stand.

Josie laughed a trill of fairy queen merriment. "Well," she said finally, coming damn close to Aunt Greta's wry smile, "I guess you could call it that."

Clearly her camping companion was over the dead Leslie. "So where am I going to get myself to in this...vessel?"

"Charlie's renting a houseboat from the marina. The meetings will take two days. He's got to show them nesting sites. Wade figures you should try Point of No Return ballpark early this afternoon."

"Can't he just take me?" Don't whine, Cameron.

Josie's hand fingered the bandana twist as she shook her head. "He's got trouble back home. His building in Toronto is melting down. Literally. The air conditioning blew and the HVAC workers are on strike." She stepped into the Lund. "I've got time to get you through the basics, Val, depending on how fast you pick it up, and then I've got to get back to Wade's."

"So what is it today, cook or cleaning lady?"

Bandana Girl actually wrinkled her nose. "It's more like what you'd call miscellaneous. Don't you ever do anything for your boss beyond the job description?" Val looked closely at her innocent expression, trying to determine whether Decker had told her to work in a crack about the unreasonable demands of pathetically beloved bosses.

Josie looked up at her expectantly. "Are you coming?"

Val stepped inside, scrambled to keep her balance, and sat next to her teacher. As the boat rocked, a tattooed word appeared between Josie's buoyant little breasts: HERE. And when she reached hard for a life jacket, another tattooed word edged into view, low over her left hip: HERE. A map of secret delights? A GPS for her erogenous zones? Places where Decker had planted his lips?

For forty-five minutes Josie took her through all the steps to starting out, which went from squeezing the bulb, starting in neutral, choking, pulling the cord, shifting into reverse, shifting into forward, and steering. Val failed the pulling the cord part of the lesson while Josie was barking out suggestive things like "snap it" and "rip it" and she was only imagining her fingers clamped around Peter Hathaway's nose. But when she switched to picturing her ripping, snapping hand on Wade Decker's shirt, the motor kicked right in and Josie moved to the middle seat.

When Val gave it some gas the boat lurched forward away from the dock, slamming across the small waves at an alarming speed. She was afraid to shift her steering arm or let go of what Josie Blanton had called the tiller, so they were on a breakneck course. Josie was yelling to slow down and was patting the air down like a Jets cheerleader at halftime.

Val twisted her wrist and the boat jerked and flew faster, so she twisted her wrist in the opposite direction, which met with a look of long-suffering approval from Bandana Girl, who then pointed violently to the right.

Val pulled her tiller hand in hard against her, which meant they turned left, fast enough to pitch Josie Blanton off her seat, her legs flying up like an overturned potato bug. Val took a quick look to see if any more HEREs appeared, but apparently she'd have to ramp up the out-of-control boating experience in order to get that piece of information.

The return trip to Peter Hathaway's dock was docile. Josie named the five things you have to have on board according to Ontario Boating Regulations—whistle, bailer, thirty-meter buoyant line, paddle, and life jacket—and Josie slipped a shoal map into a plastic case and tied it to one of the stern seat struts. Docking was violent, despite Josie's sexual instructions, "Easy, easy, take it slow, that's right, no, don't speed up," and resulted in what could only be called splintering of wood.

As Josie hopped out of the boat she ticked off a few pessimistic observations—"You're not a cowboy, so don't act like one," and "Remember, boating is a serious business"—and Val realized how charming it is when twenty-two-year-olds go all parental. She'd given up the idea of hiring a flyboy to get a contract to Charlie

Cable. If Wade Decker was providing her with the tools and the skills to get the job done once and for all, she'd see it through. After all, she was now a woman with a sawed-off bleach bottle bailer. She could handle anything.

Anything except a motorboat, as it turned out.

Having wasted half an hour, after Josie left, ripping the pull cord with no success, Val cursed the boat. It turned over once, when she had the choke out, but then it died and she thought if there were some mechanical types standing around they would shake their uncombed heads and agree: "Flooded." In the end, she riffled through an old phone directory and was about to call a water taxi that advertised WE GET YOU THERE AND KEEP YOU WARM AND DRY when the phone rang.

It was Decker, calling from Toronto. "I thought you might want a heads up, Valjean."

Her mouth thinned at the sound of her full name. "Go on."

"I just got a call from Peter."

"Hathaway?" She sounded more incredulous than she thought she should.

"He's on his way up—"

"What?" What about the twenty-four hours he'd given her? "Why?"

"He said something about having to nail down Charlie Cable, no more delays. Apparently there's a rumor someone named Julian Onnedonk is after him now—"

Julian Onnedonk. The wunderkind of a small, well-funded indie press. As wily and deadly as a mongoose. No wonder Peter was dropping everything and heading north with dispatch. Damn. Why hadn't she just signed the maniac when she had been downing his loon stew? Her skin started to tingle with the kind of professional dismay she only felt when some wonderful writer was making noises about one of the "bigger boys" understanding her better. In their weird little worlds, bigger advances made them feel the love. In the world of Valjean Cameron, she wasn't quite sure what made her feel the love.

Decker went on, "You should know your boss is bringing what he called his special lady friend."

It just kept getting better and better. Somehow the note of apology in Wade Decker's voice didn't help. There wasn't enough apology anywhere to cover her fury at Peter Hathaway's overriding his own stupid ultimatum in the matter of Charlie Cable. He was dismissing whatever he could—dismissing her competence, dismissing their nights together, dismissing, well, her altogether. From Fir Na Tine. And all because he couldn't dismiss what had been so damn good about the two of them together. Her heart felt truly sore, there was nothing she could do about it, and the likelihood of losing Cable to Julian Onnedonk was only partly responsible.

Speaking took too much effort. Words were shrinking. What to do with them had departed as well. When all she could do was stare at the Hathaway floor, Decker finally jumped back in. "And he wanted to know if I could fly them from Toronto."

Ah. Val made a futile gesture. She knew better than to ask what Decker had told him. "What time will they get here?"

"Sometime late this afternoon. I've got my hands full right now."

"Did he mention me?"

A beat. "Not directly."

"Not directly? Tell me."

"I don't think—"

"What did he say, Decker?" When she couldn't quite catch what he mumbled, she interrupted. "What?"

She heard him sigh rather lavishly. "That he was surrounded by incompetents."

And there it was.

It hardly mattered that he was wrong.

It was just how Peter Hathaway saw it.

She looked around the carefully furnished cottage where there were probably mice in teapots and garter snakes in cake pans. "I suppose I've got to clear out of this place," Val said softly, more to herself.

"Don't go feeling bad about that, Val. You can stay at Caroline's until you figure out what you're going to do. For that matter, you can stay at my place—"

She felt so...exiled. Like Eleanor of Aquitaine. "I'll head back to New York as soon as I can."

"But not before tomorrow, I hope."

"What do you mean?"

"There's the gala tonight."

"Gala?"

"The fundraiser for the Youth Alliance."

"You mean the square dance?"

"Well, yes, but come on, let me take you. You can't leave the lake thinking it's all fists to the face and moose muck portages, Val."

"I don't know—"

He offered an enticement. "Charlie might even be there. So if you miss him at Point of No Return, you can catch him at the gala."

"I don't care about that."

"Now that Hathaway's getting him to sign?"

"Make no mistake, Wade," she said. "I'm getting him to sign. Me. I'm finding him. Wherever on this lake he's counting loon chicks today, I'm finding him. First."

It was a crazy matter of honor. If it was the last official thing she'd do in her career at Fir Na Tine.

"And if I then find out for sure, with or without your help, that he killed your wife," when he tried to override her, she pressed on, "I will tear the contract up."

Decker was silent.

"I appreciate the ride tonight," said Val quietly. First thing in the morning, regardless of where she spent the night, she would leave Lake Wendaban behind her forever. "I'll be ready at seven."

19

Val studied the lake map like she was planning the Normandy Invasion. Once she located Selkirk Peninsula, and then the Hathaway island, she scoured the map until her eye caught the words Point of No Return. When she gauged it jutted out into the main lake closer to town than to where she was sitting at Peter Hathaway's dining table, she let out a soft whistle. There was just no way to judge how long it would take her, puttering along in Decker's little boat.

Call Caroline drifted across her mind. A sensible notion—although Caroline seemed pretty busy—and probably altogether more sensible than trying to corner Charlie Cable at Point of No Return by herself. Even if it looked pretty much like a wide open channel all the way there. On the one hand, fewer scary shallows to hit and pitch herself clear out of the boat. On the other hand, deeper water whenever she managed—in her cowboy fashion—to pitch herself clear out of the boat.

Where could she cadge a quick ride?

Call the water taxi guy who promises to GET YOU THERE AND KEEP YOU WARM AND DRY. Does it get any better than that?

Call Kay and work in something about Iqaluit.

Call Josie and just plain pay her.

Call Luke the handyman and just plain pay him.

Call Dixon and guilt trip the guy. No, she wanted to reach Point of No Return sometime in the present millennium. Slowly,

Val folded the map to expose the route from the Hathaway cottage to Point of No Return, there on the north shore just inside the East Arm of Lake Wendaban. She glanced at the scale: one inch equaled one mile. Spreading her fingers across the route, she figured she was four miles to Point of No Return. That didn't help.

Still, she tucked the map back into the waterproof map case, then paged through the contract for *The Asteroid Mandate* to the terms. There, in the margins, she penned a fourth item to the conditions of publication. *Included in this advance, Fir Na Tine offers to publish Author's memoirs in a timely manner for which Author will receive standard royalties. Print run will be determined by the Publisher.* More than that she couldn't think through. More than that she couldn't give him. "Timely manner" allowed enough wiggle room for a total game changer to find its way into the picture, like, say, a well-placed asteroid—the real kind, not a Cable fabrication. There would be no more money up front, and she was counting on royalties being negligible. They'd keep the print run down to something smart but pathetic, and she would refuse to address anything like subsidiary rights or promotion. Some lines she could most definitely hold.

Then she stuffed the pen and the publishing contract into the waterproof map case and zipped it shut. Taking a deep breath, Val stepped outside and winced in the bright sunlight. A cloudless sky, a warm and steady breeze. At the edge of the dock, she shrugged into the bulky PFD and snapped the straps. Then, clutching the map case, she stepped tentatively into Decker's little boat, which started to rock. Val sank quickly onto the seat and grabbed the oarlock with one hand and the motor with the other.

With about as much mindfulness as she could muster at short notice, she tied the cord of the map case to the seat and then mentally ran down Josie Blanton's checklist for the care and feeding of objectionable watercraft. Squeeze gas bulb, check for neutral gear, press electric starter if too much of a pantywaist to pull cord for manual start. Bulb squeezed, gear checked, electric starter pressed. When the motor sputtered to life, Val gripped the tiller, hoping to hell she could remember complex maneuvers like right, left, forward, and backward, then sat there for a minute just letting it run.

Puttering backwards at a speed that would rival Dixon Foote, the boat suddenly tugged to a stop and the motor whirred. Horrified, Val realized she had forgotten to untie the line from the dock, so she shifted into neutral, fumbled the line free, flipped it into the boat, and started again. When nothing truly dramatic or life-threatening happened in the first five minutes, Val picked up speed, causing a couple of nearby seagulls to take off squawking as she passed.

When a sleek, faster boat closed in suddenly from the right of her, she heard Josie Blanton's voice: *Whenever you don't know what to do, slow down and don't panic.* The girl had been so impressed with her own sagacity that she added she was pretty sure Gandhi—which she pronounced Gandy—himself had said it. But since it was all Val had, she slowed down and waited to see what would happen.

The sleek silver boat, never having heard of Gandy, apparently, crossed her path at a safe distance, with a quick wave from a tall, blond woman at the helm. Once she was out of the West Arm of Lake Wendaban, Val took a long look around at the views that had opened up in the center of the lake. Without perfect weather, she'd be lost. But all she could feel was a warm, slight breeze that meant her no harm, and all she could see were a couple of little white curls of clouds.

Ahead, according to the map, but still distant, was the Point of No Return. Val squinted against the bright light, looking for a houseboat or an official-looking boat skippered and crewed by folks from whatever ministry tracked loon data. Nothing. No one. But Point of No Return sloped off into back bays, and Val kept her hand steady on the tiller and headed Wade Decker's little boat toward what she hoped was Charlie Cable, somewhere.

Part of her expected to see a water taxi carrying their archrival Julian Onnedonk, flying the flag with the golden cobra armband of his Astarte Press, cutting her off on its way to Point of No Return. For Val, nothing in the past few days had been named better, because she was going to corner crazy old Cable, get his signature, and leave the place she would never see again as fast as she possibly could.

She closed in on the Point, saw no evidence of the dreaded Onnedonk—or, maybe worse, the dreaded Hathaway, who had panicked at the mere rumor of a rival—and slowed the boat. No shoals lurked in her way. No gulls created a diversion. She rounded the point at a good distance from the shore, and there it was.

A houseboat.

A houseboat painted to look like a log cabin against a backdrop of evergreens. Like a floating mural. Perfect cover for a bestselling hermit who just wants to count loons and otherwise be left alone. Tucked up against the ragged shore, the painted cabin on the side of the houseboat looked like the kind of dark and opaque place someone like the Unabomber would call home. Val slowed down, checked the map quickly for shoals—none—and headed toward the houseboat.

Scrutinizing the shoreline, there was no handy dock to ram, so she fervently hoped all she'd have to do is somehow come alongside the houseboat and Cable would catch her line. Then she noticed him mucking around on the shore, crabbing awkwardly along some small rocks in black hip waders and a blowzy gray t-shirt, holding a clipboard. Was he alone? Were the federal loon people somewhere out of sight on the houseboat? Or not there at all? Should she have slid Caroline's rifle into the motorboat?

At that moment in time, absolutely nothing in the world scared her. Her goal was in sight. She slowed the boat and risked frightening the loon families—after all, her experience with water fowl was limited to Daffy Duck—and called out in a chipper way. The words "Yoo hoo" actually escaped her lips, probably for the first time in her life. "Charlie!" As she neared the side of the houseboat, the immediate future was dark and impenetrable. Was she going to ram the houseboat? Was she going to float right up onto the rocks? Was she going to knock Charlie Cable off his feet? Was she going to stall out the motor and drift helplessly back out to the channel—worse yet, without a signature on the bottom line?

It felt like an ecstasy of variables.

Cable stood up straighter, shielded his large, crazy-looking eyes with his hand, and bellowed, "Cameron, cut your motor and let the wind blow you in."

What wind? "Okay, Charlie!" She waved extravagantly at him.

To Val's amazement, it worked. And for the next minute, some combination of boat, waves, and breeze blew her closer to the man she was uncomfortably persuaded to think was the killer of Leslie Decker. If she, Val, had caused any homicidal interruption of Charlie Cable's loon inventory, there pretty much wasn't a damn thing she could do.

In the moment he waded out into the water to grab the boat, Charlie Cable bore a strong resemblance to his own author photo on the back of that blockbuster, *The Nebula Covenant*. He looked focused and competent, but still not at all like anyone you were likely to come across at the Starbucks on Park Avenue at 49th. Still, the man had skills. When he grabbed the boat and pulled her to shore, she suddenly appreciated his strength and utter comfort in this wilderness.

Charles Cable brought her alongside, looped her line to the houseboat's, threw one of Decker's bumpers between them, and turned slowly to face her, slowly folding his massive arms. He seemed impervious to the fact that he was standing hip-high in lake water. Glowering at her, he yelled, "Bring a contract, Cameron?"

At least she was acquainted enough with this bestselling madman to believe his glower was associated with Serious Thought. Setting aside any images of how easy it must have been to hurl a sylph like Leslie Decker through a second-story window, she went for a normal smile. "I did, Charlie." She started to unzip the map case.

"Let's get it done, then." He flung back his head and cried to the cloudless skies. "I've got the MNR meeting me here anytime now." When he slammed a beefy hand against the side of the boat, Val thought it was more a show of anxiety about the loon meeting than about anything Val herself signified.

The zipper stuck. Val nattered, "Is this a good spot, then, for loon babies, Charlie?"

"Chicks!" He bellowed with a fond look on his mug. "Chicks."

"Used to be. Used to be," he said darkly. "May be again, right here, Cameron, but not if..." He trailed off, scowling at the papers she held out to him. She watched him hang onto the boat as he patted himself rather futilely, then mumbled, "Got a pen, Cameron?" When she produced one, he stuck it between his jumbled teeth and flipped heedlessly through the contract until he exposed the last page. Then he messily folded back all the other pages and set the document on the seat ahead of her. As he clicked the pen and bent over the side of the boat, Val spoke up.

"You really should read it, Charlie," she told him. She didn't want any pushback later.

He fixed her with a look. "You leading with my memoirs?" he quizzed her.

"Yes." As she studied his face, she saw a kind of aged innocence there. All around the eyes. A man with a bad combination of strong ideals and misplaced faith. In all his years, had he been too innocent not to lash out whenever he'd finally understood that he'd been had? Or too innocent, really, even to know when he'd been had?

He grunted softly. "Trust you, Cameron, on all the other stuff," said Charlie Cable gruffly. "You'll do right by my memoirs."

"I will." And it seemed prudent to add, "We'll work together on making them the best they can be." Already her mind flashed ahead to an image of herself as a ragged galley slave, keeling over, finally, unnoticed.

Leaning over the contract, hanging onto Decker's rocking boat, Charles Cable signed with an illegible flourish, then placed a very delicate period at the end of it. "Appreciate your help, Cameron," he said, lips tightly shut, pressed into invisibility by the moment.

"And I'm editing *Asteroid*, Charlie." Better tell him now. Before Peter shows up and even the clear water of Lake Wendaban gets muddied in ways only Peter could manage. Cable looked up at her with an expression of childlike wonder she found hard to interpret. She cracked a smile. "So you're stuck with me for both."

Tickled, he pushed on the sides of the boat like he was trying to overturn a float in a swimming pool. "Well, that's just grand news."

"Peter and I fought over it," she added, hanging on for dear life.

At that the maniac of the Northwoods cackled. In that moment, behind the ignored hair and the shoddy shaving, the snaggleteeth he could never take the time to have fixed because he was out saving the world, she saw a brief shadow of the young man Charlie Cable must have been. At a time before he had to bellow at all the rest of them because they just weren't listening. Now he was at an age when crazy and idealistic and strong and completely without vanity was really kind of beautiful. Suddenly she liked him better than Peter Hathaway, who always knew what every cell visible to anyone else was doing, what it was feeling, how it was looking—and what it could do for him.

And then she remembered he was on his way up to find and sign Charlie Cable himself, chased by the specter of Julian Onnedonk. All of which meant—bearing in mind their last conversation—Val was as good as out of a job. At the end of this and every day, Peter Hathaway had no faith. No faith that Val Cameron could deliver. And it struck her that he very likely had never had any faith—and this Northwoods assignment was just a sure way of putting it to the test. The realization felt worse to her than overhearing Daria Flottner crooning nonsense to him and bathing his feet, which were really not so much to look at.

As Charlie Cable handed her the folded contract, she added quietly, "As long as I'm at Fir Na Tine, Charlie, I'm your editor." She gave him a smile that was more reassuring than she felt. In fact, holding the signed contract it had taken her days of near mythic suffering to get, she felt nothing. All she had managed was to get Peter Hathaway exactly what he had wanted in the first place—and lose her job. The truth of it seemed like just a bald metaphor for her relationship with the man who had suddenly become both her former lover and her former boss.

She had gained nothing.

"You in trouble, Cameron?"

She looked at the bestselling author, who was scrutinizing her. She took in a big breath that was just a little too noisy. "Hard to say, Charlie." It always made her nervous when someone—especially a man—caught her out in any of those many small ways she liked to keep hidden. She fixed him with a look, and said, "Are you?" Here in this remote, deserted bay, was she inviting him to confess to the murder of Leslie Decker? Had she really become just that rash?

She watched his chest take in enough air to fill out his old t-shirt in the second before it escaped in a blare of laughter that echoed around the bay. In a movement so quick she didn't even have time to flinch, Charlie Cable scooped up his clipboard, leaned in toward her, and swatted her on the head. "Me, Cameron?" He stomped around in the thigh-high water like he was seven years old and playing hopscotch. "If I'm not in trouble with someone, then I might as well be dead."

"Is that how Leslie felt?"

His face fell. "Little Leslie," he said finally. But that was all.

"Your comrade in arms."

He squinted at a distant point that could have been a past that had fallen short. "So much more we could have done."

"Before she was killed."

"Before she died."

Why was Charlie Cable splitting these particular hairs? Was he whitewashing his own involvement? "She was thrown out a window, Charlie."

A tight little shake of his head. And then he said an extraordinary thing. "She jumped."

"Why would she do that, Charlie?"

"Why would anyone kill her?" he countered.

She could certainly list the usual reasons for murder—greed, betrayal, blackmail, revenge, jealousy, convenience, love gone all sorts of wrong—but she stuck instead with his comment about suicide. It could be an interesting new possibility. One that would make her feel a whole lot better about binding Fir Na Tine to him—with or without her—by contract. "Why would she jump, Charlie?"

At that he started to breathe hard and she realized he was almost hyperventilating. "Because she was too good for this goddamn world," he shouted, right in Val's face. For an instant she felt like she had lost her hearing. The boat was rocking, but there was no sound. Overhead, seagulls slashed white, low across the sky, close enough she could see their beaks opening and closing, but there was no sound. All she could hear was the sound of her heart pounding, which felt like a dangerous surf between her ears. Over Charlie Cable's shoulder, which was way too close to her face to feel secure, she saw a blue and white boat approaching them.

Too good for this goddamn world.

Reason for suicide?

Or reason for murder? Had the goddamn world according to Charlie Cable finally destroyed something in Leslie Selkirk Decker that he killed her out of some kind of perverted love for who she had been? In his strange mind, did he have to kill her to save her?

20

She nearly collapsed with relief when she realized she could hear the motor of the approaching boat. "Here's your meeting, Charlie," Val managed to get out as he fumbled the clipboard, which clattered to the floor of Wade Decker's little boat. She stumbled over a seat to snatch it and hold it out with a shaking hand. All she wanted, all she ever wanted, was to find her way home. She was no good here. She had nothing to give. Right now all she could say for sure about Valjean Cameron was that her heart fluttered like feathers, like wings, like bird song. It was all she was, and all she had left to her.

Charlie Cable gave her a pat on the shoulder, and turned away to wave like he was signaling a rescue plane. Someone tooted a boat horn. He straightened up, the breeze that had blown her in now tossing his wild hair as he steeled himself to represent loons anywhere on this benighted planet before a committee that could make a difference. Maybe a t-shirt and hip waders were Cable's idea of dressing for success.

Val pressed the electric start button and with exquisite slowness backed away from the man who would very likely keep Peter Hathaway in business. In industry news. In serf pants and shoes of the fisherman. In something that passed for love with women who provided enough of a floor show that it took his mind off his own inner spaces. Where the problem was that maybe there wasn't really so much space, after all, when it came right down to it.

Distracted, Charlie Cable gave Decker's boat a shove away from the houseboat and actually blew her a funny little kiss, with his big paw flattened across his mouth the extravagant way kids do, covering up the whole bottom halves of their faces. Val gave the motor some gas, putting more distance between herself and the federal loon squad as they closed in effortlessly toward the rented houseboat that looked like a log cabin afloat on the lake.

Two men, two women with lots of power and inscrutable goals, coming to meet with a blockbuster writer who thought Leslie Decker had been too good for this goddamn world. Voices, back and forth, hallooing, joking, and in the end, Val wondered whether anything terribly important would come out of the meeting.

Val shifted into neutral long enough to slip the folded contract, the thing of gold that—in the end, really—had nothing to do with pleasing Peter Hathaway, into Decker's waterproof map case and zipped it shut. If she had managed to get the contract signed a couple of days ago, she would have enjoyed staring at it in a moment of quiet triumph, but not now. Everything was too late.

Including—here she smiled—Peter Hathaway.

She shifted into forward, made a wide, safe circle in a direction that surprised her, and headed toward the main channel. A distant speck to the south could have been a canoe, but too far away to tell. No confident blond skippering a silver boat with right of way. No Dixon Foote barging along imperceptibly. Behind her, the houseboat grew small, smaller, until, as she veered, Point of No Return slipped from sight along with the ministry boat.

Val bounced the boat over the little waves that were coming at her and forced herself not to think about how uncomfortable she felt in wide open spaces with no one else in sight. Was there really just no pleasing her? She didn't like Lake Wendaban when she was in the company of its residents because they were all so completely unlike her. But she didn't like the lake any better when nobody was around because the place itself was so completely unlike her. It was a sly place where anything could happen even when doors were closed and snakes still turned up in cake pans. Even when windows were closed and women were hurled through them. The wilderness just seemed like a place that could absorb an infinite amount of human fear, without ever taking pity.

As she neared the wide open channel she would follow to the West Arm, and from there to the Hathaway cottage where all she still had to do was pack, Val thought again about Leslie Decker, the woman she couldn't get any straight answers about—not from Decker, not from Charlie, not from Caroline or Kay or Martin Kelleher or even Dixon Foote. Had she been so utterly unknowable? Was she such a shifting thing that there was not a single Leslie Selkirk Decker people could agree on? Had she kept everything important about herself stashed away in such an inaccessible place inside her that it could never get out?

Val suddenly slowed, but without trying.

Was she talking about Leslie Decker...or herself?

The boat puttered along, but the motor seemed to be hacking. All she could do was glare at it. Finally, it died. Val stood, her legs apart, and huffed at the motor. She shifted into neutral and tried the electric start. Nothing. Then she ripped at the pull cord, hard, four times, with no luck. She sank down to the seat. Had Josie Blanton left out some important piece of information? For a full minute Val stared at nothing. She was completely out of ideas. Only one truth niggled at her brain: the lake was not about to let her go. It wasn't done yet with Valjean Cameron, plaything of wilderness waterways.

With a wry smile lost on everything around her, she pulled on a cord and lifted the neon orange whistle to her lips and blew shrilly until she had to come up for air. No response, but no surprise. The whistle seemed like an unbearably stupid thing to make part of the required equipment. Whistling couldn't do you any good if no one was in sight, and if someone was in sight, you wouldn't need to whistle. If she ever got off Lake Wendaban, she vowed to write a letter to the appropriate ministry of boating.

Buoyant line? Throw to what? Throw to whom?

Bleach bottle bailer? As yet, no leak.

Life jacket? Possibly, she heaved a sigh, if abandoning ship became the last resort. But last resorts were called that for what were usually very good reasons.

Oars? Yes. *Yes!* Rowing toward the West Arm had to be better than swimming, didn't it? For a moment, it felt like a true toss-up, a final indignity either way. She prepared herself to feel worse than whenever she'd get off the elliptical at the gym—not that it was a recent experience or a perfect memory. At that moment she found the finest use of wilderness. It was made for shouting into it. If it could absorb all human fear until the end of time, it could damn well absorb her frustrated screams. Val lumbered to her feet, which set the boat rocking, and with her fists at her sides, she let it rip.

She screamed because Peter Hathaway had no faith. She screamed because it had taken her five days to accomplish what she should have done in one—so then she screamed because maybe Peter Hathaway was right. She screamed because a woman like Leslie Selkirk got a guy like Wade Decker, which surprised her because she wasn't even sure what she meant by it. She screamed because she should have gone into the waterfall. Spent, she glanced down and noticed the black bulb on the gas line. With a sudden, bad feeling, she squeezed the bulb which felt as yielding as Daria Flottner's thighs. Her eye followed the line to the red plastic gas tank on the floor in the bow of the boat.

Slowly and carefully, Val stepped over seats, heading toward the tank Josie Blanton had neglected to tell her about. Bracing herself, she leaned over the tank and checked the gauge, where the black pointer flickered over the E. How could the sky still be so clear and cheerful? Face it, she was out of gas. In more ways than one. Had Wade Decker forgotten to check? Or had he assumed Josie Blanton would check? No, when it came right down to it, she herself should have checked. It just never occurred to her that she should.

In New York, gas tanks were most definitely other people's responsibility—cabbies, the MTA, limo services. If she keeled over here, she could fall out of the boat and drown. If she keeled over there, a few people might step over her, but there would be those who would call 911. And then step over her. Altogether the better option.

Val stood in the center of the gently rocking boat. In every direction all she saw was some combination of water hundreds of feet deep, treacherous shoals, islands of rock and pine that had never needed anything from humans for millions of years, and mainland impossible to tell apart from the islands.

No boaters.

Anywhere.

Well, there was nothing to do but roll up her sleeves, sit, grab the weather-beaten old oars (ah, Decker), and row. The rhythmic squeak of metal on metal. The rhythmic bang of wood on aluminum. She was just one big racket of activity. When she discovered it was hard to match her strokes, left arm, right arm, she decided she may be swerving her way back to the Hathaway family cottage, but sooner or later she'd get there.

But would she have time to change clothes before Decker picked her up for the "gala"? Could he bring something clean and corny she could wear? An A-line clunky denim skirt that comes to the middle of her calf, say? Or floppy gaucho pants and ankle boots. True wilderness chic. Did Leslie have such a thing? Or Josie?

Her upper arms were beginning to hurt when Val noticed two things. More clouds had appeared, out of nowhere. And a speck on the horizon was getting bigger. It was a boat. A red boat. With gas. And a working motor. It cut through the water, running parallel to Val, so it was too far away to notice her, and not getting any closer. Damn. It was heading straight for the West Arm. She even thought she could hear the motor, but maybe she was imagining it. Nothing to do but to flay her arms raw and head for the cottage. Stroke. Stroke. Stroke. More clouds gathered. Slowly, still, but with the uncoiling sureness of Lake Wendaban clouds that wanted to work up to a good, sudden downpour.

She could put up with anything that didn't include bears.

Hell, she already had.

Between the metal scrapes and wooden clangs of her rowing, another sound started to dominate. Val let go of the oars, and one nearly slipped out of the oarlock. As she made a grab for it, she looked around. The red boat that had been running parallel to her was now heading toward her. With her luck, it would turn out to be a waterborne cop who'd present her with a ticket for pleasure boating without a license. She would have to argue the "pleasure" part, cop or no cop, but if she needed a license, she was definitely going down.

The bow of the approaching boat was just a little too high for Val to see the skipper. So she sat, biceps aching, her hands clutching the handles of the oars, and waited to see what would happen. An official police boat would look more, well, official, she thought. As the boat came in range of her, it slowed, the bow settled, and she could see a young man with a close-shaved head in the stern. He was wearing a light purple sleeveless vest, unzipped, and baggy black nylon shorts. As he came alongside, he flashed her a smile of recognition, then turned away long enough for Val to see Go Jays across his skull.

It was Arlo.

From the bait shop.

"Hey, Miss."

"Arlo, hi," she cried, as they grabbed hold of each other's boat. "I ran out of gas."

The kid grunted in a way that suggested the very same thing had happened to him once. Then he craned his neck as he gave her boat a quick onceover. "No spare can, eh?" He easily flipped his two side bumpers between them, softening the bumps.

"No."

With a sniff and a nod, Arlo the bait boy disconnected the fuel line from his own tank. "You found Mr. Wade okay that day, then," he said, a little awkwardly.

"I did, thanks." She sat up straighter. "He helped me find Charles Cable," she explained, making a vague gesture. "My work sent me up to Lake Wendaban to get him to agree to work for us."

Arlo gave her a quick look as he grabbed the handle of the gas tank with both hands and hauled it closer to the center of his boat. "New book?"

Her eyes widened. "New book."

"Hold on now to both boats, okay?" He tipped his broad chin at her. "You hold us close."

Spreading her hands, Val clamped them tight over the rims of both boats, careful to keep her skin from getting caught as the boats slammed together. "Charlie Cable," said Arlo as he stepped first one beefy leg and then the other into her disabled boat. "Him and me do some jobs together." As he heaved his gas tank over the sides of the joined boats, he said between gritted teeth, "He knows I'm a good worker. He pays good and he loves the lake."

"Like Leslie Decker," she heard herself say.

Arlo started to say something, then thought better of it. He scowled at the gas tank as he lowered it to the seat behind her own empty tank. "I know Charlie pretty good, from the jobs him and me do."

It struck Val that the kid Arlo worked in a bait shop literally on the municipal dock, a particularly fine spot for watching people come and go. And it happened to be the place where Charlie Cable docked the boat Kay Stanley remembered having seen disappear just out of sight around the point of Selkirk Peninsula on the morning of Leslie Decker's murder.

"Kay tells me Charlie keeps a boat tied up at the dock in town."

"That he does." Arlo gripped his tank and carefully started to pour some of his gas into hers.

"The one with the Jolly Roger he flies off the—the—"

"The stern, yeah. Funny." Arlo laughed.

"It was out on the lake the day Leslie Decker died."

"Oh, yeah? Well, it wasn't Charlie."

"No?"

"Nah. He leaves the key in it. He just don't care about material things like boats and stuff."

Having seen where the man lives, she had to agree. Could

someone else have taken out the Jolly Roger boat that day? "How can you be so sure, Arlo?"

The kid actually looked around as though they could be overheard, and set a finger against his lips. "Me and Charlie was on a job together that day."

"Really?"

The kid seemed to be debating with himself. "I shouldn't say," he mumbled.

"Are you sure it was that day?"

"Yeah, when we got back to town sometime that afternoon, we heard about the—the murder." His face darkened. The admission seemed huge to Val, who couldn't understand why this alibi for Charlie Cable for Leslie Decker's murder wasn't common, boring knowledge all over the lake. What was she missing? "Charlie was broke up something terrible," Arlo said softly.

"What job were you and Charlie doing that morning, Arlo?" She didn't know how she could possibly persuade him to tell her. She could only hope he'd already forgotten he decided against letting her in on it.

Arlo gave her a long, blank look that gave nothing away but his mind seemed very active behind his unreadable expression. She was an outsider, that was for sure, and one he didn't know. All she could do was watch him come to some conclusion she was powerless to affect. "You're not from here, Miss," he said finally. She sighed and looked at her feet. In a way, she understood. "So I think it's okay to tell you."

Her breath caught.

Arlo went on, "It's the police chief."

Val was baffled.

"He calls Charlie in when it's what they call a delicate matter."

"Such as?" said Val slowly.

"The police chief and tribal chief and Charlie Cable had worked on a plan for dismantling a dam on a river on tribal land up the highway—" here he jerked his Go Jays head in the direction of a far-off town, "—which was one of them so-called delicate matters because the tribe and the whites needed to work together, but they couldn't be seen working together, if you get what I mean."

"Where did Charlie Cable come in?"

Half squatting, Arlo tipped his own gas tank over Decker's empty one, working the spout into place. As the gasoline flowed, the smell rose around them. "So the dam was bad for what he called the ecosystem downriver, which empties into the main lake, and taking it down had to be an under-the-table arrangement."

Val narrowed her eyes, trying to understand what she was hearing. "In what way?"

Arlo went on patiently, "It had to appear to the tribe and the whites alike like an act of vandalism—"

And then she got it. "So responsibility couldn't get laid off on one group or the other."

Eyeing the soft glug of the gasoline, Arlo kept nodding. "That morning, me and Charlie bushwhacked through the forest to where the dam was and spray painted some stupid graffiti to look like random kids. Then we set a couple sticks of dynamite and took out the dam. Days later," Arlo went on, "the police chief thanked us, but by then that murder was taking up his time and that was the last we heard about it. Some jobs are like that," said Arlo, like he was talking about working the stock room at IKEA, wrinkling his broad nose at her. "Nice and clean."

With a quick smile, he tightened down the cap of her gas tank and squeezed the bulb until it was tight. While he climbed back over to his boat with his tank in his arms, Val thanked him absently. All she could think about was the revelation that Charlie Cable's alibi for the murder of Leslie Decker may not be known to the rest of the lake, but it was well known to the chief of police, and that's what counted.

Val watched her best suspect burn into vapor like the mist on Lake Wendaban. If Charlie Cable hadn't thrown Leslie Decker out that window, it meant someone else had.

21

When she got back to their island, Diane Kelleher stumbled out of the canoe and tied it up to the dock with trembling hands. On rubbery legs she walked straight up the gravel path, past the flourishing geraniums, to her pottery studio. Inside, everything was the way she had left it just two hours ago, before she had decided to take a break and paddle the back bays. It was always better to be out on the water in the heat of the day.

She surveyed the studio, numb, taking in the kiln, the long work tables, clean and uncluttered, the crocks that held her glazes. The pails, the plaster bats, the old coffee cans—everything was in order. Everything that wasn't human and arrogant and full of deceit, that is. There on the wheel head was a clay face, nearly dry, most of the slip having been carefully sponged away. As she rotated the wheel, the face seemed to be turning slowly to look at her over an imaginary shoulder. When they came face to face, she was looking at a clay mask of herself, the thing she had been working on for the last day and a half without knowing why. But it felt strangely like a memento. She touched the eyes, which were still damp. The cool clay formed a membrane across the sockets.

She stood in the center of her studio, hands hanging useless at her sides. Her mind cast back to that first time, years ago, before they were married, when Martin Kelleher had brought her to Lake Wendaban and walked her around this property for sale. He spoke in that decisive way he had about his plans for what would become the Kelleher estate, pointing to the right, to the left. On the subject of this property, he was no halfway laddie, not ever. And not with Cintorix Corporation, not ever.

But with everything else in the life of a human being, if that human being was at all lucky, he was forever a halfway laddie. In anything that required Martin to see something beautiful and decent in other people's needs, especially if they did not coincide with his own, he was a halfway laddie. And for Diane March Kelleher, it had always been enough. Was it the money? Was she just that shallow? Maybe it was security, or routine, or some kind of stupid inertia on her part. Or was it just goddamn misplaced love, all these years? Diane squeezed her eyes shut tight, then opened them wide, and kept them open, forcing herself to picture what had just happened as she eased the canoe around the point of one of the small, overgrown islands just a mile from their own.

She remembered ducking underneath the branches that overhung the water as she paddled, and in the late morning light Diane could hear the katydids buzzing in the brush. There was a smell to the summer heat, colorless and powerful as it burned away the dew and left the air swollen and wonderful. Below her, where she sat in the canoe, Diane could see a smallmouth bass motionless, down about four feet, its black-striped tail waving lazily.

Around the bend was a campsite high up on the rock, tucked back into a clearing shaded by tall red and white pines. Two small motorboats were tied up there. Some instinct made Diane halt where she was, without drawing attention to herself. Then she silently paddled close enough to see a blue and yellow tent pitched on the campsite, and a clothesline strung between two trees where some skimpy clothes dangled. Nearby was a fire pit, and a makeshift table made of tree stumps and weather-beaten boards. All the marks of somebody settled in for some long-term camping.

Diane sculled closer to the shore, where she hoped she was out of sight, when she heard a noisy tent zipper pulled open and soft laughter sail out. Carefully pulling herself up to a crouch, she strained to see what was happening. A girl emerged naked from the tent, her face obscured by dark, curly hair. She stretched in that languid way a girl can when she's that young and slim and her breasts spend a lot of time in the open air. Then she stepped into a lightweight denim skirt, telling what she thought was a funny story about a boating lesson, a thumb flicking at something by one of her tattoos.

And all of a sudden Diane recognized her.

Josie Blanton.

Didn't she live in town somewhere?

Didn't she clean for Wade Decker?

And then a hand pushed aside the tent flap and Josie Blanton's partner started to climb out, awkwardly, on older legs trying to behave like younger legs in the presence of this girl. It was Martin. Diane watched him have to push himself upright—camping was something even money couldn't make easier—and, if he was a little embarrassed, he covered it by zipping his jeans in a manly way, if there could be such a thing, like he was tucking away his power supply. Which maybe he was. How long could she not breathe, wondered Diane, hidden there in the shallows? Why did she feel absolutely nothing?

Martin said something declarative to Josie Blanton that brought her, sauntering, over to him, where he fingered her nipples in that way he had, like he was trying to tune to an FM station, that had never done it for Diane. Then Josie ran her arms up around his neck and they sank into a clinch while she tried to wiggle her toes into a couple of negligible sandals. Swaying, she pulled away, and he gave her a fond spank and tried to find the head hole of his green Izod shirt. Sex always confused Martin.

As Josie Blanton pulled on a pink bandana headband, she said she was sick of doing demeaning work for rich lake people when she should be a supermodel in New York, say, or even running her own business. Diane thought that, from what she could see, the girl was doing just that. Martin murmured reassurances of some sort. Josie sounded skeptical. Martin did something she had never in their lives together heard. He pleaded. Josie seemed airy. Martin wheedled, promising her anything, Diane guessed, up to and including Diane's Noritake china and pottery studio. Josie seemed coyly unconvinced.

For this girl Our Lady of Perpetual Help got a new choir loft?

Diane headed for home. At one point, when she was out of sight, and so were they, she had a moment of acute vision, boring through the easy gauze of the sky. She lay the paddle across her lap, letting the slight breeze rock her when nothing else in her privileged life did, and she knew what she had to do.

She blamed herself for her inaction in the matter of Cintorix and whatever her husband had up his cheating little sleeve. There wasn't a person on this lake Diane liked less at that moment— including the dead Leslie Selkirk Decker, who had been dangerous until someone had ended her—than Martin Francis Kelleher. And she was the only one, anywhere, who knew what to look for, and where to look for it, to do right, in some small way, by Wade and Caroline and Charlie and all those others. All those others. Somehow, she'd hack into Martin's laptop, she'd pack a bag, make a couple of quick calls, and take herself to the landing in their fastest boat, after a quick stop at Camp Sajo. She hoped whatever papers and files she could turn over to Caroline Selkirk would be enough.

For the 9,646th dinner of these last thirty years, the halfway laddie was entirely on his own. And Diane's heart lifted when she realized it cut both ways—if he was alone, then so, so was she. If she worked fast, she could grab a Bee Burger in town before she hit the road in the Mercedes that Martin never let her drive. It might actually top the list in the settlement.

By late afternoon, Val had straightened up the Hathaway family cottage and made some calls. She washed the few dishes she had used and set them in the drainer to air dry. She swept out whatever dirt and pine needles she had tracked inside. She stripped the bed, remade it with a set of clean sheets she found in a blanket chest, happily noting they were heavy flannel. She figured she'd give Peter and the performance artist known as Daria Flottner a head start generating some heat in the bedroom on a muggy night in August. When her mind irresistibly started to play with the image, she picked up a broom and swept some more. There was nothing she could do about whatever Muffy and Lana had left in the fridge that was still there, marching past their expiration dates, so she closed the door to the fridge and left fuzzy green surprises for her former boss. She set back up the framed photos—all shots of the smiling, privileged Peter she had turned facedown. In the ash can.

She called Rocky Shore Lodge in town and booked a room.

She called the Ontario Lakeland train service and learned the train to Toronto came through at nine thirty tomorrow morning.

She called Caroline who told her, yes, she could certainly come hang out at Camp Sajo before the gala. Be happy to have her. Be nice to see her.

She called Wade Decker, left a message asking if he could please pick her up at the camp.

She called Peter Hathaway, left a message that she had a signed contract to hand off to him and that she was giving him her two weeks' notice. At the end of the day—and this was more a message to herself than to him, so she didn't include it—she'd be damned if she'd let Peter Hathaway fire her. If she ran into him at the gala, she'd tuck the signed contract into the waistband of his flowing, muslin drawstring pants. If she didn't see him before she left Lake Wendaban, then she'd set it on his desk at work.

For an exciting moment, Val wondered if Charlie Cable would follow her to her next editorial job. And would he follow her sooner than later? If Val Cameron was the kind of stand-up gal he'd insist on editing his mem-WAHRS, not to mention his space junk thriller, wouldn't he and his career come with her? Val's fingers lingered on the phone, tapping softly while she considered calling Julian Onnedonk and asking him for a job—on the strength of landing *The Asteroid Mandate* by Charles Cable. She'd let the reality of that coup flop heavy and golden in the Onnedonk boat. How particularly delicious it would be when Peter Hathaway found out that not only had Fir Na Tine not tied up Cable, but Julian the archrival wunderkind had—because of Val. Val the incompetent. Val the smitten sap. As thoughts went, it was just about as diabolical as Valjean Cameron had ever been.

It was interesting to learn she had it in her.

And interesting to learn she couldn't do it.

At least, not yet.

The prospect of leaving Fir Na Tine was terrifying. Maybe it was the way the afternoon sunlight slanted through her office window that was always just a little grimy and landed next to her laptop while she worked. Or maybe it was the way she couldn't tell whether those were cherubs or hollyhocks sculpted into beautiful old millwork running the perimeter of her office ceiling fifteen feet high, and she never wanted to know the answer. And then there were the floor stacks and stacks of colorful Fir Na Tine books that looked like they were trying to stretch all the way up to the millwork.

Her framed Matisse prints, her old Turkish flatweave rug Aunt Greta had given her for no good reason, her antique walnut credenza she had bought on Craigslist. The humidor where she kept tea bags. The brass coat rack from her grandparents' old speakeasy on Thompson Street in the Village. Fir Na Tine held the things she loved, and even though Val knew she could cart most of them away with her, wherever she went, it was terrifying to know she was tearing something apart.

Even when it was required.

Her fingers slipped off the telephone. There would be no call, yet, to Julian Onnedonk, although there was something sweet about calling him from Peter Hathaway's phone. No call yet because there was still the matter of Peter and the feelings that never seemed to lessen or change or just plain go away. She and the publisher of Fir Na Tine were a tangle of little gold links like the necklaces in her jewelry box she couldn't tease apart, and so they stayed—a chain that couldn't be worn, a heightened glimmer of no practical good whatsoever.

Val loaded her laptop, briefcase, and overnight bag into the little boat that now had half a tank of gas, thanks to Arlo. Her final act of defiance, once she was seated by the motor, was to slip on her navy Prada heels. They matched her shiner, but could she square dance in them? It hardly mattered. One foot on the battered wooden step the train conductor would set out for her, and she was as good as gone.

She was just that close to putting the whole unpleasant episode of the last few days behind her. A couple of solitary lunches in the MOMA café, after basking in their Edward Hopper collection, and Deckers both dead and alive would shrink to little pinpoints in her mind that would no longer be jangled. In a year and a half, Charles Cable would be nothing more than a black and white photo on a dust jacket, and now, finally, easy to grab.

Without a glance at the Hathaway family cottage, where Peter would soon be installing Daria Flottner and letting her love phloem ooze all over him, Val set out west toward the Selkirk Peninsula. There was still plenty of daylight, and the way she had it figured, all she had to do was get herself to Camp Sajo this one time. From there, all her transportation needs were met by Wade Decker, Ontario Lakeland train service, and Air Canada.

From LaGuardia, she was one Yellow Cab away from her home on E. 51st St. And there wasn't a cabbie anywhere in the five boroughs that would tell you WE GET YOU THERE AND KEEP YOU WARM AND DRY. They didn't have to. It was the job, man. She'd be in her own queen-sized bed with the pillow top mattress and Egyptian cotton sheets by bedtime tomorrow night. The heels felt a little snug, because her feet were swollen from the abuse they took on the canoe trip with Wade, but snug only made her love them more. She wanted to feel every leather centimeter of support the brilliant Mario Prada was offering her.

The clouds that had been bunching ominously while Arlo was sharing gas and providing Charlie Cable with an alibi for the murder of Leslie Decker were thinning out, scattering slowly in a wind she couldn't see at work. That's how high up it must be. The unobstructed sun burned up there like an ingot and started a slow descent toward the horizon. When she got close to Caroline Selkirk's ghost camp, she watched Kay Stanley turn from the garden halfway up the gentle hillside toward the lodge. Kay tossed a handful of weeds into a basket, pulled the gloves from her hands, and started down to the dock.

"How'd you learn to operate a boat?"

"Necessity," said Val. "A big fat absence of Wade persuaded me." She grabbed the warm, weather-beaten boards of the Camp Sajo dock and held on tight. "He arranged for Josie Blanton to give me a lesson."

Kay reared back at the name. "I hear she's good at lessons," she said, and then widened her dark eyes at Val. "Only I didn't know they had anything to do with boating."

Remembering Josie's *rip it, rip it, easy, easy, faster*, Val laughed. "You hear tell, do you?"

"I hear tell," she agreed, smiling at her bare feet. "Mainly from the maintenance crew." Kay rubbed a tanned forearm across her thick, short hair, and the two of them stood enjoying a silent moment together the way two women do when they've most definitely got the number on a third, who's absent. After Kay tied the line to a silver cleat, she reached for the overnight bag Val was handing up to her.

Slinging the laptop and briefcase onto the dock, Val grabbed the hand Kay offered and stepped out of the boat. As Kay slipped the white bumpers over the sides of Wade Decker's little boat to keep it from banging the dock, Val thought about her letter to Trey Selkirk all those years ago. All those years between a baby born in Iqaluit and given up, because she just couldn't do that to the Selkirks, none of them, and the domestic life here at a dying camp. A garden on Trey Selkirk's old soil. Loaves of bread baked in Trey Selkirk's old kitchen. Laundry washed, dried, folded in Trey Selkirk's old boathouse that had, one day two years ago, been the scene of his daughter Leslie's violent end. Now Kay Stanley was tending to his sole remaining daughter, Caroline, because she couldn't tend the inconvenient baby she had given up. In the hardy summer sunlight that still hadn't slipped between the trees, Val felt inexpressibly sad.

"Who's here?" she asked Kay, eyeing the sleek new boat with a motor the size of a doghouse that looked like it could sleep four.

"Diane Kelleher," said Kay, the smile evaporating. "Just came." Between them they carried Val's things up to the porch of the lodge. Luke Croy, who stood just inside the screen door with his arms folded over his tight blue t-shirt, nodded at Val and opened the door just wide enough for her to slip inside. Diane Kelleher. Martin Kelleher's wife. Martin, the leader of what he called "the environmental bloc." Martin who strong-armed cottagers into signing petitions, running for office, and passing Diane's excellent shrimp fritters, please.

What was his wife doing here?

22

In the reduced light of the Camp Sajo lodge great room, with its walls lined with framed photos of smiling young campers decades ago, stood Caroline Selkirk in the center of the empty room. Close to where Val herself had been knocked out five nights ago. In a plain green sleeveless shift, Caroline Selkirk looked about as old as the campers in the framed photos. Her fine head, with its tumble of red hair, was tipped as she listened to Diane Kelleher.

"I can't stay long," said Martin Kelleher's wife. Her brown hair was held back by a pair of sunglasses she had pushed up from her eyes. In the heavy, empty silence of the great room, her words seemed to hang there. Like the pearl drop earrings she wore. She was dressed in gray linen and the kind of glossy black sandals better off on Fifth Avenue than clambering out of big boats in the Northwoods. In an instant, glancing down at her own heels, Val knew this was a woman who was heading south.

Caroline and Diane both noticed Val at the same moment. At Caroline's look, Diane answered, "She can stay." Then Martin Kelleher's wife slid the hefty messenger bag off her linen shoulder and handed it to Caroline. "This is for you."

Caroline looked down at it. "What is it?" she asked, slowly opening the flap, revealing a stack of papers inside.

At the question, Diane Kelleher fell silent. Then she lifted her chin and said simply, "It's proof." And her slender hands, with nothing more to offer, opened wide.

"Proof?" asked Caroline, shaking her head slowly. "Of what?"

Diane Kelleher bit her lip and set a hand on Caroline's shoulder. One sweet little stroke, meant to express something that didn't seem quite clear to any of them standing there in the late afternoon summer sunlight.

"Proof that my husband is behind the illegal access roads." Diane's face started to fall apart.

Caroline Selkirk sank slowly onto the bench behind her, nearly missing it. She gave Luke a quick look of pure pain. "Martin?"

Diane went on, "I've spent the afternoon getting as much together as I could. Invoices, letters of intent, email, documents of incorporation. I hope it's enough to—"

"I don't believe it."

"But you will."

"I don't understand."

"There's a shadow company he set up through Cintorix."

"His corporation?"

"Right now the shadow company is paying a contractor to bring in the equipment and manpower to make these illegal access roads."

"But why would he do that?"

"It's all there."

"Why?"

Diane said softly, "Because he wants your land, Caroline."

"The camp?"

"He wants all of it. He wants Selkirk Peninsula."

"For what?"

"To develop, not to develop, his to decide. But first he has to own it."

"Why? Why now?" said Caroline, trying to understand. "In a year it all goes back to the Queen."

Diane said gently, "If you own it, it will."

"What are you saying?"

"Martin is rich. He gets to keep what he wants."

And there it was.

"But the petition campaigns, Diane, and the—the meetings and plans and—"

"The environmental bloc."

"Yes!"

"Or blockheads, as he calls you." She gestured to the sheaf of papers. "Page forty-three."

Caroline seemed dazed. "Why would he go to all the trouble to—"

"Merely speaking of poison," said Diane Kelleher, "poisons. If he can get you all worrying enough about the water quality and habitat destruction and threats of copper mining and clearcutting and—"

Luke put in, "Illegal access roads."

"—illegal access roads, you will sell."

Caroline shook her head obstinately. "Martin knows these people. He knows they won't sell. Their cottages go back in their families for a hundred years."

Diane said patiently, "It's because he knows them that he knows they will. They will sell. You just don't see it yet."

"How can he do all this, everything you're telling me, on his own? It's impossible, Diane. One man can't—"

"You're right," Diane said, glancing at her feet. "He had help."

One word: "Who?"

Diane stood silent. Nobody moved.

"Who?"

Diane squared her shoulders. "Leslie."

The hands gently pushed a beer well out of the way of the fireproof old metal box that had belonged to the girl called Leslie Selkirk. The bent nail Leslie had pushed through the latch felt smooth. But, then, it really wasn't a nail, after all, was it? Then, what? The hands took a soft rag and wiped it. But what had seemed like dirt and rust turned out to be tarnish, after all, and needed some real polish. But the piece of bent metal Leslie used on her Army surplus box was a piece of jewelry, it looked like—a silver stick pin, maybe, with the fastener broken off. It was finely worked with delicate rosettes. Too old to be Leslie's. Or Caroline's. Maybe Hope Selkirk's, the mother. And wouldn't it be just like Leslie to ruin a piece of silver jewelry when a two-penny common nail would do?

Before reaching for the spiral notebook, the hands set aside the ruined stick pin, then stretched out flat against the table. It was all, all of it, just ruined stick pin, wasn't it? The camp, the marriage, some reputations, other confidences. So why this ritual, this slow discovery of the extent of the damage? The wind was picking up, fluttering the loose pages the hands slid out of the metal box. *Because ritual is my answer to Leslie Selkirk Decker. Against all her careless devastation, I set this slow mindfulness. I outlived her. I outloved her. And I retreated first, without ever taking a step. The beautiful silver stick pin is ruined, but I can set it where I please. If I control the rate of these discoveries, I make her small for all of time.*

The hands turned each page of the spiral notebook until an entry appeared. It was the final entry, and there was relief in that. The last entry Leslie Selkirk made before journals became uncool or she no longer needed to justify herself. *Yesterday I was seventeen and Dad gave me a very cool underwater camera,* she wrote. *Caroline wants it, I can tell, but I told her she'll have to take five of my night shifts here at camp before I'll let her use it. I wonder if she will. She called me selfish and walked away, mad. That idiot camper Marcus Cadotte sneaks out practically every night and I'm sick of getting him back inside his cabin. That's why Caroline has to trade. He's big and fat and ugly at fourteen and he'll still be big and fat and ugly at forty. He's got crooked teeth and goofy hair and I hate the way he smells.*

He's what Mom calls a scholarship kid, which means he comes to camp for free. The more the other kids don't like him, the harder he tries, and then he ends up spilling cherry Kool-Aid pop all over that cute kid Jeremy's Upper Canada College sweatshirt. It'll never come out, that idiot Marcus. At activity time, all the other campers wait to see what Marcus signs up for so they don't get stuck with him. Mar-curse, that's what I call him. Not to his face, of course, just to Caroline. Mar-curse, Mar-curse. When the Toronto Star reporter came to do a piece on Chez Trey, Dad made me sick when he put Marcus Cadotte out in front and made a big deal out of him, how good camp was for this dear lad. He actually called him this dear lad. Was Dad being funny? Doesn't he realize kids like big fat Mar-curse will bring us down? One look at retards like Marcus Cadotte and rich Toronto parents aren't going to send their kids to this camp anymore. They're not!

Dad is a fool. Dad is a blind old silly fool no matter what everyone else thinks and I love him so much. I think Marcus sneaks out at night to catch counselors making out, but Caroline says he likes the night sky and likes to lie on the archery field in the dark, even if it's against the rules. That's what he tells her. And she believes it because she's full of shit and romance because she's screwing Wade Decker and thinks nobody knows—

The hands set down the spiral notebook.

The reader pushed back from the table.

Six o'clock. Time to get ready for the gala.

Lucky thing.

Lucky, lucky thing.

The rest of that final entry would just have to wait.

Val sat alone in the camp dining hall for an hour after she slipped out of the lodge when Caroline burst into tears. It was all too personal, and none of her business. And it seemed very odd to Val that she could make Leslie Decker's murder her business, no problem, but when it came to the kind of betrayal that scrubs clean all the old safe illusions about the woman, then no. Caroline's sobs filled the space, and Val knew she herself was one person too many.

When Luke bounded over, straddled the bench, and pulled the last of the Selkirks into his arms, Val backed quietly out of the lodge. Only Diane Kelleher was left standing, her empty hands trying to come to rest somewhere, as they cupped her own face, smoothed the linen that wasn't wrinkled, and just hung, finally, at her helpless sides.

Outside in the sweet-smelling air, Val walked over to Kay, who was standing in the garden, her broad face turned toward the sound of the cries. Val gave her a look like she didn't know where to start, and Kay held up a gloved hand. "I'll hear later," she said softly, then jerked her head up the path. Val followed, passing a tetherball court where weeds shot up, unpicked, through the cracks. Inside the camp kitchen, Kay set out cold drumsticks, sliced beefsteak tomatoes from the garden, and bread. Wordlessly, she left, and Val took a cup of coffee and a plate out to the open timbered dining room and the wall of windows overlooking the lake. From the center rafter hung the Canadian maple leaf flag, unmoving in the still August air.

From where she stood, holding her cup to her uninjured cheek, she would be able to see Wade Decker arrive. And she couldn't hear Caroline Selkirk crying. Coming to terms with the truth about Martin Kelleher, the friend she wrangled with, but they had been safe wrangles, the kind you have when you know you're on the same side. *If Charlie's still with us, then why doesn't he do more? Can one of us get elected to council and put a stop to development? Who's got the most passion for the cause, you or me?* And then she finds out he was playing her—playing them all. For years.

As for Leslie...

As for Leslie. How will Caroline Selkirk ever make sense of it? She couldn't consider the possibility that the murder was a result of anything other than robbery and random mischance. To Val, all death seemed like death by misadventure. With Leslie Decker, the misadventure had come at someone else's hands. The question was whose. And Val realized in that moment, surrounded by other people's pain, that it still mattered to her. She could go merrily ahead and publish Charlie Cable's blockbusters, but when it came right down to it, in investigating Leslie Decker's murder, Val had only really helped herself. Her own career, her own peace of mind. And it felt bad.

In a quick burst of understanding that popped and dissolved in the second she saw it whole, she knew she wanted to see it through to the end, this search for the treacherous Leslie's killer, for Wade. "It's for Wade," she said softly to herself, with a strange kind of wonder that this fact was only just this moment clear to her. She could barely carry a heavy pack, or fire up a camp stove, or even just keep her city girl misery to herself on what was probably just as difficult a trip for Decker as it had been for her—but this thing, she could do. She could get all the way to answers in the matter of his wife's violent death. This time, for Decker, the man who was only just free enough to stand naked and battered in a powerful waterfall. As she looked out over the lake from the dining room of Camp Sajo, she didn't want to think too long about why any of it still mattered. She had planes to catch.

Diane Kelleher was heading down the path from the lodge, and the slant of her gray-linen shoulders told Val that she was leaving a scene of wreckage behind her. As well as a messenger bag that held a load of sorry truths. She watched the perfidious Martin's wife stumble on a tree root and keep right on going. Tree roots were small things compared to the faithlessness of human beings.

With a pang that there was someone heading somewhere off the lake—Philadelphia, was it?—so much as half an hour ahead of her, Val sipped her coffee. Diane Kelleher's story had opened up a range of new possibilities in terms of the murder. If Arlo the bait boy hadn't provided Charlie Cable with such a snug alibi, she thought the revelation about Leslie's treachery ramped up the motive for Charlie to have hurled her in a rage through the second-story window. All these years, he had not only kept the faith, he had been jailed and made sacrifices for preserving the lake environment—shoulder to shoulder with his beloved comrade in arms, Leslie Selkirk. The Leslie who, in his mem-WAHRS, came across as a goddess activist. Fine, principled, unyielding.

But on the day Leslie died, Charles Cable was off on a secret assignment to dynamite a dam. With his spray paint and his explosives and his willing sidekick, Charlie was suddenly flung back to his radical days—at the very same time Leslie Decker was being flung to her death. *Broke up something terrible about it,* Arlo had said, when they had got the news. If not Charlie, then who? Martin Kelleher had certainly been playing a double game, and even had more to lose in terms of position in the community than the eccentric Charlie. And lose he would, because although Charlie had been blowing up dams in pursuit of an ideal, Martin had been manipulating his friends and neighbors in an underhanded land grab.

What if Leslie had the goods on him? Diane had access to files and documents and email accounts, but what if Leslie had secretly recorded her conversations with Martin, and then threatened to expose him? Was it possible Leslie Selkirk Decker had played a double game of her own? Could it be that Trey Selkirk's younger daughter was everything Charlie and Caroline had believed her to be—a passionate eco-warrior—and she had somehow cottoned to Martin Kelleher's selfish ambitions about lake property and had...daringly...set him up?

She set down her cup so hard the coffee sloshed onto her hand, then looked down at some of Mario Prada's finest work and kicked them off—then set off at a run. Out of the Camp Sajo dining hall, where nothing much ever happened anymore, and at a pretty good barefoot clip down the path to the docks. Kay was nowhere in sight and neither was Luke, probably tending to a devastated Caroline. "Diane!" called Val, waving her arms, trying to get the attention of the woman at the controls of Martin Kelleher's fancy new boat, still tied to the Selkirk dock.

Val came to a halt alongside, clutching the edge of the white half-canopy. Lined up neatly on the carpeted floor of the boat were two leather suitcases, a laptop, and three Rubbermaid bins of what looked like art supplies. Diane walked over to her. "Can you get the stern line for me, please?" The long, graceful fingers of one ringless hand lifted in the direction of the rope.

Val nodded. "Diane," she said, catching her breath as she untied the line from the silver cleat. "October, two years ago."

"Yes?"

"The weekend Leslie Decker died." Val tossed the line into the boat.

While she struggled with how to phrase the next question, Diane Kelleher crossed her arms, then squinted at the disappearing sun with a small smile. "All I can say for sure is that Martin was not at home."

"All weekend?"

"All weekend. He told me he was taking out the schooner we keep on Chesapeake Bay." Then she widened her eyes at Val. "Two years ago, I believed him."

"And now?"

She lifted her shoulders in an elegant shrug. "He may very well have been on the schooner out on Chesapeake Bay, but if he was, I doubt very much he was alone."

"And if he wasn't on the schooner?"

Diane said softly, "Then he could have been just about anywhere, couldn't he?" She held out her hand to Val, who took it. "I'll leave that to you to figure out." Her eyes narrowed. "I never believed the innuendoes about Wade."

Val's heart pounded. "Why not?"

"Leslie could only hurt him just so much, and no one ever kills from a place of indifference." Diane let go of Val's hand. "And I never believed the robber scenario Caroline is so hoping is the truth about her sister's death. Or if it was a robber, it was one we know, one of a different sort. After all these years of marriage, Val," she said finally, as she set her sunglasses in place, "I cannot alibi my husband. After everything he's done, even if I could," she gave a short laugh, "I'm not sure I would."

Val stepped away from the boat as Diane Kelleher backed it up with practiced ease, shifted, turned the wheel, and headed up the lake. Three short toots in farewell. Then, as she shifted into high and sped toward town, she passed a boat heading for Camp Sajo, shot an arm over the top of the canopy, and waved. Something kept Val on the dock, maybe the sound of the wake from Diane's boat that splashed against the pilings, maybe the quick look at her wristwatch that told her it was six thirty. Could be her date for the Lake Wendaban gala was early.

23

Wade Decker was wearing a light denim shirt and a pair of nylon cargo shorts that may have been what he wore the day she met him. He looked shaved, reasonably combed, and even the Nosekote had been rubbed in until it disappeared. She eyed those heaven-loving great legs and couldn't help notice the old pair of tennis shoes. "Thanks for the loan of the boat," she said, giving him a quick look while he reached for a colorful bag.

"No problem."

She looped the rope around the cleat and made a string of chain knots. "And thanks for the loan of Josie."

"Right."

"Girlfriend?"

He gave a short laugh. "Josie Blanton does some chores, and I pay her pretty well. But I keep her out of my bedroom, out of my board room—"

"Your what?"

"—and out of my life." Then he passed her the thin cloth bag that was two shades of pink. "Here," he said, "this is for you." Then he added, with a sniff, "For the gala."

It was from the Free People boutique. "You went shopping for me?"

With a small smile, he held up a hand. "Well, I didn't go to Toronto just to get you something pretty," he explained, "but while I was there it seemed like a good idea."

"Did you get Peter?"

"Oh, yes," he said inscrutably. "And the poet."

"Ah."

Decker looked away from her, a little embarrassed. "Since he thought you were still at the cottage, he muttered something about awkward, and said he and Darla—"

"Daria."

"—would figure something out."

So Peter Hathaway was on the lake. Any time now he would meet up with Charlie Cable and discover Fir Na Tine already had a signed contract. Decker went on, "They'll be coming to the gala, just so you know."

Val fell silent. Then she loosened the bag, reached in, and pulled out a billowy, light cotton dress with irregular layers of skirting in red and yellow paisley. The neckline was ruffled and low, but not too low, and the sleeves were roomy and came to the elbow. She held the dress up to herself. "Bohemian without being too weird," she said approvingly. Forget the Prada shoes. Not for this Colorado hippie look. Decker gave her an appraising look. "Thank you," Val said gruffly. Suddenly she felt moved, then surprised about it, and clutched the dress in a knot against her swollen cheek. "Very much," she added, trying hard not to choke. With great care, she folded her new dress, fingering the light fabric. "I've got something to tell you. Diane Kelleher stopped by."

"So I saw."

And Val went on to tell him about Martin Kelleher's deep betrayal of the cottagers on the lake, all for his own gain. The ream of incriminating papers in the messenger bag—the emails, the letters of intent, incorporation documents, invoices. At the end of it, Wade Decker's eyes were fixed on the forest of Selkirk Peninsula, outside the boundaries of Camp Sajo, as if he were trying to comprehend what motivated Martin Kelleher. "Aside from feeling sad," he said, finally, "I don't know what to tell you."

A quick smile. "You're pretty good at that."

"It's just survival, Val." And then he added so quietly she barely heard it, "Coming back is hard." She felt it cost him to tell her that. "We should get going."

She'd change into the new paisley dress in the camp office. But first she'd grab her makeup kit out of the overnight bag she'd left on the boathouse porch. As Decker followed her, she said over her shoulder, "What if Leslie set Martin up?"

Decker sighed, suddenly weary. "Please don't push me too much on Leslie Selkirk, Val."

Leslie Selkirk. As if she was just an acquaintance. Was that what Diane had meant when she talked about indifference? "What if Leslie had figured out what he was up to?"

"Just let it go, all right?"

"What if he found out..." She tried to work it out as they reached the porch of the boathouse.

"For tonight, please, just let it go—"

"—and he killed her. Right here." Val pointed toward the rocks along the side of the building.

Decker grabbed her arm and pulled her close. "I know where it happened," he said intensely. "I saw the spot. I saw the body." Breathing hard, he spoke softly, close to Val's ear. "I've known her alive, and I've known her dead, and I can tell you this much—I don't know which is worse. You," he said, releasing her arm, and patting it once, gently, "don't understand."

Maybe she didn't. Maybe, when it came right down to it, the murder was one of the less complicated things on this lake she was putting behind her for good. "I'm leaving in the morning."

His face softened. "Oh," he said. "Did you—?" And then he seemed to forget why she had come in the first place.

She folded the dress and held it in her two hands. "I got Charlie Cable's signature."

He straightened up. "Well, then," was all he could say.

Staring at her briefcase, waiting out the awkward silence, Val could picture what was inside—what she still needed to get back upstairs when nobody was looking. The file, the kaleidoscope. Probably no bearing on Leslie Decker's murder, but Val thought there might be implications for the Selkirk family as a whole. "How well did you know Trey Selkirk?" she asked.

Decker shrugged. "Pretty well, I guess. Why?"

"Did you know he had a kid? A kid other than Caroline or Leslie?"

He looked at her sideways. "What are you talking about?"

"He and Kay Stanley had a baby."

"Kay?"

There, on the narrow porch of the old Camp Sajo boathouse, she laid it out for him. The letters from Kay in her self-imposed exile in Iqaluit, hidden in the broken kaleidoscope. From the stack of photos from Trey's basket.

"It's called a wannigan," he told her. "It's how camps used to carry food on canoe trips. I've seen Trey's, up in Leslie's office. That one?"

"That one. There's the June 1981 photo of a pregnant Kay, alone with Trey Selkirk. But in all the photos after that date, no baby."

"So what happened to it?"

"In the one letter, all she mentions are her plans for the baby, something about St. John's."

"Newfoundland?"

"I don't know." Val eyed the garden by the lodge. No Kay.

"St. John's." His eyes narrowed in an effort of memory. "What was the year again?"

"1981. I figure she had the baby in September. There was the letter about the wolves..."

He leaned against the railing, where he slumped. "I'm having a bad feeling."

"Why?"

"Well, there was that kid," Decker said, biting his lip. "At camp. The summer of 1995. The kid who drowned." He looked at her, then scratched his face. "Big kid, kind of goofy, but fourteen. We're all goofy at fourteen. I played a game of tetherball with him on the lower sports field one day and he told me he came all the way from St. John's. There were whispers at camp—he was the scholarship kid." Decker let out a little laugh. "I remember Caroline joking that Marcus Cadotte was probably her dad's love child."

"Do you think she knew?"

He thought about it for a minute, then shook his head. "No. I just think she was trying to make sense of why this one kid, and only this one kid, in the history of the Selkirks owning Camp Sajo, got to come for free. All the way from bloody Newfoundland. She thought it was great—and about time." A quick look. "And you say Kay's baby was born in 1981."

Val nodded slowly, feeling colder.

Decker pushed himself away from the railing. "He'd be the right age, then, in 1995," he said softly. "So I'm wondering if Marcus Cadotte was Kay's son."

"And, if you read the letters, Trey's."

The look Wade Decker gave her was awful. It was as if he had been cast back to the day of the drowning. As if he had been present and helpless. A swift look of revulsion passed over his face. She could tell he was putting together something in his own mind, something that brought in a rush of possibilities in. "Do you think Leslie knew?" he blurted.

She stepped right in front of him. "Tell me what you're thinking. Is it about the murder?"

"It's all about the murder," he said in a strange voice. "Everything for the last two years has been all about the murder."

At that moment, the door to the old boathouse, which had been slightly ajar, opened, and Val felt horrified to see Kay Stanley standing in the doorway. "Oh, Kay..." Decker murmured, as she looked past both of them through the screen door.

She stood nodding, empty-handed, the sounds of the washing machine at work behind her. "Marcus was my son," the woman said finally, the words hanging between them in the summer air. It may have been the first time in thirty years that Kay Stanley had spoken them. What was there to remember, wondered Val, that didn't have something to do with pain? Then she looked first at Val, and then at Wade Decker. "But he wasn't Trey's," she said in a low, steady voice, wanting them to understand. "He was Charlie's."

*   *   *

The Lake Wendaban Community Center was a one-story sprawling building that had been built back in the fifties out of what Decker told her was post and beam construction. It sprawled over low boulders on the shore of an island close to the municipal docks in the town. Over the years it had changed with the times, serving as an outfitting store for wilderness adventures, a canoe manufacturing company for more wilderness adventures, a grocery store for no wilderness adventures, and a library for reading about wilderness adventures. For the past three years, as the Lake Wendaban Community Center, it had hosted modest little job fairs, amateur theatricals, political rallies, weekly bingo, and ecumenical church services.

At seven thirty on Val's last night on the lake, the sound of the bass thumped out over the water as Decker puttered them slowly along the line of boats tied up at the docks and, when there were no more slips, each other. He had loaded Val's bags into his boat, since getting her to the motel in town where she had booked a room would be easy to do when the gala ended, and he and Val talked Kay Stanley into coming with them. The gala emptied out Camp Sajo—the maintenance crew took the Sajo pontoon boat, and Kay thought Luke Croy might persuade Caroline, but she wasn't sure.

She sat serenely in front of Val, who spent a bad moment remembering her first night on Lake Wendaban, scrambling across rocking boats tied to each other for the meeting that had ended for her in unconsciousness. In some ways, she thought as she stared at a scuff on the tip of Kay Stanley's clog, it seemed like a very long time ago. As Decker sidled the boat up to a dazzling silver Stanley vessel that looked like it could transport an invading army, Kay grabbed the side. She hadn't changed out of her gardening clothes— the loose shirt and black capris seemed to be the outfit for all occasions—but she slipped into what she called her "dress clogs." Back on the porch of the Camp Sajo boathouse, Kay explained what had happened.

Charlie Cable was what you might call the love of her life. She was twenty-one and had knocked around the lake long enough to know she had no money and no prospects. He was thirty-one and wasn't smart enough to know that money and prospects, if he was going to have them, would already be on their way. She had high school and a job at the laundromat in town. He was working as the world's oldest stringer for a newspaper three hours away, and getting arrested for illegal protests over the environment was what he enjoyed instead of playing catch or taking a family out for ice cream.

These truths about Charles Cable were so very clear to Kay. Two times of almost accidental sex had happened between them, months apart. And he seemed to forget both of them. Not like a prick "forgets," and wants you to know in some cruel way that it was a mistake, when all you ever thought was that it was love and the beginning of a future together. No, with Charlie there was never any bad morning after, no careful attempt to distance himself from Kay. She could tell that for Charlie, those two nights fell somewhere between pulling off his socks and shaving his face. Natural and automatic, hardly a brain required.

So when she turned up pregnant, there was no question of telling him, of forcing a family on him—he was already starting to kick around some story ideas—but Kay wanted to give that Kay and Charlie baby a life somewhere, even if it meant the mom with nothing better than high school and a laundromat job couldn't be part of it. So she went to stay with her Auntie LeFay in Iqaluit. The only person she told was Trey Selkirk, who knew her well enough to guess it anyway, and he was a good friend to her during that time. Not even Hope or the girls knew.

It had been Trey's idea, fourteen years later, to offer the boy she had given up for adoption a place at camp that summer. But only if Kay could handle it. And she could. He was somebody else's son, she told herself, no longer hers in any real way.

And when Marcus Cadotte showed up on one of the camp buses, she thought just everyone would recognize him as Charlie

Cable's boy. Tall and fleshy and goofy, with the lumbering walk and the kind of hair no barber could tame, with the same way of scratching his chest when he was thinking, and the same way of biting his lip when he thought you were full of shit. Kay's heart sprang every time she saw the boy loping around camp. Caroline was nice to the scholarship kid.

And the other campers, well, those who knew the Cadotte kid got to come for free thought it had less to do with inability to pay than it did with "having connections"—kind of a prize the wealthy give each other—and, of course, they were right, as kids often are. Leslie either avoided him when he wasn't noticing, or fake-niced him when he was. But she was just seventeen, and fake-nice is right up there with personal grooming at that age, so Kay didn't hold it against her.

And then came the day the boy drowned.

What were the chances?

And only she and Trey Selkirk knew the dead scholarship kid Marcus Cadotte was her flesh and blood. Those two weeks before the accident, when he had been running around at camp, were the only time that child signified something other than deep and never-ending loss for Kay Stanley. Aside from those days, he was born and left. And then he died and left. And joy was compacted into fourteen days of watching him try his hand at tetherball and tennis, and watching him find a spot in a group of boys belly-whopping off the swim dock. And joy was thinking maybe he had prospects neither she nor Charlie nor Ron and Francie Cadotte knew anything about.

It all, all felt like better than enough, and she was content as she slipped the scholarship boy Marcus Cadotte a special ginger cookie she had iced with a chocolate heart, and he grinned up at her, "Say, thanks, ma'am!" and their hands touched. For the first time since the tiny hospital in Iqaluit, when five little fingers had curled around one of hers, not knowing they never would again.

When they brought the campers back that day from the water chutes, the body was in a separate chopper, alone, and Kay was frozen before grief could fully hit to tell her she was still human. And Trey Selkirk walked her over, they leaned on each other as the paramedic drew back the wet sheet like a shroud, and Kay heard herself let out a sound like a long yelp. All the other yelps inside her she forced back down because in that terrible moment she felt she was stealing a woman named Francie Cadotte's grief.

Val took in the string of lighted Chinese lanterns draped across the overhang of the Lake Wendaban Community Center: blue, red, yellow, green. Two sets of double doors stood propped open and lake people—cottagers, Ojibways, townspeople, outfitters, permanent residents, youth camp owners—streamed in, stopping at the ticket table to pay the ten dollar price of admission. Val, Kay, and Decker made their way up the sets of new wooden steps set into the rock, heading for the live music by the Finger Pickin' Pea Pickers that would any minute now turn into square dancing. Gripping all the skirting of her new dress closer to her legs to keep from catching them on the rough wood railings, Val stepped lightly in a pair of soft leather flats she borrowed from the closet in the Camp Sajo office. Caroline Selkirk was nowhere around to ask, but Decker thought she wouldn't mind.

Or, for that matter, even care.

At the table by the entrance, where the Lake Wendaban Youth Alliance banner was hung, Decker presented a check made out ahead of time that made a big impression on the ticket sellers. Through the two sets of double doors at the back, Val could see a line of barbecues set up for grilling burgers and hot dogs. A portable bar was selling beer and soft drinks.

The five-piece band was at the far end of the room that served as a bingo hall for the lake and town, and was lustily riding what even Val recognized as the "Wabash Cannonball." The sound system was strong enough to let the banjos outtalk the people clustered all around the community center, some café tables and chairs had been set around for sore feet, and a silent raffle for quilts hung over dowels suspended on the far side, away from the band.

Val recognized some players from the night she stumbled into the meeting at Camp Sajo and got knocked out during her attempt to chase down a disappearing Charlie Cable. A couple of white-haired men were wearing panama hats to keep the sun, that was getting close to setting, out of their eyes and Canoe Head t-shirts tucked into their elastic-waist pants. There were the outfitters, dressed in neutral baseball caps and tops and shorts made to dry in five minutes. There were youth camp directors and townsfolk, and all the beer was pale ale in plastic glasses.

Shelley Timms, the square dance caller, introduced herself and her handsome springer spaniel Finnegan, who was waiting for the human entertainment to begin. The caller, an energetic brunette wearing tight jeans, a pink checkered shirt, and a blue neckerchief, was exhorting all you lads and lassies to pair up for the Virginia Reel and be careful where you grab—this met with a thunderous laugh—because inappropriate feeling up will not be allowed. Appropriate feeling up is encouraged outside in back of the center, where the lights have been shot out. Another thunderous laugh. While she continued to encourage bad behavior, and Val wondered what the wide-eyed kids in the community center were making of it, she happened to get a view of the docks and saw the Water Taxi—WE GET YOU THERE AND KEEP YOU WARM AND DRY—disgorging a couple of passengers.

24

It was Peter Hathaway—she'd recognize those muslin pants anywhere—and what she could only assume was his personal peppermint foot bather, Daria Flottner. Daria was indeed bald by choice, but she sported, erupting from the boniest part of her skull, a brown rat-tail of braided hair. She appeared to be wearing a toga, like a retro Hare Krishna. In their His and Hers shoes of the fisherman, they headed for the steps, and Val felt a moment of panic. So when Decker looked at her inquiringly, pointing to the dance floor where the couples were lining up, facing each other, she practically fell into him, nodding like she'd suddenly developed a palsy.

Since the Virginia Reel was something Val thought was altogether best left to things called hoedowns and shindigs, quaint social customs occurring west of the Hudson River, she had never danced it. She looked around in another panic when the fiddle started up and Dixon Foote, next to Wade, was bobbing completely out of time from the music. "That there's my oldest girl LeeAnn, Val," he yelled over to her, and Val smiled grimly at the blond teen with a thick blue headband standing next to her.

Hands on his hips, Decker was trying to give her looks of encouragement which was a little hard to distinguish from indigestion. Then the caller took them once through the steps and she realized they were the second couple down from the head couple, which meant they'd be leading before she knew it. When the music started up in earnest, out of the corner of her eye, Val saw Peter Hathaway swagger tastefully through the doorway, surveying the gathering like Gatsby overlooking his glitzy paper kingdom. If he had cuffs instead of a loose collarless shirt made in Sri Lanka, he'd tug at them. Daria appeared beside him in a swath of fabric the color of jaundice.

Suddenly Val and Decker were the head couple. Bow, skip, elbow, skip, two hands, skip, do-si-do, skip. If she kept skipping she'd be all right. And then the slide, their solo, arms spread, holding hands, down the center of the aisle while the couples clapped them on, and Dixon Foote delivered a shrill whistle. And back the other way.

She tried concentrating on how pretty her dress was, even in borrowed shoes she'd never heard of, and she tried to figure out where Peter Hathaway had gone, but suddenly she felt swept away by the music as she and Decker reeled their way down the center, and she knew her heart felt, well, happier than when she tucked Charlie Cable's signed contract into the zippered map case and she zoomed away from him in a motorboat.

Every time she met Decker in the middle, he switched it up and held her around the waist—now even LeeAnn Foote was whistling—and she realized he had had an arm around her waist ever since she had stepped off the train in town and waited for him impatiently on the municipal dock. It surprised Val to know she had been safe all along. His color was high and his face was creased in the kind of smile she had never seen and by the time they were forming the bridge for the other couples to dance through, they were both laughing.

When the Reel finished, Decker went out to get a couple of beers, and Peter Hathaway was introducing Daria Flottner to the mayor of Wendaban, Ontario, a rough, nicely dressed fellow with a bolo tie whose eyes glazed over when she spontaneously started reciting a poem called "Tingle, Bingle, Single." Val motioned to her boss to follow her outside while Daria regaled the town council. He followed. When she turned to face him, damned if her stomach didn't flop.

Something to do with his cheekbones, something to do with

that sensual mouth that told the unspoken truth to anyone who knew better that the whole ascetic act was very far from the real man. All those late nights with difficult manuscripts and wine in their separate offices. Then there were those few times he knew just how to slip her top off her shoulders using just his thumbs while whispering to her about the early Philip Roth that became the sexiest talk imaginable.

She waited to see what he had to say.

"You survived."

"I did."

He narrowed his eyes at her. "I learned how to make sesame encrusted ahi tuna rolls." Not even glancing around for Daria. Despite the terrible phone calls, the indifference, the threats, he was asking her to bed.

She looked up and found a knot in a pine rafter high overhead. "And I learned to operate a boat."

"Motor whisperer."

"Not just yet."

"It'll come," he said, his eyes on her lips.

Were they speaking in code?

Her hand slipped into her pocket and felt the folded Fir Na Tine contract. "Did you get my message?"

"That Charlie signed? Yes." He found his office voice. "You, Valjean Cameron, held off Julian Onnedonk."

She considered it. "No, Peter. I, Val Cameron, held off...you." She produced the contract, and handed it over to him. He gave her a look of deliberate obtuseness she had seen once or twice in their many business years together: phony bafflement over how he was being treated. He took it like it was suddenly the Black Spot, or something inconsequential—both lies—and he murmured, "Good job."

"And you got my two weeks' notice."

At that he looked amused. "No need to apologize," he said, whacking her playfully with the contract. "I figured you were mad."

A waltz started up, one that seemed familiar, but Val didn't know how it could be, and the caller identified it as "Down in the Willow Garden." The sound of it squeezed her heart. "I was mad. And then I wasn't. But I stand by the message," she said, her voice getting tight as the face-to-face reality of her feelings for this man threatened to capsize her. No neon whistle, bailer, thirty-meter buoyant line, life jacket, or oars could make a difference.

He could tell. "No, you don't," he said softly.

"We'll just have to see," she said, giving him a frank look. If she stayed at Fir Na Tine, she had Peter's word she could edit *The Asteroid Mandate*. And Charlie had her word as well. But how could she ever go back to work in that office with Ivy League Ivy and the rest of the suffering staff and Daria trailing her toga and Krishna braid everywhere and—Peter himself. She didn't know what lay ahead, but she knew for sure what lay behind her. And it seemed profoundly sad that she couldn't have the career she had carefully built at Schlesinger Publishing in those charming old wainscoted offices for the past twelve years. All because she couldn't tolerate either more or less of the man she so unreasonably loved. Quitting, she suspected, was the easy part. But at least she had done it.

Stepping around Peter Hathaway, Val went back inside, crossed the dance floor, and set down the two beers Wade Decker was holding, one for her. "Dance with me," she said, "please."

"Is this like one of those pity dances, or make-him-jealous dances I remember from high school?"

She stepped into his arms. "No," she said, "maybe more like one of those oblivion dances."

"Help you to forget, eh?"

She shot him a grim look. "Maybe it's better not to."

"That'd be my advice. Did he fire you?"

"No," she said, almost philosophically. "I sort of quit."

"Which means you sort of didn't."

"I handed him the contract."

"Which may have been stupid, but you had no alternative."

"And I think he asked me to bed."

A beat. They kept waltzing. "Quitting, firing," he said, "truly the high art of seduction."

"Only it wasn't entirely clear."

Decker closed his fingers over her hand. "More's the pity. He needs to explain more fully." Val fell silent, turning, turning, letting the sweet fiddle seep inside her. The room was crowded, and the smell of burgers and beer floated across the dance floor.

Over near the quilts stood Martin Kelleher in a clutch of cottagers, where he was no doubt playing his game about needing to fight environmental desecration of all sorts. *Speaking of poison,* Diane Kelleher had said, *poisons.* And she could see, even without hearing him, that what Kelleher was telling them wasn't galvanizing them with an uplifting course of action—it was causing just the kind of sick anxiety that stood out in front of desperate minds that were wondering whether, in their golden years, they really wanted to vacation in a place where tailings from new mines would pollute the lake water, or clearcutting would lay bare formerly beautiful hillsides for two generations they'd never get to see. How long would it take before they started wondering how much they could get for their cottages?

Just as the music was bleeding to the perfect final note of what seemed to Val all waltzes, she caught sight of Caroline Selkirk, with a ravaged face, still in her stone-washed green shift, head across the floor. Luke Croy stopped halfway across and folded his arms. It was her fight. "Martin," she said, as the crowd parted and the man who had betrayed her and her family turned slowly toward her. In the silence between songs, she hauled off and slapped him hard across the face. "You bastard."

"What the hell are you—"

"Shut up!" she raged, her fists right up in his shocked face. She made a wide circle, opening her arms to the throng of cottagers. "Do you know this man is behind all the illegal access roads?"

"Caroline," he warned.

"Do you know this man has been working for years to get you to sell your property?"

A cottager blustered, "That's not—"

"What makes you—"

She whirled on Kelleher. "Your wife—who, by the way, has left you, you fool—"

He looked suddenly lost. "Diane?" he cried, his voice rising. "Where's Diane?" Beside him Josie Blanton seemed very small.

"You fool—you goddamn fool—Diane is halfway to Toronto by now."

He tried to push by her. "I don't believe you—"

Caroline Selkirk pushed him back. "She gave me so many documents about your shadow company and invoices from contractors, Martin, that you will never be able to hang onto your own place, let alone get your hands on anyone else's. Who's going to fix your docks? Who's going to bring your propane?" She drove him back. "Who's going to respond if there's a lightning strike? Who's going to keep an eye out for break-ins? Who's going to replace your roofs? Who's going to store your boats?"

When the grumbling started, Martin Kelleher looked wild. "There's work," he cried shrilly. "Work for everybody!"

Dixon Foote stepped away, shaking his head slowly.

"Is this true, Martin?" said an elderly cottager with a quaver in his voice.

Kelleher whirled. "It's not the whole—"

"But it is, Martin," shouted Caroline. "It is the whole story. Your betrayal is all you are."

His face darkened. "It was good enough for your sister."

With a cry, Caroline hauled off and slapped him again. "And now look at her," she said. At the mention of the dead Leslie, the entire room grew quiet, and the lone fiddler set down his fiddle.

Through gritted teeth, Caroline Selkirk stepped right up to Martin Kelleher, and set just two strong fingers on his chest. "This afternoon I made copies of everything Diane gave me, and before coming here tonight I dropped off a set in town at the police station." With a grim smile she added, "Let's see what they can do about those access roads."

With a pleased shout, the crowd closed in around Caroline, where Kay pulled Caroline in against her, and Martin Kelleher was left impotent outside the circle. He seemed ten years older, suddenly, and his clothes hung a little looser on his stocky frame. Even Josie Blanton had slipped away. He seemed incapable of moving, doubting which direction led to safety. One of the grillers announced more brats ready for hungry lake people—excluding Martin Kelleher, who already had enough. A cheer went up. And the band launched into something the caller Shelley Timms happily announced was "The Kentucky Rag."

Val saw an opportunity. Across the crowded dance floor was a long line of newcomers waiting to pay at the ticket table, and the dance floor seemed to be shrinking as people clustered in small groups, balancing burgers on thin paper plates. Four miles west of the community center, Camp Sajo stood empty in the gloom. She might be able to bring the matter of the murder to a head, but she wouldn't take a chance by herself. Not now. She cast a quick look at Martin Kelleher, standing like a wallflower at the dance, marginalized, here in the corner by one of the open back windows. She saw his eyes come back to life, darting around, his mind working on ways to salvage his reputation.

Val couldn't give him the time.

She tugged lightly at Decker's sleeve. Scratching his cheek, he leaned in close. "Play along," she said so quietly she wasn't sure he heard her. Then she walked across the crowded dance floor, where couples were trying to get the hang of what the caller was telling them to do, and slipped sideways past the throng at the ticket table, Decker right behind her. They made their way around the building on the wraparound deck, past people who were exercising their rights to appropriate feeling up. Nobody she recognized, not even Peter Hathaway and Daria. Toward the back, off the low deck, boozy voices sailed back at them in the shadows of the bushes. Down at the far end of the deck, heat from the busy barbecues rippled off the sizzling grills.

Val put up a hand to Decker, and positioned herself just

outside the open rear window. "I found proof," she said carefully, just loud enough to be overheard.

"What kind?" said Decker, feeling his way along. "About the access roads?"

"About the murder." When Decker had nothing to say, Val went on. "I came across it in some of Leslie's old stuff stored in the boathouse."

"What is it?"

She gave him a tight nod, letting him know he was doing just fine. "Her date book for the month she died."

"Any familiar names?"

"One in particular."

He murmured. "Tell me."

"I can't take the chance."

"So she knew—"

"I'd say so. And that's not all," Val went on, improvising the kind of proof that might provoke some nighttime activity. "There's a journal—" at that, she was surprised to see Decker wince, "—and a flash drive that will give the cops everything they need."

"Are you sure it's enough?"

Val spoke very clearly. "His life is ruined."

When Decker was at a loss where to take the conversation, she mouthed *Where?* at him. "Where did you put the proof?" he asked.

"I left it right there on the first floor, where I found it. What safer place? It's out of sight."

"Have you called the O.P.P.?"

When she figured he meant the cops, Val said, "Already did. I didn't give too much away, just said new evidence in the murder of Leslie Decker." And now for the turn of the screw. "They're meeting me there tomorrow, first thing."

"I want to be there."

"Naturally." Then she circled her hand to show him they could wrap it up.

"Let's get a beer," he said, nodding in the direction of the portable bar. When the bartender pushed two plastic glasses of pale

ale over to them with a grin, Val realized she was shaking. And in the sweltering August night, she was cold in her Colorado hippie dress Decker had bought with her in mind. Was it all just gamesmanship? And just how far out of her element had she stepped? Wordlessly, they tapped their plastic glasses together, and as Wade Decker raised his to his lips, he said softly, "Now what?"

"We give him a head start," Val said, staring into the pale ale that really had no more answers than anywhere else she looked. Their heads together in a clutch of teenage girls happily wound up over absolutely nothing, LeeAnn Foote and a couple of her friends bumped into Val. Shrieking apologies, they glided off.

Past the heads of the crowd inside the community center, clapping in time as the caller sang out, "Allemande Left," Val only wanted to be where there were bright lights and honest people and tunes she half knew. It was all more comforting than she had ever imagined. Behind her in the woods the crickets rasped in the gathering night, and one of the men cooking was cheerfully asking a Canoe Head whether he wanted grilled onions with that. But somewhere close by was something terrible, something murderous that passed itself off as normal and trustworthy and smiling. It felt deeply unfair that evil had a common face, and that was its greatest disguise. It looked like all the rest of us.

Maybe for the first time since she had stepped off the train a week ago, she was truly out of her element. Bears might leave her alone. But the man she had just alerted to some pretend evidence only she, Val Cameron, had viewed, might very well not leave her alone. And he might very well not need a second-story window to help him make his point.

"And until then?" asked Decker quietly, taking a sip.

Val turned to Wade Decker, who was cast in the kind of shadows reserved for appropriate feeling up, and she looked past him into the brightly lighted community center where the banjo and fiddles were cranking it out. "We might as well dance," said Val, more bravely than she felt.

25

An hour later, after Val spied Caroline sitting at a café table surrounded by Kay and Luke and a few cottagers, she looked around quickly for Martin Kelleher. He was nowhere to be seen. Her heart thudded a little more insistently. After a search of all likely spots, Decker came back and told her that the rest of the camp maintenance crew were accounted for, drinking in a boisterous cluster off the side deck.

The Finger Pickin' Pea Pickers were on a break and a ponytailed representative from the Lake Wendaban Youth Alliance announced the results of the silent auction of the donated quilts. *Have you ever seen such beautiful handiwork? Can't you just picture snuggling up with your honey during the long lake winters under one of these beauties?* Reliably, Dixon Foote whistled.

Val couldn't find Peter Hathaway but saw Daria Flottner nibbling on a corn cob, sitting next to the mayor's wife, a stiff-haired middle-aged gal with braces who looked like she was most definitely up to the Daria challenge. When Val crouched beside Daria and asked where she could find Peter, toga girl turned slowly and smiled beatifically in her face. Val thought she looked stoned. "Respite and nepenthe," said Daria, floating her arms skyward, brandishing the corn cob like a baton.

When Val pressed her, Daria Flottner's fingers moved sensually at the side of her shaved head, as though working through phantom locks. Val then learned that the nice camp lady apparently offered him a bed in the boathouse, and he was just so exhausted what with bringing Daria to multiple bingles well into the previous night, and with flying hither and yon, mostly yon, he was now seeking respite and nepenthe in the bed the nice camp lady had offered him, after arranging for his luscious Gift—Daria means gift, she told Val solemnly—to be brought to him later by water.

Although his luscious Gift could not quite say where. Or by whom. "Quaff, O quaff!" she sang to Val, offering her a plastic glass of beer held cupped in her two hands like a chalice. Someone, Daria no doubt, had drawn sultry red parted lips alongside her actual, colorless lips. It was against these red cartoon lips that Daria Flottner now held a finger. "Shh!" she uttered, her pupils black and large.

Disturbed, Val stood, staring down at the woman preferred by Peter Hathaway. But the only thing that mattered was that Peter Hathaway was apparently sound asleep in the darkened boathouse—with a desperate Martin on his way. She wouldn't even let herself picture the scene. Val stepped quickly back from Daria, then headed at a half-run through the crowd on her way to the entrance. It was her fault. It was all her own damn fault. All of it. Why couldn't she have just left it alone?

She dashed by Decker, who was waiting on the steps. "Wade, hurry," she called back to him as she hurried, nowhere near fast enough. Scrambling across the boats tied up to theirs, thunking softly in the indifferent night, she tried to explain what Daria had said. Moving quickly, Decker untied the boat, and all she could say from a very tight throat was, "Hurry. Please."

"Sit down, Val," was all he said, giving her an unreadable look, and then, "I'll get us there." *And keep you warm and dry.* The laughter and the bluegrass band went on without them as they pulled away from the dock, and Val felt the only thing on Earth that was holding her up was the fist clenched hard against her teeth. He held out a light mounted on a pole for night boating and motioned for her to position it in the bow. Shivering hard, she crawled over the seats and stuck it in the holder and flicked it on, the red and green glowing when nothing else in her mind was. When she climbed back to the middle, she saw he had mounted a white light in the stern.

He tossed her the dry bag. "Take the sweatshirt," he yelled. With fingers barely moving, she undid the clasps and tugged out a sweatshirt she pulled on, then snapped the bag shut. The sky clouded over, only the very brightest stars made an effort, and the moon wasn't up. Those little battery-operated lights were all they had, and Val sat hunched over, cold, as Decker flew the boat over a deep black lake he knew well. Hunched over her knees, silently keening, all she could say to herself was *no, no, no*. They had given Martin a one-hour head start. There was just no way they'd get to Camp Sajo before he did, his reputation in tatters, his wife gone, his property threatened, his freedom in question.

Ahead of them the distant sky glowed. Decker swerved at high speed into the West Arm and the glow brightened. Val couldn't get oriented. Was it still somehow the vestige of a sunset? Around them, the islands were looming black shapes, unrecognizable. Did they pass the Hathaway cottage, where Peter should himself be damn well asleep, only he thought Val was still staying there? Because she hadn't told him she had left. Oh, God.

A smell drifted high across the water toward them, getting stronger as they neared Camp Sajo. Decker rounded another island—Charlie Cable's old place?—and when they did, everything became horribly clear. In the distance, the boathouse at Camp Sajo was on fire. Against the black night the flames roared. "Holy hell" was all Decker said as he cut the motor in his approach to the dock.

"Oh, God, Wade, hurry." She started to climb out.

"Sit down."

"Peter's in the boathouse!"

"Val, sit down."

She couldn't. As they came alongside the dock, Val tumbled out, ripping her dress, and secured the line with cold, shaking hands. Fire was everywhere. She ran stumbling up to the boathouse, aware of Decker moving quickly behind her in the hellish glow. "Peter!" she yelled, not knowing where to run or how to get in. The front door knob seared her hand. She ran to a window and looked in, but the heat pushed her back.

Was he dead inside? Her heart felt blasted with loss and impotence, and her anger made her wild. Goddamn Kelleher. She started to grab at the window, but the wood was smoking and her hand jumped back. "Peter!" Through the window she saw a center beam collapse with a deafening rush.

Where was Decker?

As she tore off the sweatshirt to wrap around the metal door knob, she heard hissing and couldn't figure out what it was or where it was coming from. The door wouldn't open. Shit. It was one thing to lose the evidence, but another thing to lose the man she had loved not all that long ago. "No," she cried, tugging at the handle. The hissing grew louder. She was paralyzed by grief. "Peter!" She pounded on the burning door, as if he could let her in.

From the back of the boathouse Decker yelled, "Run!" It was far away and made no sense and all she wanted was to get to Hathaway. "Val, run!" She backed away from the boathouse, stumbling, her skin writhing with heat from the fire, her hands blackened. She backed away, weak and staggering, to look at the place that was denying her.

She couldn't get in.

And she couldn't leave.

She couldn't leave.

In the moment before the explosion, she saw Decker launch himself at her through space like all the truths since the beginning of time were located in him and she was about to learn them the hard way. He landed on her in a clutch that left no room for air, hurling them both over the rock, twisting so he'd take the brunt of the fall, as a flaming raft of exploded wood sailed over them. It felt to Val like his head and neck hit the rock hard.

When the second propane tank blew, with a grunt he pressed her under him, covering her so completely that her face was jammed into his neck as she heard the shards of shattered window glass fall like sleet around their feet. Her ribs hurt. It hurt when she breathed—and it hurt when she didn't. "He isn't in there," Decker said, his voice pained, his lips moving against her skull. "I got around to the back window."

"What—"

"Peter's not inside."

She pulled her head to the side, straining. The explosions had taken out half the cottage and spread the fire to the island. "Wade." She grabbed him, feeling his grip on her loosen. "Wade, we've got to get out of here."

He slid off her slowly, and in the sickly orange light, she got to her feet, wondering if her ribs were broken. Decker was on all fours, hardly moving. She got under his left side, flung his arm over her back, and pushed him to his feet. If they fell, she didn't think they'd be able to get up again. The sound of burning wood surrounded her and she started to cry, stumbling with Decker over the ragged rock and down to the dock, where she lowered him into one of the chairs and looked back.

She dashed to the lodge, her skin hardening and standing away from her flesh in the heat, and stumbled up the porch steps. Inside, she ran into the office, fumbled the phone, and dialed 911. Nearly yelling, she identified herself to the dispatcher and reported the fire, then flew back down the path. Bushes were crackling, the pine needle floor was smoking where the blasted pieces of the boathouse wall were spreading the fire. She couldn't look anymore. In the waves of vermilion firelight she reached Wade Decker on spindly legs, then helped him out of the shadows, where he was holding his head, moaning, and eased him into the boat.

He rolled slowly to the floor between the seats, his shirt twisted and torn. Val released the rope, threw the end into the boat, and climbed shaking into the stern. She ran a hand over her face and started the motor.

Shifting into reverse, she pulled away from the dock, rocking hard in the waves, and prayed it wouldn't conk out on her. Then she turned the bow toward the black horizon that terrified her more than staying behind. And then, with a pang, she realized she didn't know where to go. Behind her, the fire was spreading. But ahead of her was a vast and horrifying blankness. Her mind was completely empty. *Do something, damn it.*

Val shifted into neutral and they drifted for a minute while her ribs throbbed. "I can get us back to the dance," she blurted. Not even sure whether it was true.

With an effort, Decker pulled himself up far enough to grab her shaking arm. "And take a chance of running into Martin on the way?" It hadn't occurred to her. "No," he said, letting her go.

In the firelight his face was pulled out of shape from pain. Val felt alarmed. "I have to get you to a hospital." Sometimes things are just that clear. Her voice was high and unfamiliar, but it sounded like the only thing to do, and she lurched the boat forward. If they ran across Martin Kelleher along the way, maybe she could outrun him.

Decker raised himself up on his elbow. "No," he said, "I'll be okay."

Val yelled, "I have to get you to a goddamn hospital, and that's—"

He overrode her with a flash of anger. "I said no!" She felt stunned. Decker ran a hand that looked misshapen over his face. Then he hoisted himself onto the middle seat and hung his head. "Just get me out of here. I can't watch this place burn." After a moment, he looked at her pleadingly. "Take me home."

At that, Val felt angrier than she could ever remember. "Take you home? And do what? Make you a fucking cup of tea, Wade? Look at you." She flung an arm in his direction, noticing how cold she felt.

"You heard me," he said with stiff dignity, and as he turned his back to her, he added, "Just take me home."

There was a catch in his voice. Cold and scared, she puttered the boat along. "Why are you being so—"

"I've got a rifle," Decker told her with a flash of energy. "If he comes after us, at least I've got a rifle."

A rifle? What good was that going to do them? She felt her

fingers stiffen around the throttle. "I don't know how to use a rifle any more than I know how to paddle a canoe," she cried.

"But I do. My place is closer than any other option, Val. We'll wait it out—"

This time, she was louder. "—and go to the hospital first thing in the morning."

Decker straddled the seat. "So bossy," he said softly. "We'll go at first light. I promise." Then he squinted at her. "I'll be fine overnight, Val. Really. I just need to be in my own bed."

She still didn't like the plan, but she didn't like any other plan any better. "Is your goddamn collarbone broken, Decker?" She sounded like she was accusing him of trying to put something over on her.

As he started to lean back against the side, Val stuffed an extra life jacket under his head. "My guess is," said Decker, flopping a forearm over his eyes, "I'm banged up and maybe I've got a concussion." He tried to sit up. "Look, I've been in this spot before, and I came through just fine—"

"Oh, really? When?" She was hardly listening, just trying to get oriented to the boat.

"Rugby. At university. Three times. Do you want an affidavit?"

She crossed her arms. "You're a pain in the ass," she cried.

"But you have to admit," he said groggily, "a pretty fine dancer."

Scrambling over him, she opened the stowage, pulled out a flashlight, and turned it on. She was shivering from cold and fear, but Val thought she could find where they were on the map and get to Decker's—maybe not fast, but at least get there. When she heard gurgling noises, she turned the light on Decker. She gently pulled his arm away from his face and turned his head toward her. There was blood, she couldn't tell how much, where he had hit the rock with Val wrapped in his arms. With flat palms, she swallowed hard and felt his entire head, looking for God knows what, then ran her fingers over his neck. Nothing. Then she undid his shirt and peeled back the fabric. She swept the flashlight once quickly outside the boat to check their position and then turned it on Decker again.

A layer of skin had been sheared off over the right side of his collarbone, but it had already stopped bleeding. She pressed it. He jerked away with a cry and started to retch. Val set the flashlight on the seat and turned it away from his face. With cold fingers she gently buttoned his shirt and lifted him up just enough so he could turn his head away from her when he started to throw up.

"Oh shit, Val," he said.

She helped him crawl to the seat in the stern and settled him on the floor of the boat at her feet. If he had a concussion, she had to keep him conscious, although she no longer knew why. She took her place next to the motor and pulled Decker up between her legs, leaning his chest against her thigh, her arm across his trembling shoulders. With all their weight in the stern now, it was going to be a slower ride than she had hoped.

Val shifted into forward and headed the boat toward what she believed was the channel, where if she stayed steady, before too long she'd see the channel marker. She hoped to hell she was supposed to keep to the left of the red buoy. With a sudden heave, Decker clutched her thigh and threw up. She tightened her hold on him. "Sorry," he said a moment before his body jerked and he threw up again, more violently. Her eyes straight ahead, she stroked his back, and began the song where the jolly swagman was under the shade of the coolabah tree. Her teeth chattered so uncontrollably she thought they'd break.

Val rotated the tiller to pick up speed. Once she got past Veil Point they were out of the West Arm and in a wide channel that would take her straight to the opening of Lightning Bay. With both of them in the stern, the bow was riding high out of the water, flopping hard on the dark waves, then came down when the boat started to plane.

"When we get to the bay," he said with effort, "stay straight down the middle. My place is at the back."

Just ahead was a red buoy. She steered to the left of it, and she could tell it was red for the same reason she didn't need the map or the flashlight. The moon was full. The islands, the lake, the buoys, the night sky—she could pick them out in the light of the moon. With a steady turn of her wrist, she opened up the motor all the way.

She didn't cut the motor soon enough and hit Decker's dock too hard, then swung the tiller to pull in the stern and pressed the off button. Moving him gently off her leg, she stepped over him, climbed onto the dock and tied the boat up tight against the pilings. Then she climbed back in and, crouching, slipped an arm under him. With the other arm supporting his back, she tried to raise him but only fell onto her knees. She couldn't figure out how to move him forward without putting pressure on whatever part of his body was badly bruised. She wasn't sure she could.

Lifting him gently, she tugged him until his chest was against hers and she held on. His head lolled in the bend of her elbow, and together they smelled of fire and vomit. She put her mouth near his ear, her fingers splayed on his hair. "Wade," she said. "Wade, I got you home. I'm going to get you inside, but you have to help."

He turned his face toward her and looked perplexed, then he flung his arm over her and practically pulled her down on top of him. They struggled, his other hand pushing against the inside of the boat, his feet pushing him up, and she got under him again. "Let me," he whispered, and she let him go. He inched himself backwards onto the dock, finally, almost without the use of his arms, which he held clenched over his heart.

She helped scoot him back so his legs cleared the boat, then she grabbed him behind the knees and pulled him onto his side. When he started to sit up, she scrambled behind him, got her arms around his chest, and helped. He bent one knee, leaned heavily on her for support, and finally stood.

Her shoulder bracing him under the arm, they made it up the steps, flung open the door, and stumbled inside. Past the kitchen, past the sitting room where the slant of moonlight through the windows showed her the way, through the wide opening where he had to duck his head to clear the low beam, and into his bedroom.

She sat him, slumped, on the edge of the bed, then crouched on the floor in front of him and took off his shoes, setting them aside, holding his feet in her two hands to offer comfort in ways she couldn't name. To figure out where the hell to go from there. Decker injured, Kelleher roaming and desperate, and Peter— missing.

Decker set a hand on her head, and as it slowly strayed back over her hair her chin was pulled up. Squinting at her, he let his hand slide down over her ear, until one by one his fingers left her face. "I have to lie down," he said, slurred. As he stiffened his back, she could see him bite his lip, and he let himself sink back onto the mattress as she pulled his legs up.

She shoved a cushion under his head, which made him start to roll. Her hand caught the far side of his face. "Wade, help me." She couldn't get any leverage. She climbed on the bed, dragged the other cushion into position near his head and, thankful he was nodding off, straddled his chest.

With one hand she grabbed as much of his shirt as she could and yanked him toward her as her free hand shoved the cushion into place on top of the other one. She fell back at his side, her heart pounding.

"You've got to sit up, Wade." She stood up on the bed, got behind his head and, with her legs separated by the cushions, bent her knees. Gritting her teeth, she reached under his arms, figuring she had one good chance before he thrashed too much or slugged her, and tugged him long and hard while he yelled. Her heart felt splintered. Only, at the end of it, he was mostly upright, his hand limply grabbing at his hair.

Val felt weak enough to cry, only she didn't want to take the time, so she took two more pillows stashed on a steamer trunk and wedged them in behind him. His eyes were nearly slits with fatigue. Wiping her shaking hand across her mouth, she opened the windows wide. In the moonlight she could see the bay and the islands, which meant she could see Martin Kelleher when he came. Then she groped her way to the kitchen, where she put on her penlight, and scanned the shelves.

In one corner was a package of Alka Seltzer, a bottle of Robitussin, four different kinds of vitamins, some aspirin, and two plastic pharmacy bottles—an out-of-date antibiotic and Tylenol with codeine. She shook out two pills, hand pumped some water into a tin coffee cup, then filled a porcelain basin she found, and threw in a cake of soap. Back in the bedroom, Val sat next to him, and set the basin on the floor. "Open your mouth," she said quietly.

His voice was soft. "I can do it."

Val handed him the pills and the cup. His fingers managed to place the pills just inside his mouth, but his hand shook with the cup so she steadied it with her own. Then she set it down on the floor and went to the old armoire next to the trunk, pulling out what felt like a bath towel, a washcloth, and a shirt. Decker was facing the window, and she could see his chest rise and fall in the moonlight. She took the other things over to where he lay. He didn't say a word as she eased first one shoulder, then the other, out of the torn shirt and set it on the floor. She wouldn't touch his collarbone, but she could clean him up and keep him warm and awake until daybreak, when she'd get him to the nearest hospital.

26

Setting the basin on the bed, Val looked him over. His right arm had taken a hit when he had thrown up in the boat. So she soaked and soaped the cloth and washed his arm lightly, rinsing, drying, watching her own hands work. The soap was white, the cloth was white, her life was white in the moonlight. The only sounds were the soft rasp of cloth on skin, then the trickle of water back into the basin. Wherever Kelleher was tonight, she no longer feared him. Wherever Peter was, she no longer worried.

Decker said nothing.

Then she moved the basin to the nightstand while she raised him under the shoulders with one arm, holding open the clean shirt with the other. He slipped into it and they buttoned it together in silence. She worked slowly and carefully, watching her hands do something she had only ever done for herself. At last, she told him she was going to talk to him all night, which, she added, was about eight hours longer than she'd ever had to talk to any man. "By dawn," she finished, "I'll probably be naming all my grade school teachers."

He wet his lips. "You should save your best material for last."

"How do you know my grade school teachers aren't my best material?"

Decker's laugh was dry and lifeless, and he winced as he tried to change position. "Val, if Martin comes, the rifle's under the bed and a box of shells is in my underwear drawer."

She felt sacked. "Then I guess I'll use them." While he gave her a three-sentence crash course on how to load, aim, and fire a rifle, she realized it had become an imperative of her life never to have to use the information. When he was spent, his hand flopping uselessly on the thin coverlet, Val crawled into bed next to him and covered them both. The cool night air was still filling the cottage. She sat up straight, hugging her knees, her head tucked into her chest.

His hand found her right heel and squeezed it once. "Thank you."

She turned and looked at him, stricken that in his mind she was doing anything at all that required his thanks. She took the handkerchief from the nightstand and wet it in what was left of the water in the tin cup. Then she wiped off his face. Her hand was moving along his jaw when he spoke.

"It must have been the vomit."

"What do you mean?"

He managed to open one eye and look at her, nearly smiling. "I think I must have won you over with the vomit."

"Vomit will do it every time," she said, pushing back his hair with her fingers, hearing his words, *must have won you over*. She felt touched that it seemed to matter to him. That it was something he cared to do. Val settled back with a glance at her watch. 11:10. For the first hour she told him about her work at Fir Na Tine—the cheesy politics, the author stories. Then she told him about what it had been like being in college at Rutgers, classes harder than hell, occasional malnutrition, frequent cigarettes, and weekend booze. Then the radical boyfriend who slid in and out of her life even after college ended, looking for something to be radical about, until he wandered into Pakistan on an expired visa and that was the last anyone ever knew.

These things she told Decker as the room got colder and he asked questions like what kind of glasses did her Yeats and Eliot professor wear and what brand did Val smoke and what was the color of the boyfriend's hair and whether he was the first. The first.

She pulled the coverlet closer and looked past the rocking chair in the far corner of Decker's bedroom, past the walls of rough-hewn wood and silence and years—and because she was cold and weary she told him a story she had never told anyone, not even her best friend Adrian—maybe because Decker was loopy with codeine and wouldn't remember.

She told him how late on Election Night in her second year she and an acquaintance who looked like a gremlin and whose name may have been Corey—they had worked together on the Gore campaign—went back to his place for what he called losers' drinks. He shared a house with a roommate, an Agriculture student she only met for the first time that night. On her third shot of tequila poured by Corey she thought he was hoping that maybe getting laid would take the edge off his Election Night grief.

But Val, still a virgin, who had already spent a year and a half turning down his betters, was not so drunk she was about to give it all up to some transparent worm with a well-stocked bar, no matter how he voted. But she was there until morning brought sobriety, since no one was offering to take her back to the dorm, and she figured on sleeping it off by herself while she could still find a place to do it. Only by the time she made her way upstairs with the hopeful gremlin whose name really may have been Coley trailing her, a fourth tequila had sucked out her brain and ripped off her legs and she launched herself onto a bed before she passed out.

In the morning, she discovered it was the Ag student roommate's room, his bed, his random experience, and her clothes were heaped on the floor. At least, she thought in a way that flattened her worse than the hangover, he didn't seem bad-looking or mean, where he stood zipping up his jeans and checking for his wallet. He smiled at her with distraction. She got dressed quickly and when she decided she was going to feel like an asshole in any event, asked him whether she was still a virgin. "Oh, were you?" he asked, and that concluded their conversation. For all time.

She left the room looking for a place—away from there—to vomit up her own stupidity, when the gremlin named Corey or

Coley roared up to her, having apparently waited for some time. He said he was never going to talk to her again, and in the confusion at the front door he added something about her fucking someone who voted for Bush. What she felt like saying was *at least it wasn't you*, but she didn't, and she left, barely upright in the glare, never even knowing the name of the Ag student. Two blocks from where it happened she thought maybe a crime had been committed, something even worse than her own powerful stupidity, but when you've been stupid you've stoked the crime yourself, and half a block later she finally threw up on someone's tree lawn, right next to what was left of their hardy mums.

She looked at Decker, who was watching her. So much for codeine. Suddenly restless, Val felt her eyes dart away from his face. She needed something from the kitchen—or the boat, or anywhere at all—and started to move, until his hand pressed her hip back into place. "Don't run off." She looked away from him. He pressed her again. "Not any part of you."

He told her that his first time was with Caroline Selkirk. He was sixteen and she was an experienced nineteen, on the couch in the staff lounge after camp had ended. One minute they were sweeping the floor together—he worked the broom and she held the dustpan—and the next she had her hand between his legs, and what followed was like getting swept down a wash by a flash flood. His clothes sprang off his body, which seemed capable of having a life independent of his brain. What he most remembers—and this was no reflection on the estimable Caroline—was the precise moment her father, Trey Selkirk, walked in on them, where they lay curled and spent on the couch.

Caroline had pulled a tatty green and gold afghan over them, and he was still trying to catch his breath and figure out what the hell had just happened. The thing called sex, he was reflecting, was some kind of cross between naked rodeo and death by dismemberment. He'll never forget: the screen door slammed and Caroline froze; Trey Selkirk passed them to get the AM/FM radio from the table, raising one eyebrow. Then, as the screen door slammed behind her father, Decker heard himself explain, croaking, that they were just sweeping, sir.

Val laughed.

Over the next few summers, before the campers came and again after they left, he and Caroline Selkirk marked the season with what she called their annual vernal rite. Others came, for both of them; still he loved her back then with the same kind of awe you feel when a moose comes out into the open or your paycheck holds more than you were expecting. It ended, finally, when she hooked up with Peter Hathaway, the summer Decker was twenty.

Val watched him close his eyes.

His was the better story. It had passion and afghans. Hers was nothing more than inebriation and randomness. His had lasting friendship. Hers had names forgotten and names never known. Suddenly, wincing, he pulled himself up straighter, and half turned to Val. "There's a box on the kitchen table, Val," he said, his voice still loopy, but he spoke each word with great care.

"I'll get it," she told him, sliding off the bed and flicking on the little penlight. Her hearing felt acute, like it was an early warning system, waiting for the first appearance of Martin Kelleher's boat. Would she recognize the sound of his motor? No. Would Wade? Possibly. As she made her way to Decker's kitchen, she felt surprised that her dread about Martin Kelleher didn't weigh her down, didn't pull her closer to the floor she'd bleed out on if he found her.

Dread had always seemed like chain mail, something that encased you, making it harder to move a limb. Instead, all she felt was light, like everything with weight was just floating away from her, and all she was, in what could well be those hours before a terrible end, was a set of infinitely thin dragonfly wings. Was she too light to shoulder Decker's rifle, if she had to? Was she too insubstantial to pull the trigger?

She swung the light around the kitchen. There on the square wood table with a '60s green metal top was a box. Val's breath caught in her throat. It was the missing box, the box that should have been next to Caroline's and Hope's there in the boathouse. Why did it surprise her to find it here at Wade Decker's cottage? Leslie had lived here too. Only...judging by what she recalled of the lack of dust in the rectangular patch left by the missing box, Decker must have taken it away pretty recently. And, if it was here on his kitchen table, rather than stored in a closet, he must have been going through it recently too.

And now all the others—Hope's, Caroline's, Trey's basket—had burned up in the fire set by Kelleher. Were the firefighters still there? Had they saved the rest of the camp? Of all the things stored in that boathouse, Leslie Decker's metal memory box was the only thing left. Val turned the flashlight on the old battered box where the name Leslie Dungannon Selkirk had been etched a long time ago. Instead of a nail, what looked like a stick pin held the latch in place.

Lifting it carefully, for reasons she couldn't even describe— maybe out of some care for a dead woman's belongings—she carried it back to the bedroom. Out on the moonlit lake, still no sound of Kelleher's motor. The thought that he could be approaching by canoe was suddenly terrifying. No early warning. No warning at all. What if—what if he set fire to the cottage, and she and Wade were trapped? How could she get him out? She had barely been able to get him in.

Val found Decker propped up on the pillows, as vertical as he could get himself, what with a tender collarbone. First she set down the box close enough so he could reach it, and then she settled herself next to him. "Thanks," he said, without touching the box, so softly she could hardly hear him.

In the dim light from the hurricane lamp, she could see how pale he was. For a minute he looked away, and then he started shaking his head, lost in whatever thoughts made it all the way through the pain or the effects of the painkiller. Still, he didn't touch the box. Val finally asked, "Is there something you want from this box?"

When he turned to look at her, he widened his eyes, like he

wanted her to understand something, even though he couldn't explain it. She waited. He pressed his lips together, then said, "I want you to see something." Then he lifted his chin at her. "Go ahead and open it, Val."

She gently tugged the covers up higher on Decker and then opened the Army surplus box that had been his wife's. Shining the light inside, she could see it was a jumble of odd objects. First she pulled out a handful of little wobbly dolls—Weebles, maybe? And then a flat silver Ankh cross on a heavy chain. And a spiral notebook. A purple flash drive that looked rather new, wrapped in a white piece of paper labeled MY FOOLPROOF PLAN TO SAVE OUR BELOVED CAMP. And a worn brown leather billfold containing two ten dollar bills and an Ontario temporary driver's ID issued to a Jeremy Nolan from Toronto. And a camera that looked maybe twenty years old. And a ragged square from an afghan that had been cut and slashed, pinned with a corner ripped from a camp brochure. Val set all the objects on the bed and looked wordlessly at Decker.

"It's the notebook, Val. Read up to the place where she gets the camera. That's where I left off."

Carefully, Val placed all the other objects back inside the metal box, the smiling painted faces of the inscrutable Weebles staring up at her. She set the box on the floor and opened the cheap drugstore notebook, flipping through the pages, taking in the alternating entries in hot pink and peacock blue ink. A childish scrawl. Half the notebook was still unused, as if the writer had lost interest, and the few entries spanned only half a dozen years. At the moment Val started to read, she remembered Decker's words, back on the porch of a boathouse that no longer existed: *I have known her alive and I have known her dead, and I don't know which is worse.*

This, then, was Leslie Selkirk Decker. This, on the page.

At the sound of a distant motor, Val fumbled the notebook, left it open on the coverlet, and darted to the window. "I hear it," said Decker, with no anxiety. Val squinted into the dark. There, out in the widest part of Lightning Bay, was a set of night running lights.

The sound of the motor was the kind of low thrum you could almost mistake for the wind kicking up. About two seconds away from pulling the rifle out from under the bed, Val could tell that whoever was out there at night was traveling away from the bay, away from Decker's island. Not Martin Kelleher...

When she picked up the notebook, her hands were cold and shaking slightly. So she read while, beside her, Wade Decker waited. At least his breathing was less ragged. And over the pages of peacock blue and hot pink entries, Val understood. She didn't know how any of what Leslie Selkirk was had led to her murder, but at least she understood that the woman hurled through a second-story window was dangerous. Just how dangerous was the question. When she reached the line about *screwing Wade Decker and thinks nobody knows,* Val stopped reading and looked Decker straight in the eye. In the low light, he looked exposed. She leaned over the side of the bed and thrust her hand into the Army surplus box. In a second she was laying the slashed piece of ratty afghan next to him on the bed, her fingers holding up the pinned scrap:

the fucking bitch

and I do mean fucking

and I do mean bitch

"From your annual vernal rite with Caroline?"

He nodded, then winced.

"Does Caroline know what Leslie did to it?"

"No."

"What are all the other things in the box, Wade?"

"I don't know." Then with some spirit, he said, "But the wallet..."

"Jeremy Nolan."

"A popular camper." His hand plucked at the coverlet.

"The cross?"

"Marcus Cadotte. Kay's boy. I remember seeing it when we played tetherball."

"The camera? The flash drive?" Two saved objects, many years apart.

"I don't know. I only just started going through the stuff," he explained, with a heavy wave sideways, maybe in his mind seeing the box topple clear out of existence. Then he tried for a wry smile. "Not the sort of thing you can rush."

Her fingers turned over a Weeble fading with age. "How—" Her voice sounded high and faraway, and she couldn't find a diplomatic way of asking the question. "How did you end up with her?" In that moment, she couldn't even say the name. "I mean, after—"

His smile was slight. "Caroline?"

"After Caroline."

Decker squinted into the corners of the bedroom. "I think that was exactly the problem for Leslie. Everywhere she looked, she came after Caroline. She couldn't run fast enough, even though she won races. She couldn't get the Selkirk name on the front pages of enough papers, even though she managed some headlines. She couldn't be anointed to run Trey's precious camp, not when there was the exceptional Caroline. Everywhere she looked, there was Caroline." Decker pushed himself higher on the pillows while Val stayed very still. He went on: "Caroline Selkirk was exactly the girl Leslie Selkirk wanted to be. And then there I was. She was beautiful, and I was stupid. She was a firebrand, and I kept right on being stupid. The day we got married, Leslie told me, 'Caroline got you first. But I've got you last.'"

Val felt shocked. All she could do was stare at his fingers as he picked at the coverlet. "And at that moment I saw it all. I was the biggest race she could win. And all I heard from anyone who knew us both was how very lucky I was to land—they actually said 'land'— that beautiful activist Leslie Selkirk." Rubbing his eyes, he said behind his hands, "For a while there were loud fights, and louder sex, but nothing got to her. Finally, she drifted into affairs—I'm guessing Martin Kelleher was one of them—and I drifted into indifference. You can see," he widened his eyes at Val, "what a good suspect I made when she was killed."

"Why did you stay?"

"Because I was stupid." His voice came fast. "Because I was ashamed. Because I kept thinking I had to be wrong. Because, if I wasn't, if I wasn't wrong—it started to feel like some crazy kind of sacred obligation to everyone else to keep an eye on her."

Val took a breath. "Someone else saw it differently."

"Yes," he said finally. "Someone with less patience and, really, more at stake. That's how I see it."

She nodded slowly. "Well, Wade," she said, "the Virginia Reel seems like a long time ago."

He looked away. "That's what Leslie does."

"What do you mean?"

"She takes every pleasurable thing and flings it so far away you can never remember how it felt." When he tried to turn toward his nightstand, she could tell he was reaching for a box of cigars, so she climbed over him, slipped one between his lips, and lighted it. One shaking hand came up to hold it.

He pushed his hair back from his face. "Read me the rest, Val," he said, studying the tip of the cigar, but only out of habit. He couldn't seem to focus. Out on the lake, close, a loon made its three-note ghostly call. The sound settled her heart. Not every pleasurable thing could be flung away from them by Leslie Decker. But then she cleared her throat and started to read the last part of the final entry to the broken man beside her, and she wasn't at all sure:

I finally got some good pictures today with my new camera. Dad's right, candid shots are best. Of course now I'm going to have to think of something else to make Caroline do for me since night shifts won't be a problem anymore. But there's been so much excitement in camp afterwards that I can hardly think about it yet. Maybe I should have her do my laundry? Or let me out of waterfront search drills? Well, I'll think of something.

So today was day three of the trip to the waterfalls—big whoop—and same old same old. We let the kids play around in the waterfall pool for what seemed like hours. I was so bored. Alex, who's nineteen and kind of likes me, says I can go spot at the bottom of the water chute and we can start letting the kids go down the chute.

Then he gets Max and Belinda to get them to wear their life jackets like diapers. The girls always shriek and hug each other, falling all over themselves and tugging at their bikinis while the boys waddle around in their life jacket diapers going "goo goo." Off to the side that idiot Marcus is fumbling with straps and looking at the others, not wanting to make himself look any more like an idiot than he is but still none of them will want to go down the chute with him.

I follow the rushing water over the boulders, it's maybe a meter and a half deep, and not very steep at all. It just seems like fun because of the twists and turns, and the water foams up high and makes a lot of noise. It's pretty fast. So they're all out of sight back at the waterfall pool and I'm down on the rocks near the last big turn in the chute.

I crouch down in the water and go under just long enough to try out the camera. The picture's pretty sharp in the viewfinder. I take a shot of my long hair swirling all around my face. We'll see how it comes out but I'm thinking it's going to be very cool. My hair might even look like snakes!

"Ready?" Alex shouts, and then again, "ready?" I yell back ready, rolling my eyes, wondering if he can hear me over the noise of the water. All of a sudden I see a kid's legs come around the bend, then the force of the water tumbles him right over, and it's Marcus Cadotte and the life jacket slips off one of his legs—of course he wasn't doing it right—and he's flailing around and goes completely underwater. It's amazing how the water can take even a big fat kid like Marcus.

I figure he'll pop up closer to me any minute now, but he doesn't, he's such a bother, so I plunge in and look around. My snake hair is getting in the way, but I can see Marcus on the far side of the chute, pulling at his foot where it's got stuck between a couple of big rocks. His swim trunks are that blue and white Hawaiian print they were showing maybe three years ago so he *must have got them at a thrift shop. No one the size of Marcus Cadotte should wear a print like that. I look through my viewfinder at him and that swimsuit practically fills the entire frame, so I scan up and find his face.*

He sees me, his eyes are big and his mouth opens. The bubbles that come out—is he trying to say something?—make a cool shot and I think this will be the first in the Mar-curse series. He flings his body this way and that, bucking so hard I think he's going to pull his foot off. I move closer underwater and get another shot of his face, it's so expressive. I should get help, but when will I ever get a chance like this again? This is real. This is real and everything that's safe and boring is ripped away, and everything else we ever are in the world is less less less than this moment.

Marcus sinks, his bum bouncing on the rock bottom, and his arms look graceful. Marcus's arms and my hair make a kind of dance, I'm dancing with Marcus Cadotte, his eyes staring without blinking up at the sunlight on the water's surface. Three quick strokes and I'm back on shore, calling for Alex and Max and Belinda, yelling, "Stop, stop! There's something wrong with Marcus."

But two kids make it through the natural water chute, bumping up against the obstruction near the end, before Alex stops the fun and the world shuts down. Because I'm wet I later get the credit for trying to free the Cadotte kid's foot, even though we all stood around watching Alex and Belinda, the strongest swimmers, dive again and again, crying, trying to do something, to change the course of history.

They choppered us all back. Pretty cool. Not even Caroline has ever been choppered.

I wonder if we can get the Toronto Star reporter back up here to do a new piece? We can put that cute Jeremy out in front. He's got the right look for us, he really does, and it would be great to get that U.C.C. sweatshirt in the picture. I wonder if club soda would take out that Kool-Aid stain?

27

Afterward.

In the middle of the night, Val's life felt like one long afterward. There was her voice in Decker's dimly lit bedroom as she read the final entry in Leslie Selkirk's spiral notebook. And then there was afterward. Decker sank into silence as his cigar burned down—just one more pleasurable thing Leslie Decker got between— but he seemed more alert. For him, there were no surprises, not really.

But for Val, it was different. Val worried that, back home in her New York life, every melon she'd press for ripeness, every wine list she'd scan for something Chilean, every shampoo bottle she'd check for silicone before buying, and wondering whether it mattered, would get stacked against what she had read in Leslie's diary. Every smallest action would bleed into the terrible truth of a teenager letting a boy drown. Watching death happen. Seeing an opportunity to snap a picture, to dispel a boredom that went deeper than boredom. Would Val ever get past the hot pink scrawl that— afterwards—showed a chilling lack of satisfaction in the act? Wondering only about a Kool-Aid stain on a cute guy's shirt.

Afterwards, she had held up the camera and asked Decker whether this was the one. Whether the chronicle of a drowning was still on it. He couldn't say and they agreed that on it, not on it, either way was awful. *No more tonight*, she had said. And when he said, *It'll keep*, she knew he was right and she knew it was all just more afterward. She set the camera back in the Army surplus box that held horrors. And she closed the journal of someone who seemed other than completely human, and slid it back inside. Back down with Janie's Weebles and Marcus's cross and Jeremy's wallet.

Outside the open window, where mosquitoes bounced against the screen, the moon was high, and the narrow strip of its white rippling light shot across the surface of the lake to where she and Wade Decker sat in his room without speaking. Her eyes stared into the white light, wondering whether what the two of them had discovered gave her any new insight into the murder. It had to. The death of Marcus Cadotte had been a terrible event in the lives of anyone who had loved the boy. And a terrible mark against the camp, which had never fully recovered.

The Selkirks had survived it, somehow, and surely Caroline's new annual vernal rite that had nothing to do with sex—opening a summer camp, year after year, with dwindling numbers—was an act of such cockeyed hope that she couldn't have held her sister responsible for what Caroline herself didn't even see as a failure. And Charlie Cable hadn't known that Marcus was his son—hadn't known Marcus at all, for that matter. And although Kay knew and loved him, her tale to Val about the discovery of Leslie's body made it clear that she loved Leslie as well.

She couldn't bring Martin Kelleher into the picture for Leslie's death based on what she had done to Marcus. It just didn't work. On some level, Caroline had loved her sister. And Kay Stanley had loved her. And, of course, Charlie had revered her in that innocent warrior way he had. The Leslie who triumphed in that newspaper photo of the two of them on Parliament Hill after an important vote. The Leslie who had genuinely worked to preserve the lake environment, before she seemed to shift her allegiances to the devious Martin.

If she had, then why had she? Was she sick of watching the historic Camp Sajo sink slowly to its death, the way she had watched Marcus when she was just seventeen? Sick of being pulled down with it? Just plain wanting out and seeing what seemed like the only way—sell off Selkirk Peninsula and Camp Sajo to Martin Kelleher—of pulling her poor, misguided sister out with her, without her even realizing it?

Just as she was slipping the stick pin through the latch of Leslie Selkirk Decker's little box of horrors, she remembered the flash drive, and pulled it out. MY FOOLPROOF PLAN FOR SAVING OUR BELOVED CAMP, rubber-banded around the drive. How could Leslie have been plotting with Martin to sell off all the Selkirk property on the one hand, and yet coming up with foolproof plans to save it on the other? It struck Val that to Leslie maybe saving the property meant something other than retaining ownership. Maybe, for her, it was still all about the environment, a throwback to her eco-warrior days shoulder to shoulder with Charlie Cable.

She handed Decker a glass of water and left him in the room lit partly by the hurricane lamp and partly by the pale moon. He seemed restless. So was she. As soon after dawn as she could handle the boat comfortably, she'd get him to the nearest hospital. With her penlight in one hand and Leslie's flash drive in the other, she quietly let herself out of the cottage and headed down the path to Decker's boat.

It was three a.m. and even the night seemed drained, like it had gone on too long. She kept her eyes on the path, feeling all around her the strange heavy emptiness of summer nights. A rustle off to the left, a snap off to the right. On the dock, she lifted her laptop out of Decker's boat and carried it back up to the cottage. A quick check found Decker still awake, still silent, his head turned toward the moonlight.

Val powered up the laptop in Decker's kitchen, her eyes squinting against the bright screen, and inserted the flash drive with the foolproof plan for saving their beloved camp into the USB port. The directory showed just one file: *InCubeOps.docx*. Surprised, Val sat back. What on Earth was Leslie Decker doing with the file for one of Schlesinger's biggest sellers? She opened the file.

InCubeOps:
America's Secret Program to Destabilize its Allies
by
Anonymous

The book had been published five years ago, with Peter Hathaway as the editor who had acquired it. And the only one who knew the identity of Anonymous. Twelve printings, one sequel, and a Pulitzer Prize. It was one of those dramatic exposés that combines a high moral tone with a fast, sexy prose style. Not too high and moral to kill sales, not too fast and sexy to be dismissed. Anonymous had hit all the right notes: government plot, covert dickishness, bewildered allies, intimidated enemies, policy wonk clubbishness, and scores of "necessary casualties." All in service to what some stolen, highly classified documents termed "geopolitical redistricting." Anonymous even managed to trot some sexual intrigue into the mix.

Not at all Val Cameron's kind of story—but certainly Peter Hathaway's. It was his prize and he guarded it more closely, he'd have them all believe, than the U.S. government had guarded the whole InCubeOps secret program. On the strength of this find, and because Anonymous wasn't turning up, he was booked on the major news magazine shows, and finally given his own imprint. It had made his career.

And here the file was, in Leslie Decker's hands.

Even Val hadn't seen the book in manuscript form.

In the semi-darkness, she poured herself a glass of water and took a little tour around Decker's cottage kitchen. Her eyes strayed over the canned goods stacked neatly on the open shelves, over the cooking utensils hung up on a pegboard. She sipped. Then she sat and stared again at the prose on her screen. And in the next moment, she grew cold very quickly.

What if this book was a work of fiction? The government had denounced it loudly when it came out, but when that only made people believe it was all true, it had distanced itself quickly and refused, ever after, to comment. Had Leslie Selkirk Decker written this book? Was that it? Had the dangerous woman who watched, unperturbed, as a peer drowned, who had stolen keepsakes, who had managed her own treacherous covert operation with the acquisitive Martin Kelleher, been capable of this story? The girl with the childish scrawl in hot pink. The girl with a deadly conversational style. The girl who had taken a knife to the afghan her fucking bitch sister had used to cover up herself and Leslie's own object of desire. Could such a woman have written this book that had yielded millions in sales? Was that her foolproof plan to save their beloved camp?

Was she Anonymous?

Did Peter Hathaway know? Had he encouraged her, brought her along, played nursemaid to the project as she wrote? She recalled Caroline's telling her that the Camp Sajo office had been temporary space for different cottager friends—including Peter Hathaway, who had spent a month with them, when he needed an office and his cottage was being re-roofed and logs were being replaced. That must have been about half a dozen years ago, and Val remembered that month he had tried telecommuting from his cottage.

Was that when he had worked out a secret deal with Leslie Decker, who was watching the Selkirk family camp head toward bankruptcy? Or had the strange, perfidious Leslie really stayed anonymous, even to him, and submitted the work to Peter Hathaway at Schlesinger Publishing Company just because she knew him from years and years on Lake Wendaban? But where was the money? She remembered the Toronto Dominion deposit slips in Leslie's office for thirty and forty grand—a start? But there was only a single question that gripped Val: Could Leslie Decker have written such a hefty book without Wade's knowing about it?

Yet here was the file.

Val scrolled down, through the Track Changes, where it was clear to her it was the author, not the editor, making changes. In one margin: *Too far-fetched? Should I pull back here, maybe change the name of the French contact from Henri to Henriette? Make it female?* Val kept scrolling down. In another margin: *If anyone ever catches me on this Tony Blair thing, I can say I met him at a conference back in 2005, and that I was Anon's source on this.*

Page after page, Val saw paragraphs deleted, self-questionings about word choice, corrections of punctuation, tough marginal questions about how to represent sources, and ongoing monologues about troubling passages. *Won't be my last chance to fix this section!* Midway through the revision of *InCubeOps* Val came across one of the writer's marginal comments that made her breath catch in her throat: *Get Val to fact-check these dates. Whole section needs verisimilitude.*

Val?

Val had never met Leslie Selkirk Decker.

And she found it hard to believe that the woman who stole keepsakes of her heartless triumphs knew the word *verisimilitude.* The dates Anonymous had needed fact-checking covered a miserable series of bombings in Paris that was part of the so-called InCubeOps operation but had been chalked up to Islamic militants. *Get Val to fact check these dates—*

Get Val.

And then her shoulders drooped.

It was Peter. Not Leslie.

Peter Hathaway had written *InCubeOps.*

The twelve printings, the sequel, the talk shows, the Pulitzer, the publishing coup, the imprint of his own, the...hoax.

His career had been built on a hoax.

But why had he given the file to Leslie Decker? What service could she possibly—

She couldn't. And he didn't.

Val's mind worked slowly, but she stayed with where it was taking her. Leslie Selkirk had come across the file, somehow— maybe *InCubeOps* was what Peter Hathaway was working on in the office at Camp Sajo—and had made herself a copy of it on this flash drive. If she had cagily asked Peter what he was working on, he might have laughed it off, shrugged it off, telling her, oh, just some boring work stuff—memos, you know the kind of thing.

And when she had checked out the file she had copied, sometime later, when she was alone, Leslie Decker, the Leslie who may not have known the word *verisimilitude* but who knew just how long it took a fourteen-year-old kid to drown, that Leslie Decker had indeed found a foolproof plan to save her beloved camp—the camp she had doomed when she let Marcus Cadotte die.

She blackmailed him.

She couldn't have written that book.

But she could damn well blackmail the man who did.

And the purple flash drive with just one file, wrapped in a victorious note—MY FOOLPROOF PLAN TO SAVE OUR BELOVED CAMP—was just another one of this unfinished human's trophies. Like a camera. A cross. A wallet. Some toys. Who would care? Who would look? Foolproof, save, beloved, exclamation points. Just another half-cracked Leslie plan that would only end in vapor, like all the others. Who would possibly know that the woman who had protested with Charlie Cable and plotted with Martin Kelleher had finally hit pay dirt?

With this one small weapon, this flash drive, Leslie Decker could do more to Peter Hathaway, in a sense, than she had ever done to anyone else. He was without a doubt her masterpiece. She was stealing a bigger wallet than Jeremy Nolan's and watching a man drown horribly that, for him, had nothing to do with a clumsy, sneakered foot stuck between two unforgiving underwater boulders.

Very carefully, Val saved and closed the file, ejected the flash drive, and zipped it into the inside pocket of her briefcase. 4:33 a.m. She wondered if she would always remember that time. Had she tumbled down the rabbit hole? Or finally climbed her way out? She turned off her laptop. While she waited for it to shut down, she shivered, and remembered the top she had stashed in her briefcase. Still there? Her hand pulled out the book weighing it down—the advanced reading copy of *Cling!* that she had mistakenly packed at the Hathaway cottage—and set it on the smooth green metal of Decker's table. By the time she got the top over her head, the trembling was worse, and the top wasn't helping.

Her ribs hurt.

Her heart hurt.

Cling! The hare-brained advice for a new millennium.

Val picked it up. Not the hardcover first edition. The ARC. What was it doing at the Hathaway cottage? She remembered the publication of *Cling!* was timed early in the new year—new approaches, new ways of looking at life, great for self-help sales—so the ARC must have been released early in the fall, probably October. A slip of paper fluttered to her lap. The receipt for gas at a Husky station about an hour south of Lake Wendaban, dated October 6, two years earlier, 8:03 a.m. A Visa charge, lots of asterisks, ending with the four digits 7942. Hathaway's card—she had used it when he had her pick up sushi at Haru on West 43rd just a little over a week ago. *No time to hand-roll our own,* he had told her.

And then Val had to hold onto the kitchen table to keep herself from shaking violently in the surge of truth that swept over her. Two years ago, Peter Hathaway had come to the lake on the morning Leslie Decker had died. She stood up stiffly from the table. Then, with no more information than she had, and no more information than she needed, she walked slowly in the dark to the bedroom, where she calmly told Wade Decker just who had murdered his wife.

28

When morning was nothing more than a lessening gloom across the horizon, Val got Decker to the municipal landing in the boat. It was a rough ride in a cool drizzle and she was as glad as she was going to be on that particular day that she had helped him into a black rain jacket. The hood obscured his face, but even another shot of the Tylenol with codeine hadn't helped with the wind-whipped waves. At the landing, Dixon Foote was waiting for them next to a white Honda pickup truck he had pulled close to the water. When she had gotten Decker's boat as close to the dock as she could without banging it up or splintering the wood, Dixon grabbed the line and pulled them close.

Val heard a low, exhausted rumble in the distance, the kind of thunder that seems to be rolling through on its way to somewhere else. "Thanks, Dix," said Decker as the slowest barge operator on the lake helped him out of the boat. How long would it take him to get Wade Decker to the hospital half an hour east in a town called Catawba?

"If it's any consolation, Wade," he said, "you look like hell."

"You sure know how to sweet talk a guy."

Val spoke up. "Camp Sajo?" she asked quietly.

Dixon Foote sniffed. "Fire boat got there fifteen minutes after you called it in. So did half the lake. Quite a sight," he reminisced, "all those fire pumps. About half an hour later, the MNR flew over and water bombed it."

"And—?" She just couldn't handle any more bad news.

"Boathouse is gone." That she already knew. As he reported, Dixon Foote spread his strong legs and crossed his arms. "About a half-acre of forest. Camper cabin closest to the docks was hit bad." Decker squinted at him. "What about the lodge?"

Dixon Foote nodded. "Lodge was spared," he said expansively, and Val felt a rush of joy that Caroline's office and all the framed camper pictures throughout the decades were unaffected. It felt like a place of goodness, despite the brawl, a place where the deathless smiling faces of campers who'd come to Chez Trey were saying something about youth and joy. Caroline Selkirk would be needing that. For that matter, they'd all be needing that.

The two men started over to the pickup, then Dixon Foote stopped short. "Oh," he said to them both, "Martin Kelleher showed up with his fire pump." He lifted his chin. "We turned him away."

Val opened the door on the passenger side.

Decker stood leaning against the door. In a low voice, he said, "Valjean, what are you going to do?"

And she knew he meant about Peter Hathaway. "I'm going to keep him from leaving town." That's why they had set out from Lightning Bay at dawn. And that's why she had enlisted help from the slowest barge operator on the lake.

He gave her a long look. "You're going to go to the cops."

A small smile. "That too."

"First," he said with some spirit.

"I won't be stupid." She gave his sleeve a pat. "There's no more stupid left for me to be." Unconvinced, Decker eased himself gingerly into the Honda and gave her a grim look. "Besides," Val added, "I've got my weapon."

"The rifle."

"Arlo," she said, perfectly seriously. Decker grunted, which she knew was about as much of a laugh as he could manage. Dixon Foote slammed himself in behind the wheel, starting up the engine and the windshield wipers as Decker lowered the window. His hand shot out and settled against the side of her head, where the rain had drenched her hair, and he mouthed *thanks*. "Now go get yourself fixed up," she said, giving the side of the truck a sporty little slap.

Val stepped back, surprised when the Honda roared off like a creature let out of its cage, tires squealing, kicking up gravel and dust. In a matter of five seconds, they were out of sight. So the slowest barge operator on the lake saved all of his speed for the roads.

By nine a.m. Val had taken up her position in Bob's Bait Shop, having spent two hours at the low, squat building that housed the Ontario Provincial Police. She had left the flash drive, the uncorrected page proof of *Cling!*, and the Husky receipt with them. She had put them in touch with Ivy League Ivy, who was actually at her desk on time and agog to be asked by foreign cops to lay her hands on Hathaway's date book from two years ago and to expect a visit from the NYPD shortly, who would have a search warrant.

In the low, yellow-sided building just up from the Lake Wendaban Community Center, Val was wired, fed a sugary pastry wrapped in plastic, and offered several cups of coffee and a towel to dry her hair. They discussed the obvious, that it had been Hathaway who had overhead her ruse about evidence and set fire to the Camp Sajo boathouse, the site of the murder of Leslie Decker. And what Val couldn't tell them was that the reason he didn't follow up the arson with an attempt on Val was a truth that shrank her: with Valjean Cameron, he could brazen it out. She was just that smitten, and just that easy to bring around with pillow talk and plausible explanations for everything—including murder.

The rain slowed.

The time did not.

The bus south would come through at ten, the train half an hour earlier, and Val was sure Peter Hathaway—in the absence of a car rental agency and his pilot, Wade Decker—would opt for the earliest way out of town. She fingered the hidden wire nervously as the dispatcher plopped a yellow slicker rain hat on her head.

They'd be close, they assured her.

And on her way back to the municipal dock, all she heard was the sound of her shoes—her borrowed dancing shoes from the gala that seemed a very long time ago—crunching on the wet gravel. Borrowed shoes, borrowed hat, wired for sound, dressed in her pretty new dress ripped in three different places—Val felt like an assortment of parts, too assorted even to be scared. She wasn't, at the moment she stepped into Bob's Bait Shop, much of anything at all. Except wet.

Arlo, who was dumping fresh leeches into the tank, looked up and smiled. Val brought him into the picture in three sentences. *Peter Hathaway killed Leslie Decker. When he comes, find a reason to leave the shop. The cops will be close.* Arlo met these revelations with barely raised eyebrows and no drama whatsoever. He decided he'd need to go take a piss when Hathaway turned up, and Val said it was as good a reason as any.

Val spent the next hour paging sightlessly through back issues of *Walleye World,* and Arlo waited quickly on two wizened customers who ordered two pints of night crawlers. Through the shop window, Val watched intently as a few boats docked, and a few other boats cast off and veered away up the lake. In the misty rain, a couple of workers in rain gear unloaded lumber from a flatbed delivery truck parked close to the water. Just before nine o'clock, she placed a phone call, and set a weapon other than Arlo behind the counter.

At 9:05 Val saw a boat slowly approach the landing, flying off its stern a Canadian flag and...a Jolly Roger. Charlie Cable? And when it sidled up to an available spot at the dock, she saw two heads. Two close-shaved heads. And in a flash she knew how Peter Hathaway had gotten unobserved to Camp Sajo the morning of October 6, two years ago. He had taken the boat Charlie Cable leaves unattended, keys in it, at the municipal dock. The boat Kay Stanley had seen slipping out of sight around Selkirk Peninsula when she discovered the body...

Daria Flottner first set a small bag on the dock, and then a Hudson Bay shopping bag Val recognized from the Hathaway cottage. So she and Peter must have spent the night there, once he realized Val had decamped. Did he arrive smelling like gasoline?

Smoke? Would she even notice? If she did, was it a turn-on? Hatless, Peter Hathaway tied up Charlie Cable's boat, which was when Val stepped out of the bait shop and half crossed the landing. "Peter!" she called.

Glancing up, he saw her, and she tried to keep a neutral expression on her face. He had to think she was onto him, which she was, and his look was inscrutable. When would his snow job begin? He just might put her off until he could alight on what Leslie Selkirk would have called "a foolproof plan," and she couldn't let that happen. She called out, "Martin Kelleher tried to burn down the camp."

She motioned to him to meet her in the bait shop. As she started to turn away, she saw his mind working, trying to process this new wrinkle. Then he pointed Daria Flottner, still in her Krishna togs, toward the Lake Wendaban Community Bulletin Board at the far side of the landing. Maybe he was promising her a poetry slam or handcrafted ribbons for her Krishna braid, but she loped off to check out the board, and he followed Val.

Inside the bait shop, Val took a big breath to steady her nerves, grateful for the cheerful smile Arlo gave her. As Peter Hathaway opened the door, Arlo announced he had to take a leak, and lumbered out. Val stepped behind the counter and turned to face the man she had worked alongside for the past twelve years. If she could reduce it to that—and maybe that's all it had ever been—she stood a chance of getting through the next few minutes.

He fixed her with a crooked smile. "Martin, eh?"

"How could you do it?" Her voice sounded so plain.

"Do what?" he asked, and she watched his mind settle on the easiest explanation. "Bring Daria? Val, Val," he smiled at his sandals, "you've really got to—"

"Not Daria. Leslie."

His expression changed. "Leslie?"

"How could you do it?"

"What are you—"

It was hard to catch a breath. "How did it feel?"

"With Leslie?" Peter Hathaway stared. "You're paranoid. I never had Leslie."

Was it truly all he ever thought about? "That's not what I'm—"

His cool blue eyes crinkled at her. "You're such a jealous little thing, aren't you?"

"How did it feel, Peter, when she went out the window?"

He stepped back. "You're crazy."

When he started to walk away, she pulled the rifle out from behind the counter and cocked it. Never did she think she'd find that sound of quick, sliding metal so unmistakable and so reassuring.

He whirled. "What the hell—"

Val was pleased to see that her hands were steady. "I found it all, Peter," she told him. "I found the flash drive she used against you. *InCubeOps*. It must have killed you to call yourself Anonymous," she said softly. "Where's the pleasure in that?"

A beat. Then he started to sneer. "You don't—"

"Oh, I do. Truly I do. You wrote that piece of shit book and passed it off as fact."

He snapped. "It won a Pulitzer."

She topped him. "But in the wrong category. It was pure fiction. Pure career-grabbing fiction, Peter. And now I've got what Leslie so smartly made for herself—" she looked at him right down the sight line, "—a copy of the manuscript. On her flash drive."

His jaw worked. "Where is it?"

Val nearly laughed. "Nowhere you'll find it."

"Put down the goddamn gun."

She had to provoke him harder. "How much did she get out of you before you just couldn't do it anymore? Before you arranged to meet her here, to plead with her. Is that how it went?"

It worked.

"The little bitch was bleeding me, Val, you have to understand. There was no end to it. Thirty, forty grand—"

"You made millions."

He shouted, "I earned them! She was a thief who wanted to

save that broken-down pile she called a camp. She wanted to unload Selkirk Peninsula, all right, but she damn well wanted to keep the camp."

"Why?"

"How do I know? She was crazy!"

"*Why?*"

His eyes were wild. "To prove to her sister she could save the place. Save the place when Caroline couldn't. Crazy little bitch had my balls in her fist, Val."

"What do you mean?" Say it, *say* it.

"Fir Na Tine," he shouted. "Everything I'd worked for. I pleaded with her. I hit her. I kept hitting her and she still wouldn't give me the goddamn flash drive. And finally I picked her up and told her it was her last chance."

Her heart was racing. "And then what?"

With a cry, Peter Hathaway overturned the magazine rack. When it clattered to the floor, the magazines slid out, and he kicked the metal rack away from himself in a rage. Val jumped but kept the rifle steady. "She said she'd never give it up—you should have seen her face—and then I sent her flying."

"Right through—"

"The goddamn window," he screamed. "You're so right." Across the counter of Bob's Bait Shop, the two of them stared at each other, breathing hard. He pushed his shaking hands across his scalp. "Fir Na Tine, Val," he said, finally, with a small sob. "You know how wonderful it is. You love it too."

"Yeah, those little Domino sugar packets in the stock room."

"Don't mock me!" he cried.

"That I won't do, Peter. I've got just one demand."

His eyes narrowed. This he understood. "What is it? Money?"

"You're calling the CEO of Schlesinger Publishing and you're resigning." She wanted Peter Hathaway gone from Fir Na Tine before the news about the murder and the *InCubeOps* hoax broke.

His eyes were huge. "You've got to be kidding."

"I'm not."

"No way," he said coldly, "no fucking—"

"Do it."

"Fuck you," he said, with terrible energy. Then, liking the sound of it so much, he said it again. "Fuck you."

She nearly broke. "Do it!" she shouted.

"I killed that woman for this goddamn job," he said reasonably, trying to make her understand. "She was a terrible person."

Like he'd performed a public service. "Maybe so," said Val. "But now all she gets to be is dead." With the tip of the rifle's barrel, Val edged the base of Bob's Bait Shop phone across the counter toward Peter Hathaway. Then she prodded the handset, which had been lying on its side next to the base. "Pick it up, Peter," she said quietly. "It's for you."

With a dazed look, like he had been invited to insert his hand into a basket of vipers, Peter Hathaway, wunderkind of Fir Na Tine, held the phone to his ear. "Yes?" he said dully.

Val noticed that Arlo was casually standing guard outside the bait shop and the two workers who had been unloading the shipment of lumber were heading quickly toward Bob's Bait Shop, stripping off the jackets that had covered their uniforms. She almost cried with relief that they had been close, after all, but she didn't lower the rifle as Henry Schlesinger fired Peter Hathaway from a thousand miles away.

Caroline Selkirk was crouched in the smoldering ashes, sifting through them with blackened hands. By late morning the rain had stopped, and Arlo let Val off on the Camp Sajo dock that hadn't been damaged. After the cops took Peter Hathaway away, rounding up a bemused Daria Flottner on the way, Go Jays had flipped the sign on the Bob's Bait Shop to CLOSED and taken Val to Honey Bee Mine for poutine. There she sobbed over her plate loaded with fries, melted cheese, and gravy while he talked about the best bait for catching pickerel. When he said he would give her a ride to Camp

Sajo, she went, because she couldn't think of anything better to do, and he and Kay Stanley moved her bags to one side of the double sleep cabin.

But Val couldn't move past the dock. Luke Croy and Dixon Foote were circling the camper cabin that had partially burned, assessing the damage. The maintenance crew were raking what was left of the half acre of brush beyond the destroyed boathouse. The rocks where Leslie Decker had fallen that day were covered in debris. In the middle of the ashes sat Caroline, her shoulders heaving, her fingers picking up little bits of twisted metal wreckage she turned over in her hands.

Behind her, the camp laundry machines were blackened, melted humps. All that remained of the storage were metal bed springs, poking out from blackened wood debris. And the second-story apartment Leslie Decker had used, where she had fought with Peter Hathaway and lost for good, was air. And the air smelled pungent and charred, which made sense to Val on that particular day.

Val stepped through the ashes, her footfalls stirring up strange little puffs of smoke, like a battlefield. All that was missing were the dead and dying, but maybe she just didn't look hard enough. Next to Caroline was a fire-welded mess of metal boxes that Val thought might be the Army surplus memory boxes of Hope and her older daughter. Trey's basket was gone. Leslie's box of horrors was still at Decker's place, and Val knew that when he recovered he would bring it to Camp Sajo to show his sister in law and Kay.

Val stopped in front of Caroline Selkirk, who looked up at her with a ruined face. "She hated this place, and I never knew it. She worked behind my back."

And Val thought of the woman who, beaten, held aloft by the man she had been blackmailing to get the money to save the camp she herself had practically destroyed when she let a camper drown, wouldn't give up the one small thing that might have saved her life. "Caroline," was all Val could say in that moment, "it's not the whole story."

Angry, Caroline dug her hands into the ashes. "But she plotted with Martin—"

And all Val felt suddenly was wearier than she had ever been in her life. "It's not the whole story. You'll see." As she turned away to make her way up the blackened path to the double sleep cabin, where she thought she could sleep for two days straight, she saw Charlie Cable arguing with Kay on the porch of the lodge. Then the big man set off down toward the docks, ungainly with what looked like fright, his arms pushing off things she couldn't see. Without a word to Val, he untied a small open steel boat with peeling red paint that looked like it had been a workhorse in its day, and fell into it. His yells made no sense and he slammed the little motor into gear and headed off up the lake.

Kay Stanley drew alongside Val, who looked at her. Then: "Marcus," was all Kay said. Together they watched Charlie Cable, bestselling author of *The Nebula Covenant*, get far enough out in the lake that he could slam the tiller to the left and ride in wide pointless circles. And finally he cut the motor and struggled to his feet, where he stood alone in the white misty morning, wailing. The sound of his cries spread to each shore.

Placidly, Kay Stanley, in her black capri pants and loose top, lifted her head and walked purposefully down to a camp boat. Val followed, untying the ropes as Kay started the motor. Then, with a steady hand, she headed across the water toward the other boat. She pulled alongside, tied the boats together, and stepped easily into the red steel boat, where she put her competent arms around the man standing there wailing, all alone.

Later Val learned Decker had arrived, bandaged.

No concussion.

Broken clavicle.

Footsteps on the narrow deck. His, she thought hazily.

Nearby a door closed.

Somebody set meals in a basket outside her door.

Val dreamed of nothing.

At night, with no flashlight, she staggered to the john.

Somebody had mended her Colorado hippie dress.

Somebody had washed and pressed it as well.

From outside came the smell of a cigar.

Val dreamed of nothing.

And then by the second night she sat straight up in the camp bed, her eyes blinking in the dark. Val looked at the clock. 1:54. She felt wide awake and disturbed. Outside her window the crickets rasped and the air felt cool and heavy. She got out of bed, slipped into a light robe someone had set on the wall hook and looped the sash, then opened her cabin door. Tapping softly at the frame of Decker's screen door, which was ajar, Val looked inside. The bed was made. Where was he? Alarmed, she dashed around the porch.

"Wade!"

Sitting on an Adirondack chair in the dark, he said, "I'm right here, Val."

"I was afraid you had gone."

"Where would I go?"

"I don't know."

"It's all right," he said, "go back to sleep."

With a little shiver, she said, "You haven't been to bed."

"No."

"Why not?"

He was silent. "I thought I'd have a cigar," he said finally. "And listen to the crickets."

"It's nearly two."

"I've had more than one."

Her heart pounded. "Do you want some company?"

The tip glowed. "I think you should go back to bed, Val."

"Why?"

He answered carefully. "Because I think you're heartbroken."

There was a catch in her voice. "And sleep helps."

"It passes the time."

"So does curiosity." She stepped closer to him.

"Only it doesn't satisfy."

"Which is why you're out here smoking."

"I'm thinking," he said as he blew a spiral of smoke, "of four tequilas and a nameless Ag student."

"I see." She searched for his face in the dark. "You're not nameless."

He stood up. "Not yet. But names get forgotten by the heartbroken. I know," he said quietly. "I've forgotten plenty."

She understood. "Good night, Wade."

"Good night." As he passed her in the dark, he squeezed her shoulder and moved lightly down the steps. It was extraordinary. She watched him move across the yard, trailing cigar smoke, his shadow darker than the trees. She listened to the sound of his step on the gravel path leading down to the lake, and before she couldn't hear it anymore, went back inside to her own room, where she slipped off the robe and slid under the sheets. It was the first time she had been turned down before she even knew what she was offering.

She felt herself smile. She could sleep now.

So could he.

29

At Sands Point Seaplane Base on Long Island, Wade Decker was slowly carrying Val's bags out of the Cessna and setting them on the dock, and Val found herself remembering the evening, just a week ago, when they had to leave the Cessna behind and set out for Charlie Cable's by canoe. He had lowered supplies out of the plane then too. *Where you begin is where you end.* For some reason, it all just felt inadequate, so she studied the orange wind sock and the fuel pump at the end of one of the docks, glinting in the sun high overhead.

She fussed with her briefcase, checking the clasp as though there might be something wrong with it, delaying the goodbyes, the moment when he'd climb back inside the Cessna and float a turn away from her. Decker had insisted on flying her home, or as close to home as he could get her, and now he had. She'd take the train into the city. He'd fly to Toronto for the night. Plans laid, lives resumed.

The last of the bags set down, Decker swung himself down to the dock and came toward her. Even in the heat, Val felt chilly in her aqua top and print skirt, and her shoulders hunched. When he pulled her in for a hug, she stood there stiff with her head down. All she could do was shake her head without even really knowing why. Her cheek found a place over his collarbone, where she was careful not to press.

She could feel and smell the rough bandage underneath his shirt and she was swamped with feeling she didn't know how to handle. It had something to do with sorrow at his injury. But it had something to do, too, with the strange awe she always felt at touching the skeletal part of another human being. Like placing fingertips on mortality and the patient and abiding dust. Maybe it was as close as she could get. To anyone.

With his arms around her, he rocked her once. "Come on, Val," he said with a small laugh, "just hug me back."

And because there was something in the way he said it that sounded a little unsure, her arms shot up around his neck and she squeezed hard, more to keep herself from saying that she just that minute realized she was going to miss him all to hell. They both got jumpy from the pressure and were caught between hanging on and springing apart.

They let go.

"It's my ribs," she said without thinking.

"It's my collarbone."

"What a couple of liars," she said, shaking her head.

"The worst."

She glanced away. "I wish I'd gone in the waterfall." It felt like a very big admission.

"I know," he said. "Next time."

Her heart lifted. "Oh, no," she said, "more SpaghettiOs."

Decker crossed his arms. "Listen," he said. "I don't just manage the building on Bay Street. I own it." The nasal whirr of a seaplane taking off made her realize they were just trying to fill the time. With two fingers he brushed the hair back from her face. "I've got this charity dinner dance thing in Toronto in October," he said. "You'd hate it."

"In that case, I'll be there."

He laughed. "Back to the frozen North?"

Val thought about it. "Latitudes are relative," she found herself saying. Then she looked west toward Manhattan, where her apartment was out of sight, that place with triple locks, where she'd hidden for years. A place where she cultivated meals alone and rejoiced at jackhammers in the street below and longed for old age to overtake her so she would never have to share the tender parts of her with anyone else.

Val knew what was coming, so she raised her face to him, her hands behind her back. Slowly leaning in, Decker kissed her without touching her. It was a thing of inexpressible lightness, like a dragonfly on the clear green water of a northern lake, like a bat's wings, like a needle of lightning in a distant thunderhead. She didn't move, neither did he, then they grinned at each other and she bit her lip.

"Take care of that collarbone," she offered.

He stepped back. "Should be perfect by October."

"Ah."

"Able to resume normal activity," he added, and realizing how it sounded, blushed.

"Charming," she heard herself say, with a fond, high detachment, her eyes narrowing at him in the bright daylight.

Scratching his cheek, Decker leaped back onto the Cessna's float and climbed inside. "I just figured out how to annex this goddamn country, Val," he called to her.

"How?"

The engine sputtered and revved, the prop whirling. "One citizen at a time." His eyes settled on her as she watched him touch two fingers to his lips and slowly extend them to her. *One citizen at a time.* She gave him a small nod, and calmly wondered how many times in her life Wade Decker would sing her to sleep. It was a new idea, one that would get her through the next two months of dinner dishes and endless fall afternoons staring out of her office window. She would let her mind sweep back over the sight of Decker running toward her in the moment before the door took him down, Decker standing joyful in the waterfall, Decker swinging her in the Virginia Reel—not even the summer night as alive as the man with his hand on her waist.

She was wrong. It wasn't a new idea, it was an idea so old that it existed before speech, before the first creatures crept out of the primordial mud and looked around, before the great black waters were sailed or tenanted—before, even, the first light that made possible something even better than the fine old integrity of all things. Nothing was separate. Nothing ever was. Val touched two fingers to her lips and extended them to Wade Decker, who was pulling the plane around in a sunlit watery path that could never be Lake Wendaban, and let him go.

SHELLEY COSTA

An Edgar nominee for Best Short Story, Shelley Costa is the author of *You Cannoli Die Once* (Agatha Award nominee for Best First Novel) and *Basil Instinct*. *Practical Sins for Cold Climates* is the first book in her exciting new mystery series. Shelley's mystery stories have appeared in *Alfred Hitchcock Mystery Magazine*, *Blood on Their Hands*, *The World's Finest Mystery and Crime Stories*, and *Crimewave* (UK). She teaches creative writing at the Cleveland Institute of Art. Visit her at www.shelleycosta.com.

Henery Press Books

And finally, before you go...
Here are a few other lively books
you might enjoy:

GIRL MEETS CLASS

Karin Gillespie

(from the Henery Press Chick Lit Collection)

The unspooling of Toni Lee Wells' Tiffany and Wild Turkey lifestyle begins with a trip to the Luckett County Jail drunk tank. An earlier wrist injury sidelined her pro tennis career, and now she's trading her tennis whites for wild nights roaming the streets of Rose Hill, Georgia.

Her wealthy family finally gets fed up with her shenanigans. They cut off her monthly allowance but also make her a sweetheart deal: Get a job, keep it for a year, and you'll receive an early inheritance. Act the fool or get fired, and you'll lose it for good.

Toni Lee signs up for a fast-track Teacher Corps program. She hopes for an easy teaching gig, but what she gets is an assignment to Harriet Hall, a high school that churns out more thugs than scholars.

What's a spoiled Southern belle to do when confronted with a bunch of street smart students who are determined to make her life as difficult as possible? Luckily, Carl, a handsome colleague, is willing to help her negotiate the rough teaching waters and keep her bed warm at night. But when Toni Lee gets involved with some dark dealings in the school system, she fears she might lose her new beau as well as her inheritance.

Available at booksellers nationwide and online

Visit www.henerypress.com for details

LOWCOUNTRY BOIL

Susan M. Boyer

A Liz Talbot Mystery (#1)

Private Investigator Liz Talbot is a modern Southern belle: she blesses hearts and takes names. She carries her Sig 9 in her Kate Spade handbag, and her golden retriever, Rhett, rides shotgun in her hybrid Escape. When her grandmother is murdered, Liz high-tails it back to her South Carolina island home to find the killer.

She's fit to be tied when her police-chief brother shuts her out of the investigation, so she opens her own. Then her long-dead best friend pops in and things really get complicated. When more folks start turning up dead in this small seaside town, Liz must use more than just her wits and charm to keep her family safe, chase down clues from the hereafter, and catch a psychopath before he catches her.

Available at booksellers nationwide and online

Visit www.henerypress.com for details

THE DEEP END

Julie Mulhern

The Country Club Murders (#1)

Swimming into the lifeless body of her husband's mistress tends to ruin a woman's day, but becoming a murder suspect can ruin her whole life.

It's 1974 and Ellison Russell's life revolves around her daughter and her art. She's long since stopped caring about her cheating husband, Henry, and the women with whom he entertains himself. That is, until she becomes a suspect in Madeline Harper's death. The murder forces Ellison to confront her husband's proclivities and his crimes—kinky sex, petty cruelties and blackmail.

As the body count approaches par on the seventh hole, Ellison knows she has to catch a killer. But with an interfering mother, an adoring father, a teenage daughter, and a cadre of well-meaning friends demanding her attention, can Ellison find the killer before he finds her?

Available at booksellers nationwide and online

Visit www.henerypress.com for details

A MUDDIED MURDER

Wendy Tyson

A Greenhouse Mystery (#1)

When Megan Sawyer gives up her big-city law career to care for her grandmother and run the family's organic farm and café, she expects to find peace and tranquility in her scenic hometown of Winsome, Pennsylvania. Instead, her goat goes missing, rain muddies her fields, the town denies her business permits, and her family's Colonial-era farm sucks up the remains of her savings.

Just when she thinks she's reached the bottom of the rain barrel, Megan and the town's hunky veterinarian discover the local zoning commissioner's battered body in her barn. Now Megan is thrust into the middle of a murder investigation—and she's the chief suspect. Can Megan dig through small-town secrets, local politics, and old grievances in time to find a killer before that killer strikes again?

Available at booksellers nationwide and online

Visit www.henerypress.com for details